PENGUIN CLASSICS

THE PARTY

FOUNDER EDITOR (1944–64): E. V. RIEU

ANTON PAVLOVICH CHEKHOV, the son of a former serf, was born in 1860 in Taganrog, a port on the sea of Azov. He received a classical education at the Taganrog Secondary School, then in 1879 he went to Moscow, where he entered the medical faculty of the university, graduating in 1884. During his university years he supported his family by contributing humorous stories and sketches to magazines. He published his first volume of stories, *Motley Stories*, in 1886 and a year later his second volume, *In the Twilight*, for which he was awarded the Pushkin Prize by the Russian Academy. His most famous stories were written after his return from the convict island of Sakhalin, which he visited in 1890. For five years he lived on his small country estate near Moscow, but when his health began to fail he moved to the Crimea. After 1900, the rest of his life was spent at Yalta, where he met Tolstoy and Gorky. He wrote very few stories during the last years of his life, devoting most of his time to a thorough revision of his stories for a collected edition of his works, published in 1901, and to the writing of his great plays. In 1901 Chekhov married Olga Knipper, an actress of the Moscow Art Theatre. He died of consumption in 1904.

RONALD WILKS studied Russian language and literature at Trinity College, Cambridge, and later Russian literature at London University where he received his Ph.D. in 1972. He has also translated 'The Little Demon' by Sologub, and, for the Penguin Classics, *My Childhood*, *My Apprenticeship* and *My Universities* by Gorky, *Diary of a Madman* by Gogol and two other volumes of stories by Chekhov, *The Kiss and Other Stories* and *The Duel and Other Stories*.

CHEKHOV

THE PARTY

AND OTHER STORIES

TRANSLATED WITH AN INTRODUCTION BY
RONALD WILKS

PENGUIN BOOKS

Penguin Books Ltd, Harmondsworth, Middlesex, England
Viking Penguin Inc., 40 West 23rd Street, New York, New York 10010, U.S.A.
Penguin Books Australia Ltd, Ringwood, Victoria, Australia
Penguin Books Canada Ltd, 2801 John Street, Markham, Ontario, Canada L3R 1B4
Penguin Books (N.Z.) Ltd, 182–190 Wairau Road, Auckland 10, New Zealand

This translation first published 1985

Copyright © Ronald Wilks, 1985
All rights reserved

Made and printed in Great Britain by
Richard Clay (The Chaucer Press) Ltd
Bungay, Suffolk
Set in 10/11pt Monophoto Bembo

Except in the United States of America,
this book is sold subject to the condition
that it shall not, by way of trade or otherwise,
be lent, re-sold, hired out, or otherwise circulated
without the publisher's prior consent in any form of
binding or cover other than that in which it is
published and without a similar condition
including this condition being imposed
on the subsequent purchaser

Contents

Introduction

The Party, the first story in this selection of five, was published in 1888, in the journal *Northern Herald*. In this very perceptive study of a woman in the later stages of pregnancy Chekhov has drawn on his medical experience to great effect. With much subtlety and accuracy he portrays the tensions and conflicting emotions of his heroine, Olga Mikhaylovna, wife of an ultra-conservative president of the local council. Peter, her husband, is intolerant, a snob and inveterate liar, and his quarrelling with his wife is the direct cause of a miscarriage.

The party is being held to celebrate his name-day, and the humid, stifling weather provides a perfect background to the irritability of the pregnant wife, who escapes into the garden from the interminable banquet and argumentative guests. There is something quite ominous about the stagnant air, the stillness of nature, the clouded sky, threatening rain, the hay with its cloying scent.

The story was a great success – especially with the ladies, as Chekhov stresses in his letters: 'With my *Party* I have satisfied the ladies . . .'; and 'Really, it's not bad being a doctor and understanding what you're writing about. The ladies say that the labour is truly described.' However, some critics complained that the story showed a lack of 'tendency' or positive stance on social questions, but in its seeming lack of 'tendency' the story is quintessentially Chekhovian, with the emphasis on mood and portrayal of emotion. Indeed, in a letter to Pleshcheyev (a minor poet and critic) Chekhov was quick to answer these criticisms:

Surely you can see some tendency in my last story. Once you told me that the element of protest is absent from my stories, that there are no sympathies or antipathies in them ... If I like my heroine Olga Mikhaylovna, a liberal lady who has attended lectures, then I don't hide it in the story ... it's not conservatism and liberalism that I'm weighing up against each other – these aren't the important thing for me – but the falsity of the heroes against their truthfulness. Peter Dmitrich lies and plays the clown in court, he's dull and hopeless, but I cannot conceal that by nature he's a nice gentle man. Olga lies at every step, but there's no need to hide the fact that this lying is painful for her.

It is the motivation of his characters that primarily interests Chekhov, not imparting a social message such as critics and readers of his day were apt to look for. Olga's condition, together with the heightened awareness it brings, makes her see the hypocrisy and pretentiousness of the society surrounding her, and in the end both she and her husband come face to face with the grim truth of the elemental realities of birth and death. This is of course a typically Tolstoyan theme, and in a letter to the editor Suvorin, written six years later, Chekhov admits that at the time of writing *The Party* he was to some extent under Tolstoy's spell. It is interesting to note that, in this story and in *Anna Karenina*, the respective heroines are suddenly struck by an ugly physical feature of their husbands, Anna conceiving a strong hatred for Karenin's ears and Olga noticing how ugly the back of her husband's neck is. And in both stories a pregnant heroine talks to peasant women.

Like *A Case History* and *Three Years*, *A Woman's Kingdom* (1894) has a factory background, which is shown from the point of view of the factory owners. This story is compressed into a very short period of time – Christmas Day – and tells of the frustrations and isolation of the factory owner – here a woman. As in *A Case History* (see *The Kiss and Other Stories*, Penguin Classics, 1982), the heroine is portrayed sympathetically, not as a cruel exploiter but as a sensitive person embarrassed by her own wealth. She feels guilty because of her wealth and unhappy at the social isolation that this very wealth brings her. Herself the daughter of a working man, she finds it difficult to cope with the status that wealth has given her, and clearly she hankers after the 'simpler' days when she lived in a cramped room, running errands for her family and suffering material hardship. In language reminiscent of Zola and Gorky, Chekhov personifies the foundry as a monster:

Those high ceilings with iron girders, dozens of huge, rapidly turning wheels, drive-belts and levers, the piercing hiss, the screech of steel, clattering trolleys, the harsh breath of steam; faces that were pale, crimson, or black with coal dust, shirts wet with sweat; the glitter of steel, copper and fire; the smell of coal and oil; the wind that was scorching and cold in turn – all this made the place seem like hell to her. She thought that the wheels, levers and hot, hissing cylinders were trying to break loose from their couplings and destroy people, while anxious-looking men ran around without hearing each other, fussing with the machinery in an attempt to bring its terrible movements to a halt.

Chekhov's father had worked at the Gavrilov factory in Moscow, and subsequently Chekhov gained an intimate knowledge of factories and the lives of factory workers in the Melikhovo district. *A Woman's Kingdom* is a fine study of alienation and frustration. The heroine seems quite rootless and unable to mix at any level. She does not seem able to communicate with the workers, experiences several painful, embarrassing scenes with them (for instance, when she goes on an errand of mercy to the Chalikov household). Nor is she at home with the preposterous Krylin and Lysevich, who belong to the educated class and who are both well-off. Like the suffering, frustrated girl in *A Case History*, the heroine of this story is seemingly condemned to a life of loneliness and social isolation. Obviously, marriage would provide a solution and she pines for this, envying all the married women in the town. She retorts angrily to her lawyer Lysevich's suggestion that, instead of vegetating, she should indulge in debauchery, take a lover for each day of the week and become the perfect *fin de siècle* woman – sophisticated, corrupt, decadent – when she maintains:

Personally, I don't recognize love without the family. I'm lonely, lonely as the moon in the sky above – a waning moon, what's more ... I want to escape as far as possible from musk, your occultism and *fin de siècle* hocus-pocus ... I want a husband and children.

Pimenov, the strong, very masculine workman towards whom she feels attraction, might possibly provide that family life for which she yearns. But she herself realizes that not only is the social gap far too great – their characters and whole personal make-up are worlds apart:

... she could not help imagining Pimenov dining with Lysevich and Krylin. And then Pimenov's subservient, stupid appearance struck her as pathetic, helpless, and filled her with revulsion. Only now did she understand clearly – and for the first time that day – that all she had thought and said about Pimenov, about marrying an ordinary workman, was senseless, absurd and opinionated.

There seems to be no way out of the impasse, and Anna is doomed to remain imprisoned and isolated by the very wealth that lies so heavy on her conscience.

My Life, the longest story in this selection, was first published in 1896. The title caused Chekhov much trouble, and he expressed particular dislike for the 'My', preferring what he considered a less pretentious title, *In the Nineties*. However, the editor of the journal in which this story was published persuaded him to retain the present title, with the subtitle *A Provincial's Story*. The background is very probably Taganrog, Chekhov's birthplace, and there are several features of the story linked to the author's childhood: like Chekhov, the story's hero Misail Poloznev catches and torments wild birds, has a loathing for Greek as taught at school, and suffers humiliating beatings from a tyrannical father. Originally the story was severely mutilated by the censors, who cut the scene with the Governor and the son's final confrontation with his father. These were later restored.

My Life can aptly be called a *Bildungsroman* – it has the richness of characterization and narrative interest of a short novel – and describes the journey to manhood of the rather dull, but upright and honest Misail Poloznev; and it is set in a typical stagnating, provincial small town, in all its squalor, physical and mental:

No public gardens, no theatre, no decent orchestra ... Rich, educated people slept in stuffy, cramped bedrooms on wooden beds crawling with bugs, children were kept in disgustingly dirty rooms called nurseries and even old and respected servants slept on the kitchen floor, covered in rags. On fast days the houses reeked of borshch and on others of sturgeon fried in sunflower oil. They ate nasty food and drank unwholesome water.

The narrator and principal character Misail rejects this society and refuses to work in some government office or bank with its deadening routine, opting for the simple Tols- toyan life of manual labour. This brings him into sharp conflict with his dogmatic and tyrannical father, an inept architect infected by the general atmosphere of corruption all round. After working on the railway, Misail becomes a house-painter and then, after his marriage to Masha, daugh- ter of a grasping thick-skinned engineer in charge of the railway that is being constructed close to the town, settles down to 'till the soil'. However, Misail and his wife are cheated and robbed mercilessly by the peasants, who are portrayed here as sharply and vividly as their counterparts in *Peasants* and *In the Gully* (see *The Kiss and Other Stories*); and their efforts to build a school for village children are sabotaged. Frustrated in her attempts to help the peasants and to live peacefully on the land, Misail's wife leaves him and goes to America. In the end, after a final show-down with his father, accusing him of dishonesty, of stifling at birth 'Anything at all bright and lively', Misail returns to a life of manual labour, and in this we can see Chekhov's criticism of the Tolstoyan doctrine of the simple life. The chief ex- ponent of this doctrine in the story is Dr Blagovo, who makes the hero's consumptive sister pregnant and then abandons her. In his view, physical labour is unworthy of a free man, and he asserts several times that it is not for intellectuals to waste their time and talents on heavy physical labour:

I climb a ladder called progress, civilization, culture. I keep climbing, not knowing precisely where I'm going, but in fact this wonderful ladder alone makes life worth living. But you know why you are living – so that some people stop enslaving others, so that the artist and the man who mixes his colours both have the same food to eat. But this vulgar, sordid, grey side of life – aren't you revolted, living for that alone?

In Dr Blagovo's arguments with Misail (who advocates the simple life of manual labour and rejects the refinements of civilization) Chekhov is attacking Tolstoy's well-known doctrine of 'simplification', his claim that nearly every type of higher intellectual activity is unnecessary, an immoral luxury. It is difficult not to agree with Blagovo when he states that human progress would be in grave danger if the 'élite' were to waste its time breaking stones. That the adoption of the simple life, tilling the soil among peasants, brings no tangible results at all, has no effect, is clearly evidenced by Masha and Misail's own experiences, and the wife is quick to point out that all their efforts are futile: they have been living and working only for themselves, and Masha urges her husband: 'abandon your narrow sphere of activity and act directly on the masses'. But Misail reverts to his manual work, left to himself and to look after his dead sister's little girl.

An Unpleasant Business was first published in Suvorin's *New Times* in 1888, and for the collected edition of his works Chekhov made extensive cuts. In this story an overworked hospital doctor loses his temper and strikes a drunken medical orderly in the face, in the full view of the patients. Surrounded by incompetence and corruption he attempts to fight the system but in the end is forced to accept things as they are. Here there is a strong element of farce and some excellent comic touches – in the opening scene, for example, when the drunken orderly tries to show that he is sober. There is an almost Gogolian description of the ridiculous judge who, 'after many years' service as electoral officer . . . had reached senior rank in the civil service, but had never relinquished his uniform or military habits.

He had the long whiskers of a chief of police, piped trousers, and his every action and word was imbued with martial elegance.' Some similarity can be seen between the hero of this story, Dr Ovchinnikov, and Vasilyev in the final story of this collection, *A Nervous Breakdown*: both try to do battle against what they consider to be wrong or evil in society, against what their antagonists consider to be absolutely normal. Any protest they offer is rendered ineffectual and stifled by the dead weight of an uncomprehending, bigoted society: one cannot defeat 'the system'.

In 1888 the promising young writer Vsevolod Garshin committed suicide, and leading authors of the day decided to publish a collection of stories in tribute. Chekhov had great admiration for Garshin and wrote *A Nervous Breakdown* as his contribution to the collection. In his accompanying letter to Pleshcheyev, editor of the collection, Chekhov expressed doubts that this story, concerning a young student who visits a brothel, would be suitable for 'family reading' and feared that it might suffer at the hands of the censors. However, the story appeared without any cuts when the collection was published in 1889.

Chekhov wrote about this story: 'As a doctor I think that I have given an accurate description of mental suffering, according to all the rules of psychiatry. As far as the girls are concerned — in this field I was once a great expert . . .' After publication, he commented: 'The Literary Society [where he read the story], students, Pleshcheyev, girls, etc. praised my *Nervous Breakdown* to the skies, but only Grigorovich noticed the description of the first snow.'

The lucid, terse prose of this story is typical of the author in whose memory it was written. Moreover, the young student Vasilyev, who visits a brothel for the first time, is horrified and succumbs to impotent despair, is truly in the Garshin mould in his moral purity, naivety and hypersensitivity. The effect on Vasilyev of the visit (in the company of two extrovert fellow-students) is traumatic and leads to what may be termed a Tolstoyan awakening of conscience. Now he can see nothing but evil and corruption in a society which condones the institution of prostitution; even the arts and sciences are condemned as a pack of lies and falsehood. After his experience, Vasilyev is filled with love and sympathy for the suffering, and feels the urge to redeem fallen women, to preach to their customers – even to the cab-drivers who take them to their destination. But he does not have the strength for this kind of action, suffers a mental breakdown and is taken to see a psychiatrist by his anxious fellow-students.

The alley named 'S—' in the story was the notorious Sobolev Alley in Moscow, and Chekhov refers to it directly in a letter of this time to Suvorin: '. . . prostitution is the most terrible evil. Our Sobolev Alley is a slave-owners' market.' Although Chekhov later commented that, in his story, he said a lot about prostitution but decided little, *A Nervous Breakdown* is clearly a strong attack on an institution tolerated by the State. In the final scene, where Vasilyev is crudely questioned by a bumbling psychiatrist, who cynically accepts that prostitution is part of society and that nothing can be done about it, Chekhov shows his detestation for psychiatry. All the psychiatrist does is fob Vasilyev off with some palliatives, never remotely approaching the heart of the matter.

The Party

I

After the eight-course feast, with its interminable conversation, Olga Mikhaylovna went out into the garden. They were celebrating her husband's name-day, and she was completely exhausted by her duty to keep smiling and talking, by the clatter of dishes, by the servants' stupidity, by the long breaks during the meal and by the corset she had put on to conceal her pregnancy from the guests. She wanted to get right away from the house, to sit in the shade and to relax by thinking about the child that was due in about two months' time. She was always prone to thoughts like these whenever she turned left from the main avenue into the narrow path. Here, in the dense shade of plum and cherry trees, dry branches scratched her shoulders and neck, cobwebs brushed her face while she conjured up visions of a small creature of indeterminate sex, with vague features. And then she would feel that it was not the cobwebs but the tiny creature that was affectionately tickling her face and neck. When the thin wattle fence appeared at the bottom of the path, and beyond it the pot-bellied hives with earthenware roofs, when the motionless, stagnant air became filled with the scent of hay and honey and she could hear the gentle buzzing of bees, that tiny creature would take complete possession of her. She would sit pondering on a bench near the plaited osier hut.

This time too she walked as far as the bench, sat down and began to think. But instead of that tiny creature it was the big people she had only just left who filled her mind. She was deeply worried that she, the hostess, had abandoned her guests, and she remembered her husband Peter's and Uncle Nikolay's arguments over lunch about trial by jury, the press, and women's education. As usual, her husband had argued to flaunt his conservative views in front of the guests, but mainly so that he could disagree with her uncle, whom he disliked. But her uncle contradicted him, finding fault with every word to prove to the assembled guests that, despite his fifty-nine years, he, her uncle, still preserved the mental agility and liveliness of a young man. By the end of the dinner Olga herself could stand it no longer and began a clumsy defence of higher education for women – not because any defence was necessary, but simply to annoy her husband, whom she thought had been unfair. The guests found this argument very tiresome, but felt that they should intervene and make endless comments, although not one of them cared a scrap about trial by jury or women's education.

Olga was sitting on the near side of the wattle fence, just by the hut. The sun lay hidden behind clouds, the trees and air had a gloomy look, as though it was going to rain; but it was still hot and humid. The sad-looking hay that had been cut under the trees on St Peter's Eve remained ungathered. With its withered, many-coloured flowers, it gave off an oppressive, sickly scent. Everything was quiet. Beyond the fence bees buzzed monotonously.

Suddenly there was the unexpected sound of footsteps and voices. Someone was coming down the path towards the beehives.

'It's so close!' a woman's voice came. 'What do you think, is it or isn't it going to rain?'

'It is, my treasure, but not before tonight,' languidly answered a very familiar male voice. 'We're in for quite a shower.'

Olga reasoned that if she quickly hid in the hut they would move on without seeing her and she would not have to talk or force a smile. She gathered in her skirts, stooped and went inside. Her face, neck and arms were immediately immersed in air as hot and humid as steam. But for the humidity, the stifling smell of rye, dill and osiers that quite took her breath away, this thatched hut with its dim interior would have made the perfect hiding-place from her guests, where she could think about that little creature. It was cosy and quiet.

'What a lovely spot!' a female voice said. 'Let's sit down here, Peter.'

Olga peered through a chink between two osier plaits and saw her husband Peter with one of the guests, Lyubochka Sheller, a seventeen-year-old girl just out of boarding-school. With his hat pushed over the back of his head, and feeling heavy and lazy from too much wine, Peter sauntered along by the fence, kicking some hay into a little heap. Pink from the heat and pretty as ever, Lyubochka was standing with her hands behind her back watching the languid movements of his large, handsome body.

Olga knew that her husband was attractive to women and she did not like to see him with them. There was nothing really remarkable in Peter's lazily kicking hay into a pile on which he and Lyubochka could sit down and indulge in idle gossip; nor was there anything really noteworthy in the fact that pretty Lyubochka was looking at him so sweetly. Yet Olga felt annoyed with her husband and both frightened and pleased at the thought of being an eavesdropper.

'Sit down, my enchantress,' Peter said as he sank on to the hay and stretched himself. 'That's it. Now, tell me something interesting.'

'Well, really! You'll only fall asleep as soon as I start.'

'Fall asleep? Allah forbid. How could I fall asleep with such pretty little eyes looking at me?'

There was nothing remarkable, either, in her husband's words, in his sprawling over the hay in the presence of a lady, with his hat pushed over the back of his neck. Women had spoilt him — he knew that they were attracted to him and he had developed a special tone when talking to them, which, as everyone said, suited him. He was behaving towards Lyubochka as with any other woman. But Olga was jealous all the same.

'Please tell me,' Lyubochka said after a brief silence, 'if it's true what they say, that you're facing prosecution.'

'Me? Yes, it's true, I'm now looked upon as one of the criminal fraternity, my precious.'

'But why?'

'For nothing at all . . . it was mainly . . . it's mainly because of something to do with politics,' Peter said, yawning. 'It's the struggle between Left and Right. I'm a reactionary old stick-in-the-mud and I was bold enough to use — in official communications — expressions that such infallible Gladstones as our local Justice of the Peace Mr Kuzma Vostryakov (and Mr Vladimir Vladimirov too) found offensive.'

Peter yawned again and went on, 'In this society of ours you may disapprove of the sun, the moon or anything you like, but God help you if you say anything about liberals! Liberals are like that toadstool over there — if you touch it accidentally it will shower you with clouds of dust.'

'What happened to you, then?'

'Nothing much; it was all a storm in a teacup. Some wretched schoolmaster — a loathsome type of clerical origin — filed a suit before our J.P., Mr Vostryakov, against an innkeeper for slander and assault in a public place. According to the facts, both schoolmaster and innkeeper were blind drunk, both behaved equally nastily. Even if there had been a case to answer, both parties were at fault anyway. Vostryakov should have fined both of them for breach of the peace and thrown them out of court — and that would have been the end of the matter. But we don't do things that way! We always want to classify, to stick labels on people — the individual and facts take second place. However terrible a scoundrel your schoolmaster may be, he's bound to be right, for the simple fact that he's a schoolmaster. But innkeepers are always in the wrong just because they're innkeepers — they always grab what they can. Vostryakov sentenced the innkeeper to a term in prison, the innkeeper appealed to the Assizes who solemnly upheld Vostryakov's verdict. Well, I spoke my mind . . . got rather worked up about it . . . that's all.'

Peter spoke calmly, with a casual irony, but in fact he

was terribly worried about the impending trial. Olga remembered how he had come back from those ill-fated proceedings and had tried desperately to conceal his despondency and feeling of dissatisfaction with himself from the servants. Being an intelligent man, he could not help thinking that he had gone too far in expressing disagreement – and how he had been forced to prevaricate to hide this feeling from himself and others! How many futile discussions had taken place, how much grumbling and forced laughter at things that were not at all funny! And when he learned that he had to stand trial, he had suddenly become weary and dejected, and begun to sleep badly and taken to standing by the window more often, drumming his fingers on the panes. He was too ashamed to admit to his wife that he was feeling depressed, and this had annoyed her.

'I hear you've been away, in Poltava,' Lyubochka said.

'Yes,' Peter replied. 'I got back two days ago.'

'I bet it was very nice there.'

'Yes, it was nice, very nice in fact. I must tell you, I happened to arrive just in time for the haymaking, which is the most idyllic time of year in the Ukraine. Here we have a large house, with a large garden, but what with all these servants, all the rushing around, it's quite impossible to see any haymaking. But on my farm down in the Ukraine forty acres of meadow open out before your eyes, you can see reapers from every window. There's mowing in the meadows and the garden, there's no visitors, none of this rushing around, so you just can't help seeing, hearing and feeling anything but haymaking. There's the smell of hay outdoors and in, scythes clatter away from dawn to dusk. The dear old Ukraine's a charming country, really. Believe me, when I drank water at those wells with their sweeps and filthy vodka at Jewish taverns, when the sound of Ukrainian fiddles and tambourines wafted over to me on calm evenings – then I was tempted by the enchanting thought of settling down on my farm and living a life miles away from these Assizes, smart conversations, philosophizing women and interminable dinners.'

Peter was not lying. He had been feeling depressed and he was really dying to get away from it all. He had gone to Poltava only to escape from his study, the servants, his friends and everything that would remind him of his wounded pride and his mistakes.

Lyubochka suddenly leapt up and waved her arms in horror.

'Oh, a bee, a bee!' she screamed. 'It's going to sting me!'

'Don't be silly, of course it's not!' Peter said. 'What a little coward you are!'

'No, no, it's going to!' Lyubochka cried, looking round at the bee as she quickly made her escape.

Peter followed her, his feeling of tenderness mingled with sadness as he watched her go. Looking at her he must have thought of his farm in the south, of solitude and – who knows? – perhaps he was even thinking how warm and snug life on his farm would be if that young, pure, fresh girl who was unspoilt by higher education, who was not pregnant, had been his wife . . .

When the voices and footsteps died away, Olga left the hut and set off towards the house. She wanted to cry and by now felt extremely jealous. She understood how tired Peter was, that he was dissatisfied with himself and ashamed; and people who are ashamed always avoid close friends more than anyone else and open their hearts only to strangers. She also understood that Lyubochka, like all those other women now drinking coffee in the house, posed no threat to her. But it was all so incomprehensible, so frightening, and Olga had now come to feel that Peter only half belonged to her.

'He has no right,' she muttered, trying to find the reason for her jealousy and her annoyance with her husband. 'No right at all. I'm going to let him know where he stands. This instant!'

She decided to find her husband right away and tell him the facts of the matter. The way he attracted women and sought their approval, as though it was a gift from heaven, was unspeakably degrading. He was behaving dishonourably when he gave perfect strangers what by right belonged to his wife, when he hid his heart and conscience from her and bared them to the first pretty face that came along. What had she done wrong? Finally, she was sick and tired of his lying. He was perpetually posing, flirting, saying what he did not mean and trying to appear other than he really was or should have been. What was the point of this prevarication? Was that sort of thing right for a respectable man? His lying was an insult to himself and to those to whom he dissimulated; and he did not care what kind of lies he told. If he could keep posing, showing off at the Bench, expatiating at dinner about the prerogatives of power just to spite her uncle, couldn't he see that it only went to show that he did not give a damn for the court, for himself or for anyone listening to him or watching?

As she came out on to the main avenue Olga tried to give the impression she was performing some domestic duty. The men were drinking liqueurs and eating soft fruit on the terrace. One of them, the examining magistrate, a stout, elderly gentleman, a clown and wit, must have been telling some rather risqué story since he suddenly pressed his hands to his fat lips when he saw the mistress of the house and sat back in his chair, eyes goggling. Olga did not care for their clumsy, overbearing wives, their gossip, their over-frequent visits, their adulation of her husband – whom they all hated. But now, when they were sitting there having drinks after a good meal, and showed no sign of leaving, she found their presence quite nauseating. But she smiled warmly at the examining magistrate and wagged a threatening finger at him so as not to appear ungracious. She crossed the ballroom and drawing-room smiling, making out that she was on her way to give orders to the servants and make some arrangements. 'I hope no one stops me, God forbid!' she thought, but she forced herself to stop for a moment in the drawing-room to listen – out of politeness' sake – to a young man playing the piano. After standing there for a minute she shouted 'Bravo, bravo, Monsieur Georges!', clapped twice and went on her way.

She found her husband in his study. He was sitting at his

desk pondering something. His face had a stern, pensive, guilty look. This was not the Peter who had been arguing during the meal and whom the guests knew, but someone quite different – exhausted, guilty, dissatisfied with himself – whom only his wife knew. He must have gone into the study for some cigarettes. An open case lay before him, full of cigarettes, and one hand was resting in the desk drawer. He seemed to have frozen at the moment of taking them out.

Olga felt sorry for him. It was as clear as daylight that he was exhausted, worried and perhaps engaged in a battle against himself. Olga silently went over to the desk. Wanting to prove to him that she had forgotten the arguments over dinner and that she was no longer angry, she shut the cigarette case and put it in his side pocket.

'What shall I tell him?' she wondered. 'I'll say that deceitfulness is like a swamp, the further you go in, the harder it is to get out. Then I'll tell him: you've been carried away by that false role you've been acting out, you've gone too far. You've insulted people who were devoted to you and did you no harm. So please go and apologize to them, have a good laugh at yourself and you'll feel better. And if you want peace and solitude, let's go away from here together.'

When his eyes met his wife's, Peter suddenly assumed that indifferent, gently mocking expression he had worn at dinner and in the garden. He yawned and stood up.

'It's after five,' he said, glancing at his watch. 'Even if our guests take pity on us and depart at eleven, that still leaves another six hours. That's something cheerful to look forward to, need I say!'

Whistling some tune, he slowly left the study, walking in that familiar, dignified fashion. His unhurried footsteps could be heard as he crossed the hall and drawing-room, then his supercilious laugh as he called out 'Bravo, bravo!' to the young man at the piano. Soon the footsteps died away – he must have gone out into the garden. Now it was no longer jealousy or annoyance that took hold of Olga, but deep hatred for the way he walked, for that insidious laugh and tone of voice. She went over to the window, looked out into the garden and saw Peter walking down the avenue. One hand was in his pocket and he was snapping the fingers of the other. His head tossed slightly backwards, he solemnly ambled along, apparently very pleased with himself, the dinner, his digestion and nature all around.

Two small schoolboys – the sons of Mrs Chizhevsky, a landowner – who had just arrived with their tutor, a student in white tunic and very narrow trousers, appeared on the path. When they came up to Peter the boys and the student stopped, probably to congratulate him on his name-day. Exquisitely twitching his shoulders, he patted the children's cheeks and casually offered the student his hand without looking at him. The student must have praised the weather and compared it to St Petersburg's, since Peter replied in a loud voice, as if addressing a bailiff or court witness instead of a guest, 'Eh! Is it cold in St Petersburg then? Here, my dear young man, we have a salubrious climate and an abundance of fruits of the earth. Eh, what's that?'

Placing one hand in his pocket and snapping the fingers of the other, he strode off. Olga gazed at the back of his neck in amazement until he was lost to sight behind the hazel bushes. How had that thirty-four-year-old man acquired the solemn walk of a general? Where did that ponderous, impressive gait come from? Whence that authoritarian vibrancy of voice, all those 'What!'s, 'Well, sir!'s and 'My dear fellow!'s?

Olga remembered going to court sittings, where Peter sometimes deputized as president for her godfather, Count Alexis, to escape the boredom and loneliness at home during the first few months of her marriage. Seated in the president's chair in his uniform, with a chain over his chest, he underwent a complete transformation, what with those grandiose gestures, that thunderous voice, those 'What, sir?'s, those 'Hmm's, that casual tone. All normal human qualities, everything natural to him that she was used to seeing at home, had been swallowed up in grandeur. It was not Peter sitting in that chair, but some other man whom everyone called 'Your honour'. The consciousness of the power he wielded did not allow him to sit still for one minute, and he was always on the look-out for some opportunity to ring his bell, to scowl at the public, to shout … And where did he acquire that shortsightedness and deafness? He had suddenly become myopic and deaf, frowning imperiously as he told people to speak up and to come nearer the bench. From those lofty heights he could not distinguish faces and sounds at all well, and if Olga herself had approached him at these moments, he would most likely have shouted 'What's your name?' He talked down to peasant witnesses, yelled so loud at the public that they could hear him out in the street, and his treatment of barristers was quite outrageous. If a barrister approached him, Peter would sit sideways to him, squint at the ceiling to make it plain that the lawyer was not needed in court at all and that he had no wish either to listen to him or to acknowledge his existence. But if a shabby-suited solicitor happened to speak, Peter was all ears and sized him up with a devastatingly sarcastic look that seemed to say 'God, what lawyers we're afflicted with these days!' 'Just *what* are you trying to say?' he would interrupt. If some barrister with a florid turn of phrase ventured to use some word of foreign origin and said 'factitious' instead of 'fictitious', for example, Peter would suddenly come to life and ask 'What's that? What? Factitious? What does *that* mean?' Then he would issue the pompous admonition 'Don't use words you don't understand.' And when the barrister had finished his speech he would come away from the bench red-faced and bathed in perspiration, while Peter would settle back in his chair, celebrating his victory with a complacent smile. In the way he addressed barristers, he was imitating Count Alexis to a certain extent, but when the latter said 'Will counsel for the defence please be quiet?', for example, the remark sounded quite natural, as if a good-humoured old gentleman were speaking, but with Peter it was rather coarse and strained.

II

People were applauding – the young man had finished playing. Olga suddenly remembered her guests and hurried into the drawing-room.

'You play delightfully,' she said, going over to the piano. 'Delightfully. You have a wonderful gift! But isn't our piano out of tune?'

At that moment the two schoolboys and the student came in.

'Heavens, it's Mitya and Kolya!' Olga drawled joyfully as she went to meet them. 'How you've grown! I wouldn't have recognized you! But where's your mother?'

'Many happy returns to our host,' the student said breezily. 'I wish him all the best. Mrs Chizhevsky sends her congratulations and her apologies. She's not feeling very well.'

'How unkind of her! I've been looking forward all day to seeing her. When did you leave St Petersburg?' Olga asked the student. 'What's the weather like there?'

Without waiting for an answer she looked affectionately at the boys and repeated, 'How they've grown! Not so long ago they used to come here with their nanny, and now they're already at school! The old get older and the young grow up. Have you had dinner?'

'Oh, please don't worry,' the student said.

'Now you haven't eaten, have you?'

'Please don't worry.'

'Surely you must be hungry?' Olga asked impatiently and irritably, in a rough, harsh voice. She did not mean to speak like that and she immediately had a little coughing-fit, then smiled and blushed. 'How they've grown!' she said, softly.

'Please don't worry,' the student said yet again. He begged her not to go to any trouble; the children said nothing. It was obvious all three were hungry. Olga led them into the dining-room and told Vasily to lay the table.

'Your mother is so unkind,' she said, making them sit

down. 'She's completely forgotten me. She's not very nice at all . . . you can tell her that. And what are *you* studying?' she asked, turning to the student.

'Medicine.'

'Oh, I have a weakness for doctors, you know! I'm very sorry my husband isn't one. What courage you must have, to do operations, for example, or to dissect corpses! It's terrifying! You're not afraid? I think I'd die of fright. Of course, you'll have some vodka?'

'It's all right, please don't bother.'

'After that journey you simply must have a drink. I like a drink sometimes, even though I'm a woman. Mitya and Kolya can have some Malaga. It's not very strong, don't worry. What fine young men they are, really! Even ready for marriage.'

Olga talked non-stop. She knew from experience that with guests it suited her better and was in fact far easier to do the talking than to sit listening. When one is talking there's no need to be alert, to think of answers to questions and keep changing one's expression. But she accidentally raised some serious question and the student embarked on a long speech, so that she had to listen whether she liked it or not. The student knew that at some time she had been to a course of lectures, so he tried to look serious when speaking to her.

'What's your subject?' she asked, forgetting that she had already asked this.

'Medicine.'

'Oh, yes. So you're going to be a doctor?' she asked, getting up. 'That's good. I'm sorry I never went to lectures on medicine. Now, have your dinner, gentlemen, and then come out into the garden. I'll introduce you to some young ladies.'

Olga remembered that she had been neglecting the ladies for some time. She went out and looked at the clock: it was five to six. She was amazed that the time was passing so slowly and horrified that there were still six hours to midnight, when the guests would leave. How could she kill these six hours? What should she say? How should she behave towards her husband?

There wasn't a soul in the drawing-room or on the terrace – all the guests had wandered off to different parts of the garden.

'I really ought to suggest a walk to the birch grove, or boating before tea –' Olga thought, hurrying to the croquet lawn, where she could hear voices and laughter. 'And I must make the old men play cards.'

Grigory the footman came towards her from the croquet lawn carrying some empty bottles.

'Where are the ladies?' she asked.

'In the raspberry canes. The master's there as well.'

'Oh, good heavens!' came the furious cry from the croquet lawn. 'If I've told you once I've told you a thousand times! If you want to know your Bulgarians you must go and see them. You can't tell from the newspapers.'

Either because of this shout or something else, Olga suddenly felt dreadfully weak all over, especially in the legs and shoulders. She had no wish to speak, listen or move.

'Grigory,' she said listlessly, after a great effort, 'when you're serving tea or something please don't come bothering me, don't ask me questions and don't talk to me about anything. You can do it all yourself . . . and don't make a noise with your feet. I beg you to do this. I can't, because . . .'

She did not finish and walked on towards the croquet lawn. But on the way she remembered the ladies and went in the direction of the raspberry canes. The sky, the air and the trees were still just as gloomy, threatening rain. It was hot and close; huge flocks of crows, sensing bad weather, cawed as they wheeled over the garden. The nearer the paths were to the kitchen garden, the more neglected, dark and narrow they became. Over one of them that lay hidden in a dense thicket of wild pears, wood-sorrel, oak saplings and hops, great clouds of tiny black midges swarmed around her. Olga covered her face with her hands and tried hard to imagine that little creature . . . But all that came to mind

were Grigory, Mitya, Kolya, the faces of the peasants who
had come offering congratulations in the morning.

Hearing footsteps, she opened her eyes. Uncle Nikolay
was fast approaching.

'Is that you, my dear? So glad to see you,' he said, panting.
'I'd like a couple of words with you.' He wiped his red,
clean-shaven chin with his handkerchief, then suddenly
stepped sharply backwards, clasped his hands and opened
his eyes wide. 'My dear, how long is this going on for?' he
said breathlessly. 'I'm asking you, isn't there a limit? I don't
mean the demoralizing effect of his police sergeant's views
on our little circle or the way he insults all that is finest and
noblest in me and in all honest, thinking men. I'm not
talking about that. But he could at least behave civilly.
What's the matter with him? He shouts, growls, shows off,
acts the little Bonaparte, doesn't let anyone get a word in
edgeways. What the hell! Those grand gestures of his, that
imperious laugh, that condescending tone! Who does he
think he is, may I ask? Who *does* he think he is? He can't
hold a candle to his wife, he's just a landowner lucky enough
to have married money. Another of those *nouveau riche*
upstarts. A cad and a rotter! I swear by God, either he's
suffering from megalomania or that senile half-cracked
Count Alexis is actually right when he says that children
and young people take a long time to mature these days and
carry on playing cabbies and generals until they're forty!'

'That's true, so true,' Olga agreed. 'Please let me pass
now.'

'And where do you think it will all lead?' Uncle went on,
barring her way. 'How will playing the bigot, acting the
inquisitor finish? He's already facing prosecution, oh, yes!
I'm delighted! Look where all his ranting and raving have
landed him – in the dock! And not just the local Assizes, but
the High Court of Justice! I can't think of anything worse
than that! What's more, he's quarrelled with everyone.
Today is his name-day party, but just look who's given it a
miss – Vostryakov, Yakhontov, Vladimirov, Shevud, the
Count – none of them have turned up. And who could be

more of a die-hard reactionary than Count Alexis – even
he's not here. And he'll never come again, you mark my
words!'

'Oh, heavens, what's all this got to do with me?' Olga
asked.

'To do with *you*? You're his wife! You're clever, you've
been to university, and it's in your power to make an honest
worker out of him!'

'They don't teach you at lectures how to influence difficult people. I'll have to apologize to all of you, it seems, for
having attended lectures!' Olga said sharply. 'Listen, Uncle,
if your ears were bombarded all day long by someone practising the same scales, you wouldn't sit still and you'd run
away. The whole year, day in, day out, I hear the same old
thing, the same old thing. Heavens, it's high time you felt a
little pity for me!'

Uncle pulled a very serious face, gave her an inquisitive
look and curled his lips into a mocking smile.

'So that's how it is!' he chanted in his senile voice. 'I'm so
sorry, madam!' he said with a stiff bow. 'If you yourself
have fallen under his influence and changed your convictions, then you should have said so earlier. I'm sorry,
madam!'

'Yes, I have changed my convictions!' she shouted. 'That
should make you happy!'

'So sorry, madam!'

Uncle ceremoniously bowed for the last time – sideways
on – drew himself in, clicked his heels and left.

'The fool,' Olga thought. 'I wish he'd clear off home.'

She found the ladies and young people among the raspberry canes in the kitchen garden. Some were eating the
raspberries, while others who had had their fill were
wandering among the strawberry beds or nosing around in
the sugar-peas. Just to one side of the raspberry canes, near a
spreading apple tree that was propped up on all sides by
stakes pulled out of an old fence, Peter was scything the
grass. His hair was hanging over his forehead, his tie had
come undone, his watch-chain was dangling loose. Every

step he took, every sweep of the scythe showed skill and enormous physical strength. Near him stood Lyubochka, with their neighbour Colonel Bukreyev's daughters Natalya and Valentina – or, as everyone called them, Nata and Vata, anaemic and unhealthy, plump blondes of about sixteen or seventeen in white dresses and strikingly alike. Peter was teaching them to scythe.

'It's very simple,' he was saying. 'All you have to know is how to hold the scythe and to take it calmly – I mean, not exerting yourself more than you need. Like this . . . Would you like to try now?' he asked, offering the scythe to Lyubochka. 'Come on!'

Lyubochka awkwardly took the scythe then suddenly blushed and burst out laughing.

'Don't be shy, Lyubochka,' Olga shouted, loud enough for all the ladies to hear and know that she had returned to them. 'Don't be shy. You have to learn. Marry a Tolstoyan, he'll make you wield the scythe.'

Lyubochka raised the scythe but burst out laughing again, which so weakened her she immediately put it down. She was both embarrassed and pleased that she was being spoken to like an adult. Nata, without smiling or showing any shyness, picked up the scythe with a serious, cold look, took a sweep and got it tangled up in the grass. Without smiling either, as serious and cold-looking as her sister, Vata silently picked up the scythe and plunged it into the earth. These operations completed, the sisters took each other by the arm and silently walked over to the raspberry canes.

Peter laughed and joked like a small boy, and this mischievous, childish mood, when he became excessively good-humoured, suited him far more than anything else. Olga loved him that way. But the boyish behaviour did not usually last long, which was the case this time. Having had his little joke he thought that he should introduce a note of seriousness into his playfulness.

'When I use a scythe I feel healthier, a more normal person, I can tell you,' he said. 'If you tried to force me to be satisfied solely with the life of the mind and nothing else

I think I would go mad. I feel that I was not born for the cultural life! I should be reaping, ploughing, sowing, training horses.'

Peter started talking to the ladies about the advantages of physical labour, about culture, then turned to the harmfulness of money, to landed property. As she listened to her husband, for some reason Olga thought of her dowry.

'Surely the time will come,' Olga thought, 'when he won't be able to forgive me for being the richer. He's proud and touchy. Perhaps he'll come to hate me because of his great debt towards me.'

She stopped by Colonel Bukreyev, who was eating raspberries while participating in the conversation.

'Please join us,' he said, stepping to one side for Olga and Peter. 'The ripest ones are over here. And so, in Proudhon's opinion,' he went on, raising his voice, 'property is theft. But I must confess that I don't accept Proudhon and don't rate him as a philosopher. As far as I'm concerned the French are no authorities on the matter, blast them!'

'Well, I'm a bit weak on my Proudhons and Buckles,' Peter said. 'If you want to discuss philosophy, then my wife's the one. She's been to university lectures and knows all these Schopenhauers and Proudhons backwards.'

Olga felt bored again. Once more she went down the garden along the narrow path, past the apple and pear trees, and again she appeared to be on some very important mission . . . Here was the gardener's cottage. Barbara, the gardener's wife, and her four small boys, with their big, close-cropped heads, were sitting in the doorway.

Barbara was pregnant too and the baby was due, according to her calculations, by Elijah's Day. After greeting her, Olga silently surveyed her and the children and asked, 'Well, how are you feeling?'

'Oh, all right.'

Silence followed. It seemed that both women understood each other without the need for words. Olga pondered for a moment and then said 'It's terribly frightening having your first baby. I keep thinking that I won't get through it, that I'll die . . .'

'I thought that, but I'm still alive. You can worry about *anything* if you want to.'

Barbara, who was pregnant for the fifth time and a woman of experience, was rather condescending to her mistress and seemed to be lecturing her as she spoke, and Olga could not help sensing her authoritarian tone. She wanted to talk about her fears, the child, her sensations, but she was scared Barbara might think this trivial and naive. And so she remained silent, waiting for Barbara to say something.

'Olga, let's go back to the house!' Peter shouted from the raspberry canes.

Olga liked waiting in silence and watching Barbara. She would have willingly stood there silently until night-time, although there was no need to. But she had to move on. The moment she left the cottage Lyubochka, Vata and Nata came running towards her. The two sisters stopped about two yards away, as if rooted to the spot, but Lyubochka ran and threw herself round Olga's neck.

'My dear, my darling, my precious!' she said, kissing Olga's face and neck. 'Let's go and have tea on the island.'

'The island, the island!' echoed the identical, unsmiling Vata and Nata simultaneously.

'But it's going to rain, my dears.'

'It's not, it's not!' Lyubochka shouted, making a tearful face. 'Everyone wants to go, my dearest, my treasure!'

'Everyone's decided to have tea on the island,' Peter said, coming up to them. 'Now you make the arrangements . . . we'll all go in the rowing-boats, and the samovars and everything else can follow with the servants in the carriage.'

He took his wife by the arm and walked along with her. Olga wanted to tell her husband something nasty, hurtful – about the dowry even – and the more bluntly the better, she thought. But she pondered for a moment and said, 'Why hasn't Count Alexis come? What a shame.'

'I'm only too pleased he hasn't,' Peter lied. 'I'm sick and tired of that old fool.'

'But before lunch you just couldn't wait for him to come!'

III

Half an hour later the guests were crowding along the bank near the posts where the boats were moored. There was much talk and laughter and so much unnecessary fuss that all the seating went wrong. Three boats were full to over-flowing, while two others stood empty. The keys for these boats had been mislaid and people ran incessantly from river to house in search of them. Some said that Grigory had them, others said that they were with the estate manager, others thought it would be a good idea to send for the blacksmith to break the locks. And everyone spoke at once, interrupting and drowning each other's voices. Peter impatiently paced along the bank shouting, 'What the hell's going on here? The keys should always be kept on the window-sill in the hall. Who dared take them away? The manager can get his own boat if he likes.'

In the end the keys were found. Then they discovered that they were two oars short. Once again there was a loud commotion. Peter, tired of walking up and down, jumped into a kind of long, narrow canoe hollowed out from a poplar and pushed off so hard he nearly fell into the water. One after the other, the boats followed amid loud laughter and screams from the young ladies.

The white, cloudy sky, the trees along the bank, the reeds and the boats with people and oars were mirrored in the water; deep down under the boats, in that bottomless abyss, was a different sky, where birds flew. The bank where the estate was rose high and steep, and was densely wooded, while the other sloped gently, with green meadows and gleaming inlets. After the boats had travelled about a hundred yards, cottages and a herd of cows appeared from behind the willows which sadly leant over the gently sloping bank. Now they could hear songs, drunken shouts and the sound of an accordion.

Here and there along the river darted the boats of fishermen who were setting up their nets for the night. In one boat some tipsy amateur musicians were playing homemade fiddles and a cello.

Olga sat at the rudder, smiling warmly and talking nonstop to entertain her guests, at the same time giving her husband sideways glances. His boat was ahead of all the others as he stood up working away with one oar. That light, sharp-nosed boat, which all the guests called 'an old dug-out' – for some reason Peter called it *Penderakliya* – moved swiftly. It had a lively cunning look and seemed to bear a grudge against that clumsy Peter – it was only waiting for the right moment to slip away from under him. Olga watched her husband, and she was revolted by his good looks that were universally admired, by the back of his neck, by his posing, by his familiar manner with women. She hated all the women who were sitting in the boat, envied them, and at the same time was in fear and trembling lest disaster struck and the shaky boat capsized.

'Don't row so fast!' she cried and her heart sank. 'Sit down in the boat, we all know how brave you are!'

And the others in the boat worried her too. They were all ordinary, decent people, but now the lot of them struck her as peculiar, evil. She could see nothing but falsehood in each one. 'Now,' she thought, 'that young man with the auburn hair and gold-rimmed spectacles and fine beard rowing away. He's a rich, smug, perpetually fortunate mother's little pet, everyone thinks he's honest, free-thinking and progressive. It's hardly a year since he took his degree and came to live in the country, but already he's proclaiming "*We* community workers". But before the year's out he'll be bored too, like so many others, he'll depart for St Petersburg, and to justify his flight he'll tell them everywhere that local councils are a waste of time, that he's terribly disenchanted. His young wife in that other boat simply has her eyes glued on him and she's convinced that he's a "servant of the community", but within one year she too will come to believe that local councils are useless. And that stout, immaculately shaven gentleman in the straw hat with the broad ribbon and with an expensive cigar between his teeth – he's fond of saying, "It's time we stopped daydreaming and got down to a real job of work!" He has Yorkshire pigs, Butlerov beehives, rape seed, pineapples, a creamery and a cheese dairy, and Italian double-entry book-keeping. But every summer he sells some of his forests for timber, mortgages parts of his land so that he can spend the autumn with his mistress in the Crimea. And there's old Uncle Nikolay, who won't go home, despite being angry with Peter!'

Olga looked at the other boats, where she could discover only boring cranks, hypocrites or idiots. She thought of everyone she knew in the district, but could not call to mind one person about whom she could say or think anything that was good. All of them seemed undistinguished, colourless, stupid, narrow-minded, shifty and heartless. Either they did not say what they meant or they did not do what they wanted to. She was stifled by boredom and feelings of despair. She wanted suddenly to stop smiling, leap up and shout, 'I'm sick of the lot of you!', jump out of the boat and swim ashore.

'Come on, let's all give Peter a tow,' someone shouted.

'Give him a tow! Give him a tow!' the rest joined in. 'Olga, give your husband a tow!'

While she sat at the rudder, Olga had to seize the right moment and deftly catch hold of the chain at *Penderakliya*'s bows. As she leant over, trying to grasp it, Peter frowned and gave her a frightened look.

'Mind you don't catch cold!' he said.

'If you're scared on my account and the baby's then why do you torment me?' Olga thought.

Peter admitted defeat, but not wishing to be towed, he leapt from *Penderakliya* into a boat already bursting at the seams. He did this so clumsily that the boat listed sharply and everyone screamed with horror.

'He only jumped like that to please the ladies,' Olga thought. 'He knows how impressive it looks . . .'

Her arms and legs began to tremble, for which the feeling

of jadedness, irritation, the forced smiles and the discomfort that she felt all over her body were to blame, she thought. To hide this trembling from her guests she tried to raise her voice, laugh, keep moving. 'If I suddenly burst into tears,' she thought, 'I'll tell them I have toothache.'

Now the boats at last put in at the 'Isle of Good Hope' – this was the name of the peninsula formed by a sharp bend in the river; it was covered with a copse of ancient birches, oaks, willows and poplars. Tables with steaming samovars were already in position under the trees, and Vasily and Grigory, in tail-coats and white knitted gloves, were busy near the crockery. On the far bank, opposite the 'Isle of Good Hope', stood the carriages that had brought the provisions, and baskets and parcels of food were being ferried from them to the island in a boat very similar to *Penderakliya*. The expressions of the footmen, coachmen – even of the peasant sitting in the boat – were solemn, festive, the kind one usually finds only among children and servants.

While Olga was making the tea and pouring out the first glasses, the guests busied themselves with fruit liqueurs and sweetmeats. Then followed the usual tea-time chaos, so trying and exhausting for the hostess. Grigory and Vasily had hardly served the tea than hands holding empty glasses were reaching towards Olga. One guest asked for tea without sugar, another wanted it strong, a third weak, a fourth said 'No more, thank you.' And Olga had to commit all this to memory and then shout, 'Ivan Petrovich, are you the one without sugar?' or 'Who asked for it weak?' But the guest who had asked for weak tea without sugar simply forgot what he had asked for, being carried away with the pleasant conversation, and took the first glass that was offered. Dejected figures wandered like shadows not far from the table, pretending that they were looking for mushrooms in the grass, or reading labels on boxes – these were the ones for whom there weren't enough glasses. 'Have you had some tea?' Olga would ask, and the guest in question would tell her not to worry and say, 'I don't mind waiting', although the hostess would have preferred her guests to hurry up instead of being prepared to wait.

Some of them were deep in conversation and drank their tea slowly, holding on to their glasses for half an hour, while others, especially those who had drunk a great deal over dinner, did not leave the table but drank glass after glass, so that Olga had a job refilling them. One young humorist sipped his tea through a lump of sugar and kept saying, 'Sinner that I am, I love to spoil myself with the Chinese Herb.' Now and then he sighed deeply as he asked, 'Please, just one more little dish-full.' He drank a lot, noisily crunched his sugar, thinking this was all very funny and original, and that he was giving a superb imitation of a merchant. No one appreciated that all these little things were sheer torture for the hostess: in fact it would have been difficult for anyone to guess, since Olga managed to keep smiling amiably and engage in idle tittle-tattle.

She was not feeling well, though. The crowd, the laughter, the questions, the young humorist, the flustered servants who were run off their feet, the children running round the table – all this irritated her. And she was irritated by the fact that Vata looked like Nata, Kolya like Mitya, so that it was impossible to tell which of them had had tea. She felt that her strained, warm smile was turning into a nasty scowl and that she would burst into tears at any moment.

'It's raining!' someone shouted.

Everyone looked up at the sky.

'Yes, it really is,' Peter confirmed, wiping his cheek. The sky let fall just a few drops – it wasn't really raining yet, but the guests abandoned their tea and began to hurry. At first they all wanted to go back in the carriages, but then they changed their minds and went towards the boats. On the pretext that she urgently had to see to supper, Olga asked if they minded if she travelled back on her own, by carriage.

The first thing she did when seated was to give her face a rest from smiling. She drove scowling through the village and gave bowing peasants angry looks. When she arrived home she went to the bedroom by the back entrance and lay down on her husband's bed.

'Good heavens!' she whispered, 'what's the use of all this hard labour? Why do these people hang around here pretending they're having a good time? Why all these false smiles? I don't understand, I just don't understand!'

She heard footsteps and voices. The guests had returned.

'They can do what they like,' Olga thought. 'I'm going to lie down a little longer.' But the maid came into the bedroom and said, 'Madam, Marya Grigoryevna's leaving.'

Olga leapt up, tidied her hair and rushed out of the room.

'Marya, what's wrong?' she asked in an offended voice, going up to Marya Grigoryevna. 'Why the rush?'

'I *must* go, my dear, I simply must! I've stayed too long already. The children are waiting for me at home.'

'You're so naughty! Why didn't you bring them with you?'

'My dear, I'll bring them over one day in the week if you like, but as for today . . .'

'Oh, yes!' Olga interrupted, 'I'd be delighted. Your children are so sweet. Give them all a kiss from me. But honestly, I'm quite offended. Why the hurry, I just don't understand!'

'I must be going, I really must . . . Goodbye, my dear, and look after yourself. In your condition . . .'

And they kissed. After seeing her guest to her carriage, Olga joined the ladies in the drawing-room. There the lamps had been lit and the men were just sitting down to cards.

IV

At a quarter past twelve, after supper, the guests began to leave. Olga stood at the porch to say goodbye.

'Really, you should have brought a shawl,' she said, 'it's getting rather chilly. I hope you won't catch cold!'

'Don't worry, Olga,' the guests replied as they climbed into their carriages. 'Well, goodbye. Remember, we're expecting you. Don't let us down!'

'Whoa!' said the coachman, holding back the horses.

'Let's be going, Denis! Goodbye, Olga.'

'Give the children a kiss from me!'

The carriage moved off and immediately vanished in the darkness. In the red circle cast by the lamp on the road, a new pair or team of three impatient horses would appear, their coachman silhouetted with hands stretched out in front of him. Once again there were kisses, reproaches and requests to come again or to take a shawl. Peter ran back and forwards from the hall, helping the ladies into their carriages.

'Drive straight to Yefremovshchina,' he told the coachman. 'It's quicker if you go by way of Mankino, but that road isn't so good. You might overturn . . . Goodbye, my dear! *Mille compliments* to your artist friend!'

'Goodbye, darling Olga. Go inside now or you'll catch cold. It's damp.'

'Whoa! Up to your tricks again, eh!'

'Where did you get these horses from?' Peter asked.

'From Khaydarov, during Lent,' the coachman answered.

'They're superb!'

Peter slapped the trace-horse on the croup. 'Well, off with you! Safe journey!'

Finally the last guest departed. The red circle on the road flickered, drifted off to one side, dwindled and vanished – Vasily had taken the lamp away from the front door. Previously, when they saw their guests off, Peter and Olga usually performed a jig in front of each other in the ballroom, clapped their hands and sang 'They've gone, they've gone, they've gone!' But Olga did not feel up to that now. She went into the bedroom, undressed, and climbed into bed.

She thought that she would fall asleep immediately and that she would sleep soundly. Her legs and shoulders ached horribly, her head was reeling from all that talk and once again she felt strangely uncomfortable all over. Covering her head, she lay still for a little while, then stole a glance at the icon-lamp from under the blanket, listened to the silence and smiled.

'Good, good,' she whispered, tucking in her legs, which

she felt had grown longer from all that walking. 'I must sleep, sleep.'

Her legs would not stay under the blankets, her whole body felt uncomfortable and she turned over on the other side. A large fly flew around the bedroom, buzzing and restlessly beating against the ceiling. She could also hear Grigory and Vasily treading carefully as they cleared the tables in the ballroom. Olga felt that only when those noises stopped would she feel comfortable and able to fall asleep. And once again she impatiently turned over.

She could hear her husband's voice in the drawing-room. One of the guests was probably staying the night, because Peter was telling someone in a loud voice, 'I wouldn't say that Count Alexis is a trickster. But he can't help giving that impression, since you all try to see him as other than he actually is. His eccentricity is misinterpreted as originality, his familiar manner as a sign of good-heartedness, and because of his complete lack of any views you take him for a conservative. Let's even go so far as to admit that he's a conservative of the purest stamp. But what is conservatism, all things considered?'

Furious with Count Alexis, with his guests and with himself, Peter unbosomed himself. He cursed the Count, his guests, and was so annoyed with himself he was prepared to hold forth or preach a sermon on any subject. After showing his guest to his room, he paced the drawing-room, walked around the dining-room, then up and down the corridor and around his study, then once more around the drawing-room, after which he went into the bedroom. Olga was lying on her back with the blanket only up to her waist (she was feeling hot now) and sullenly watching the fly banging against the ceiling.

'Do we have someone staying overnight, then?' she asked.

'Yegorov.'

Peter undressed and lay down on his bed. He silently lit a cigarette and he too started watching the fly. His face was gloomy and uneasy. Olga looked at his handsome profile for about five minutes without saying a word. For some reason she felt that if he were suddenly to turn his face towards her and say 'I feel so depressed, Olga,' then she would have burst into tears or laughed, and she would have felt better for it. Her legs ached and her whole body felt uncomfortable – from nervous tension, she thought.

'Peter, what are you thinking about?' she asked.

'Oh, nothing,' her husband answered.

'You've started keeping secrets from me lately. That's not right.'

'Why isn't it?' Peter replied dryly, pausing briefly. 'We all have our own private lives, therefore we must have our secrets.'

'Private lives, secrets . . . that's only words! Do you realize that you're insulting me?' Olga said, sitting up. 'If you feel depressed, why do you hide it from me? And why do you find it more convenient to confide in strange women rather than talk to your wife? In fact I heard you pouring out your heart this afternoon to Lyubochka, near the beehives.'

'Well, congratulations. I'm delighted you heard.'

This remark meant 'Leave me in peace, don't disturb me when I'm trying to think.' Olga flared up. All the annoyance, hatred and anger which had been accumulating in her during the day suddenly seemed to boil over. She wanted to say exactly what she thought about it all to her husband there and then, without waiting until the morning; she wanted to insult him, have her revenge. Trying hard not to shout she said, 'Just try and see how terribly, terribly vile all this is! I've felt nothing but hatred for you all day long – it's all your fault!'

Peter sat up too.

'Terribly, terribly vile!' Olga went on, beginning to shake all over. 'You've no need to congratulate *me*! You'd better congratulate yourself! It's a downright disgrace! You've taken your lying so far, you're ashamed to be in the same room as your wife. You're such a phoney! I can see right through you and I understand every step you take!'

'Olga, when you're not feeling too well again, please warn me. I can go and sleep in the study then.'

With these words Peter took a pillow and walked out of the bedroom. Olga had not anticipated this. For several minutes – speechless, her mouth wide open, and trembling all over – she looked at the door through which her husband had disappeared, trying to understand the meaning of it all. Was it one of those tricks resorted to by dishonest people during an argument, when they are in the wrong, or was it a deliberate insult to her pride? How was she to take it? Olga remembered her officer-cousin, a nice cheerful young man who often laughingly told her that when 'my good lady wife starts nagging me at night', he usually took a pillow and went away whistling to his study, leaving his wife looking stupid and ridiculous. This officer was married to a rich, frivolous, silly woman whom he did not respect and could barely tolerate.

Olga leapt up from the bed. She thought that now there was only one course of action – to dress herself as quickly as she could and leave that house for ever. The house was her property, but that was hard luck for Peter. Without first asking herself whether it was necessary, she dashed into the study to tell her husband about her decision (the thought 'Woman's logic!' flashed through her mind) and say something offensive and sarcastic by way of farewell.

Peter lay on the couch and pretended he was reading the paper. A lighted candle stood on a chair nearby and his face lay hidden behind the paper.

'Please explain the meaning of this, I'm asking you!'

' "Please explain . . ." ' mimicked Peter, not showing his face. 'I'm fed up, Olga! Word of honour, I'm worn out, and I don't feel up to it right now . . . We can quarrel tomorrow.'

'No, I know you only too well!' Olga continued. 'You hate me! Yes, yes! You hate me for being richer than you! You'll never forgive me for that and you'll always tell me lies.' (The thought 'Woman's logic' flashed through her mind again.) 'I know you're having a good laugh at me now . . . I'm even convinced that you only married me for social status and those vile horses . . . Oh, I'm so unhappy!'

Peter dropped his paper and sat up. He was stunned by this unexpected insult. He smiled as helplessly as a child, looked at his wife in bewilderment and, as if warding off blows, held out his hands to her and said pleadingly, 'Olga!'

Expecting her to say more horrible things, he leant hard on the back of the couch, and his whole body looked just as helpless and childish as his smile.

'Olga, how could you say a thing like that?' he whispered.

Olga came to her senses. Suddenly she was aware of her mad love for that man, remembering that he was Peter, her husband, without whom she could not live one day, and who loved her madly too. She burst into loud sobs, in a voice that did not sound like hers at all, clasped her head and ran back into the bedroom.

She slumped on to the bed and the room echoed to the sound of broken, hysterical sobbing, which suffocated her and cramped her arms and legs. Remembering that a guest was staying about three or four rooms away, she buried her head under the pillow to smother the sobs, but the pillow slipped on to the floor and she almost fell herself as she bent down to pick it up. She tried to pull the blanket up to her face, but her hands would not obey her and convulsively tore at everything she tried to grasp.

She felt that all was lost now, that the lie she had told to insult her husband had smashed her life to smithereens. Her husband would never forgive her – the insult she had inflicted on him was not the kind to be smoothed away by caresses or vows. How could she convince her husband that she herself did not mean what she said?

'It's all over, it's finished!' she cried, not noticing that the pillow had once again slipped on to the floor. 'For God's sake!'

By this time her cries must have wakened the guest and the servants. Next day the whole district would know about her hysterics and everyone would blame Peter. She made an effort to control herself, but her sobs grew louder by the minute. 'For God's sake!' she shouted in a voice hard to recognize as hers and not understanding just why she was shouting. 'For God's sake!'

She felt that the bed had collapsed under her and that her legs had become tangled up in the blanket. Peter came into the bedroom in his dressing-gown, carrying a candle.

'Olga, that's enough!' he said.

She raised herself to her knees, screwed up her eyes in the candlelight and said between her sobs, 'Please understand, please understand!'

She wanted to tell him that the visitors, the lies that he and she had told, had exhausted her, that now she was inwardly boiling. But all she could say was 'Understand, *please* understand!'

'Come on, drink this,' he said, giving her some water.

Obediently, she took the glass and began to drink, but the water spilled over and trickled down her hands, breast and knees. 'How dreadfully ugly I must look now!' she thought. Peter silently put her back in bed, covered her with the blanket, took the candle and left.

'For God's sake!' Olga shouted again. 'Peter, you *must* understand!'

Suddenly something gripped her so violently beneath the stomach and back that her tears were cut short and she bit the pillow in pain. But the pain immediately subsided and she burst out sobbing again.

The maid entered, inquiring anxiously as she straightened the blanket, 'Madam, my dear madam, what's wrong?'

'Clear out of here,' Peter snapped as he went over to the bed.

'Please understand, please understand,' Olga began.

'Olga, I beg you, calm yourself!' he said. 'I didn't mean to offend you. I wouldn't have left the bedroom if I'd known you would take it like this. I just felt depressed. I'm telling you this as an honest man.'

'Please try and understand . . . you lied, I lied . . .'

'I *do* understand . . . Well, that's all right now. I do

understand,' Peter said tenderly, sitting on the bed. 'You spoke in the heat of the moment, it's understandable ... I swear I love you more than anything in the world and when I married you the thought that you were rich never entered my mind. My love had no bounds ... that's all, I assure you. I've never needed money and I've never known its value, so I can't appreciate the difference between your position and mine. I've always thought that we were both equally rich. And that remark about my acting deceitfully in small matters. Up to now my life has been run on such frivolous lines that somehow it's been impossible to manage without petty lies. Now *I* feel low too. Let's stop this conversation, for God's sake!'

Olga felt a sharp pain again and grasped her husband's sleeve.

'Oh, such a dreadful pain!' she said hurriedly. 'It's terrible!'

'To hell with all these visitors!' Peter muttered as he stood up. 'You shouldn't have gone to the island today!' he shouted. 'And I'm a fool for letting you! God in heaven!'

He scratched his head irritably, waved his arm as if to wash his hands of the whole matter and left the room.

Afterwards he came back several times, sitting on the bed and talking a great deal, gently and angrily in turn. But Olga hardly heard a thing. The sobs alternated with terrible pains, each new one sharper and more prolonged than the last. At first she held her breath and bit the pillow during the spasms, but then she began to produce ear-splitting, obscene shouts. Once, when she saw that her husband was near, she remembered that she had insulted him and without asking herself if she was being delirious or if it really was Peter, she seized his hand in both of hers and started kissing it.

'Both you and I lied ...' she began, trying to excuse herself. 'Please understand, *please*. They've tormented the life out of me, I've no more patience ...'

'Olga, we're not alone!' Peter said.

She raised her head and saw Barbara kneeling by the chest of drawers, taking the lower drawer out — the top ones had already been removed. When she had done this, Barbara stood up, flushed from her efforts, and started opening a small chest with a cold, solemn look on her face.

'Marya, I can't open it,' she whispered. 'Perhaps you can do it for me.'

The maid Marya, who was digging out some wax from a candlestick with some scissors to make room for a new candle, went over to Barbara and helped her open the chest.

'I don't want anything left shut,' Barbara whispered. 'Open that little box as well.' She turned to Peter and said 'You should send for Father Mikhail, sir, to open the altar doors. You must!'

'Do what you like,' Peter said between short gasps, 'only get a doctor or midwife as soon as you can, for God's sake. Has Vasily gone? Send someone else as well. Send your husband!'

'I'm in labour,' Olga realized. 'Barbara,' she groaned, 'it will be still-born.'

'It'll be all right, ma'am, it'll be all right,' Barbara whispered. 'With God's help it'll live.' (It seemed she was incapable of saying 'it will'.)

When Olga came to, after another stab of pain, she was no longer sobbing or tossing about, but moaning instead. She could not help moaning, even in the intervals between the pains. The candles were still burning, but daylight was already breaking through the shutters. Most likely it was about five o'clock. A strange, very meek-looking woman in a white apron was sitting at a round, bedroom table. From her posture it was obvious that she had been there a long time. Olga guessed that she was the midwife.

'Will it soon be over?' she asked and detected a special, unfamiliar note in her own voice which she had never heard before. 'I must be dying in labour,' she thought.

Peter came gingerly into the bedroom in his day-time clothes and stood at the window with his back to his wife. He raised the shutters and looked out.

'How it's raining!' he said.

'What's the time?' Olga asked, just to hear that unfamiliar tone in her voice again.

'A quarter to six,' the midwife answered.

'But what if I really am dying?' Olga wondered as she looked at her husband's head and at the windows with the rain beating against them. 'How will he live without me? Who will he drink tea with, dine with, talk to in the evenings, sleep with?'

And he struck her as a little orphan. She felt sorry for him and wanted to tell him something pleasant, affectionate, comforting. She remembered that he was intending buying some hounds in the spring but she had stopped him as she thought hunting was a cruel and dangerous sport.

'Peter, go and buy those hounds,' she groaned.

He lowered the blind and went over to the bed, meaning to say something, but at that moment Olga had a spasm and she produced an obscene, piercing shriek.

She was numb from all the pain and the repeated shouting and groaning. She could hear, see, speak at times, but she understood little and was aware only of feeling pain or that she was about to feel it. She had the impression that the party was long ago, not yesterday, but a whole year, that this new life of pain had lasted longer than her childhood, high school days, courses of lectures and marriage put together, and that it would carry on like that for ages and ages, without end. She saw them bring the midwife her tea, call her to lunch at noon and then to dinner. She saw how used Peter had become to entering, standing for a long time by the window and leaving, how some strange men, her maid and Barbara had taken to coming in and out. All Barbara could say was 'it'll be, it'll be', and she became very angry whenever anyone closed the drawers in the chest. Olga saw the light change in the room and at the windows — at times there was twilight, then it was dim, as in a mist; at others, there was bright daylight, as at dinner the day before, then twilight once again. And each of these changes appeared to last as long as her childhood, her high school days, the university courses . . .

In the evening two doctors – one bony, bald, with a wide reddish beard, the other swarthy and Jewish-looking, with cheap spectacles – performed an operation on Olga. She was completely indifferent to those strange men touching her body: no longer did she feel any shame, she had lost her will-power, and anyone could do what he liked with her. If at that moment someone had attacked her with a knife or insulted Peter, or deprived her of her right to that little creature, she would not have said one word.

She was given chloroform for the operation. Afterwards, when she woke up, she still had the pains and they were unbearable. It was night. Olga remembered a similar night, with its peace, icon-lamp, midwife sitting motionless by the bed, the chest with its drawers pulled out, Peter standing at the window, but that was long, long ago . . .

V

'I haven't died,' Olga thought when she became aware of her surroundings again and the pains had gone.

A bright summer's day looked in through the two wide-open bedroom windows. Sparrows and magpies chattered incessantly in the garden outside.

The drawers in the chest were shut now; her husband's bed had been made. There was no midwife, no Barbara, no maid in the bedroom, only Peter standing motionless as before at the window, looking into the garden. There was no crying child, no congratulations or rejoicing, and clearly the small creature had been still-born.

'Peter!' Olga called out to her husband.

Peter looked round. A long time must have passed since the last guest had left and Olga had insulted her husband, since Peter had become noticeably thinner and pinched-looking.

'What's the matter?' he asked, going over to the bed.

He looked away, twitched his lips and smiled like a helpless child.

'Is it all over?' Olga asked.

Peter wanted to reply, but his lips trembled and his mouth twisted like an old man's – like toothless Uncle Nikolay's.

'Olga,' he said, wringing his hands, and suddenly large tears gushed from his eyes. 'Olga! I don't need your money, courts . . .' (here he sobbed) 'differing opinions, those guests, your dowry . . . I don't need anything! Why did we lose our child? Oh, what's the use of talking!'

He waved his arm in defeat and left the bedroom.

But Olga did not care about anything now. Her head was muzzy from the chloroform, she felt spiritually drained. The dull indifference to life that had come over her when the two doctors were performing the operation had not deserted her.

A Woman's Kingdom

I

Here was a thick wad of banknotes from her forest manager: he had enclosed fifteen hundred roubles with his letter – the proceeds of winning a court appeal. Anna Akimovna disliked and feared such words as 'appeal', 'winning' and 'court'. She knew that justice had to be administered, but for some reason, whenever Nazarych, her works manager, or her forest manager – two inveterate litigants – won a case for her, she always felt bad about it and rather ashamed. And now too she felt apprehensive and embarrassed, and she wanted to put those fifteen hundred roubles away somewhere, out of sight.

She thought regretfully about women of her own age (she was twenty-five) who were busy in the house, who slept soundly because they were tired, and who would wake up tomorrow in truly festive mood. Many of them were long since married and had children. Somehow she alone was obliged to bury herself in these letters like an old woman, making notes on them, penning answers and then doing nothing the entire evening, right up to midnight, except wait until she felt sleepy. All next day people would be wishing her merry Christmas and asking for favours, and the day after that there was bound to be some trouble at the works – someone would be beaten up or someone would die from vodka and she would feel somehow conscience-stricken. After the holidays Nazarych would dismiss about twenty workers for absenteeism and all twenty would huddle together bare-headed at her front door. She would feel too ashamed to go out to them and they would be driven away like dogs. And everyone she knew would talk about it behind her back and send her anonymous letters, saying that she was a millionairess, an exploiter, that she was ruining people's lives and squeezing the last drop out of them.

Over there was a pile of letters that had been read and put to one side. They were appeals for money. The people here were hungry, drunken, burdened with large families, ill, humiliated, unrecognized. Anna had already specified on each letter that one man was to get three roubles, another five. These letters would be taken to the office today, where the dispensation of charity – 'feeding-time at the zoo' as the clerks called it – would take place.

They would also distribute, in fiddling amounts, four hundred and seventy roubles – this was the interest on the capital that her late father had left to the poor and needy. There would be nasty pushing and shoving. A queue, a long file of peculiar-looking people with animal-like faces, ragged, frozen stiff, hungry and already drunk, would stretch from the factory gates right down to the office. Hoarsely they would call out the name of their 'mother', their benefactress, Miss Anna Glagolev and her parents. Those at the rear would jostle the ones in front, those in front would swear at them. The clerk would grow tired of the noise, swearing and general wailing, leap out of his office and cuff someone's ear – much to everyone's enjoyment. But her own people – workers who had been paid their wages without any holiday bonus and had already spent the lot, down to the last copeck – would be standing in the middle of the yard looking and laughing, some enviously, others sarcastically.

'Industrialists, especially women, feel more for beggars than their own workers,' Anna thought. 'That's always the case.'

Her glance fell on the wad of money. It would be nice to hand out this unnecessary filthy lucre to the workers tomorrow, but one couldn't give them something for nothing, otherwise they would ask for more the next time. And what did those fifteen hundred roubles in fact amount to, since there were more than eighteen hundred workers at the factory, not counting wives and children? Perhaps she could pick out someone who had written a pleading letter, some miserable wretch who had long lost any hope of a better life, and give *him* the fifteen hundred roubles. The poor devil would be stunned by the money, as if he'd been struck by a thunderbolt, and perhaps would consider himself happy for the first time in his life. This thought appeared original, amusing and entertaining. She picked one letter at random from the pile and read it. Some clerk by the name of Chalikov, long jobless and ill, was living in Gushchin's house. His wife was consumptive and there were five young daughters. Anna was very familiar with that four-storey building belonging to Gushchin where Chalikov lived – and what an evil, rotten, unhealthy place it was!

'I'll give this Chalikov something,' she decided. 'But I'd better take it myself rather than send it, to avoid any unnecessary dramas.'

'Yes,' she reasoned, hiding the fifteen hundred roubles in her pocket, 'I'll go and have a look and perhaps fix the little girls up with something too.'

Cheered at this thought, she rang the bell and ordered the horses to be brought round.

It was after six in the evening when she got into her sledge. The windows in every factory block were brightly lit and this made the enormous yard seem very dark. Electric lamps glowed by the gates, in the remote part of the yard, near the storehouses and workers' huts.

Anna disliked and feared those dark, gloomy blocks, storehouses and workers' huts. Since her father died she had only once visited the main block. Those high ceilings with iron girders, dozens of huge, rapidly turning wheels, drive-belts and levers, the piercing hiss, the screech of steel, clattering trolleys, the harsh breath of steam; faces that were pale, crimson, or black with coal dust, shirts wet with sweat; the glitter of steel, copper and fire; the smell of coal and oil; the wind that was scorching and cold in turn – all this made the place seem like hell to her. She thought that the wheels, levers and hot, hissing cylinders were trying to break loose from their couplings and destroy people, while anxious-looking men ran around without hearing each other, fussing with the machinery in an attempt to bring its terrible movements to a halt. They showed Anna some object which they respectfully explained. She remembered a piece of white-hot iron being drawn out of the furnace in the forge shop; how an old man with a strap round his head and another – younger, in a dark-blue blouse with a chain on his chest, angry-faced and probably a foreman – struck a piece of iron with hammers, making golden sparks fly in all directions; and how, a little later, they had rolled an enormous piece of sheet iron in front of her with a sound like thunder. The old man stood to attention and smiled, while the younger one wiped his wet face on his sleeve and explained something to her. And she could still remember a one-eyed old man in another section scattering filings as he sawed the piece of iron, and a red-haired workman in dark glasses and with holes in his shirt working away at the lathe making something from a piece of steel. The lathe roared and screeched and whistled, and all this noise made Anna feel sick and as if something were boring into her ears. She looked and listened without understanding, smiled graciously and felt ashamed. To earn one's living and receive thousands of roubles from a business one didn't understand and which one couldn't bring oneself to like – how strange this was!

Not once had she visited the workers' blocks, where there was said to be damp, bedbugs, debauchery, lawlessness. Amazingly, thousands were spent every year on their upkeep, but if the anonymous letters were to be believed, the workers' lot deteriorated with every year that passed.

'Things were better organized when Father was alive,' Anna thought as she drove out of the yard, 'because he was a factory worker himself and he knew what had to be done. But I know nothing and only do stupid things.'

Again she felt bored and no longer pleased at having

made the journey. The thought of that lucky man, suddenly to be showered with fifteen hundred roubles like manna from heaven, did not seem original or amusing any more. Going to see this Chalikov while a million-rouble business at home gradually declined and fell apart, while the workers lived worse than convicts in their blocks – that was a stupid act and it meant she was trying to cheat her conscience. Workers from the neighbouring cotton and paper mills were crowding along the high road and across the nearby fields on their way to the lights in town. Laughter and cheerful conversation rang out in the frosty air. As she looked at the women and young ones, Anna suddenly yearned for simplicity, roughness, overcrowding. She vividly pictured those far-off times when she was a little girl called Annie, sharing her mother's blanket, while their lodger – a laundress – worked away in the next room. From the adjoining flats she could hear laughter, swearing, children crying, an accordion, the buzzing of lathes and sewing-machines which penetrated the thin walls, while Akim, her father and jack-of-all-trades, did some soldering at the stove or drew plans, or worked with his plane oblivious of the cramped conditions and the noise. And now she had a strong urge to wash and iron, to run back and forwards to shop and pub as she had done every day when she lived with her mother. Rather be a worker than a factory owner! Her large house with its chandeliers and paintings, her footman Misha with his coat and tails, and small, velvety moustache, the grand Barbara, the toadying Agafya, the young people of both sexes who came almost every day to beg for money and with whom she always felt somewhat guilty, those civil servants, doctors, ladies dispensing charity on her behalf, flattering her and at the same time despising her humble origin – how boring and alien all this was!

She came to the level-crossing and barrier. Houses alternated with vegetable gardens. Here at last was the broad street where Gushchin's celebrated house stood. The normally quiet street was very busy, as it was Christmas Eve. A great deal of noise came from the pubs and bars. If some stranger to the district, someone from the middle of the town, had driven down the street, then he would have seen only filthy, drunken, foul-mouthed people. But Anna, who had lived in the district from childhood, imagined she could see her late father, then her mother, then her uncle in the crowd. Her father had been a gentle, vague soul, something of a dreamer, carefree and light-headed. He had no liking for money, position or power. He often used to say that working men had no time to think of holidays or going to church. But for his wife, he might never have observed the Fasts and would have eaten meat during Lent. In contrast, her Uncle Ivan had been a man of steel. In everything that was connected with religion, politics or morals he had been strict and unbending, and made sure that not only he himself practised what he preached, but the servants and his acquaintances too. Heaven help anyone coming into his room without making the sign of the cross. He kept the luxurious apartment where Anna now lived under lock and key, opening it only on special holidays, for important guests, while he himself lived in that poky little icon-filled room which was his office. He believed in the Old Creed, always entertaining bishops and priests who believed as he did, although he had been christened and married and had buried his wife according to the rites of the Orthodox Church. He did not like his brother Akim – his sole heir – for his frivolous attitude, calling it simple-minded and stupid, and for his indifference to religion. He had treated him badly, just like a workman, paying him sixteen roubles a month. Akim would speak to his brother most respectfully, and at Shrovetide went with his whole family to prostrate himself before him. But three years before he died Ivan relented, forgave him and told him to engage a governess for Anna.

The gates to Gushchin's house were dark, deep, and had a terrible stench about them. Men could be heard coughing near the walls. Leaving her sledge in the street, Anna entered the yard, where she asked the way to flat No. 46, where Chalikov the clerk lived. She was directed to the last door on the right, on the second floor. In the yard, and near the last door, even on the staircase, there was the same terrible smell as at the gates. In her childhood, when her father was a simple workman, Anna had lived in similar houses. Then, when her circumstances changed, she often visited them as a charity worker. The filthy narrow stone staircase with a landing on each floor, the greasy lamp in the stair-well, the stench, the slop-basins, pots, rags outside doors on the landings – all this she was long familiar with. One door was open and she could see Jewish tailors, wearing caps, sitting on top of tables and sewing. She met people on the stairs, but she did not think for one moment that they could do her any harm. She feared workmen and peasants, whether drunk or sober, as little as her own cultivated friends.

Flat No. 46 had no hall and opened straight into the kitchen. Factory workers' and craftsmen's flats usually smell of varnish, tar, leather or smoke, depending on the occupant's trade. But flats belonging to impoverished gentlefolk and clerks can be recognized by their dank, rather acrid smell. Hardly had Anna crossed the threshold than she was enveloped in this revolting stench. A man in a frock-coat was sitting at a table in one corner, his back to the door – most probably Chalikov himself. With him were five little girls. The eldest, broad-faced and thin, with a comb in her hair, looked about fifteen, while the youngest was a plump little girl with hair like a hedgehog and not more than three. All six were eating. Near the stove, with an oven-fork in her hands, stood a small, very thin, sallow-faced woman in a skirt and white blouse. She was pregnant.

'I didn't expect such disobedience from you, Liza,' the man said reproachfully. 'It's a disgrace! Would you like Daddy to give you a good hiding? Yes?'

When she saw a strange lady on the threshold, the thin woman shuddered and put down her oven-fork.

'Vasily!' she called out in a hollow voice, after a moment's hesitation – as though she could not believe her eyes.

The man looked round and jumped up. He was a bony, narrow-shouldered person with sunken temples and a flat chest. His eyes were small, deep-set, with dark rings round them; his nose was long, bird-like and slightly twisted to the right; his mouth was wide and his forked beard and clean-shaven upper lip made him look more like a footman than a clerk.

'Does Mr Chalikov live here?' Anna asked.

'That's right, lady,' Chalikov replied gruffly, but then he recognized Anna and cried out 'Miss Glagolev! Miss Anna!', and suddenly he gasped for breath and threw his arms up as if scared out of his wits. 'Our saviour!'

Groaning and mumbling like a paralytic as he ran over to her (there was cabbage on his beard and he smelt of vodka), he laid his forehead on her muff and seemed to lose consciousness.

'Your hand, your divine hand!' he gasped. 'It's a dream, a beautiful dream! Children, wake me up!'

He turned towards the table and waved his fists.

'Providence has heard our prayers!' he sobbed. 'Our rescuer, our angel has come! We're saved! Children, on your knees! On your knees!'

For some reason Mrs Chalikov and the girls – with the exception of the youngest – began hurriedly clearing the table.

'You wrote that your wife was very ill,' Anna said, and she felt ashamed and annoyed. 'I won't give him that fifteen hundred,' she thought.

'That's her, that's my wife!' Chalikov said in a shrill, woman's voice, and he seemed about to burst into tears. 'There she is, the poor woman, with one foot in the grave! But we're not complaining, ma'am. Death is better than a life like that. Die, you miserable woman!'

'Why is he putting on such an act?' Anna wondered indignantly. 'I can see right away that he's used to dealing with rich people.'

'Please talk to me properly, I don't like play-acting,' she said.

'Yes, ma'am. Five orphans round their mother's coffin, with the funeral candles burning! You call *that* play-acting! Oh, God!' Chalikov said bitterly and turned away.

'Shut up!' his wife whispered, tugging him by the sleeve. 'It's a terrible mess here, ma'am,' she said to Anna. 'Please forgive us. Please understand . . . it's a family matter. It's so overcrowded, but we mean no offence.'

'I won't give them the fifteen hundred,' Anna thought again.

To make a quick escape from these people and that acrid smell, she took out her purse and decided to leave them twenty-five roubles — and no more. But suddenly she felt ashamed of having travelled so far and having troubled these people for nothing.

'If you like to give me some paper and ink I'll write straight away to a doctor, a very good friend of mine, and tell him to call,' she said, blushing. 'He's a very good doctor. And I'll leave you some money for medicine.'

Mrs Chalikov hurriedly began wiping the table down.

'It's filthy in here! What are you doing?' Chalikov hissed, giving her a vicious look. 'Take her to the lodger's room. Please, ma'am, go into the lodger's room, if you don't mind,' he said, turning to Anna. 'It's clean there.'

'Mr Osip says no one's to go into his room!' one of the little girls said sternly.

But Anna had already been led out of the kitchen, through a narrow, intercommunicating room, between two beds. From the position of these beds she could tell that two people slept lengthways on one of them and three crossways on the other. The next room, where the lodger lived, really was clean. There was a tidy bed with a red woollen cover, a pillow in a white case, even a special little holder for a watch. There was a table covered with a linen cloth, and on this stood a milky-white inkpot, pens, paper, framed photographs — all neatly arranged. And there was another table, which was black, with watchmaker's instruments and dismantled watches neatly laid out on it. On the walls hung little hammers, pincers, gimlets, chisels, pliers and so on. And there were three wall clocks, all ticking away. One of them was quite huge, with the kind of fat pendulum weights you see in taverns.

As she started on the letter, Anna saw a portrait of her father, and one of herself, on the table in front of her, which surprised her.

'Who lives here?' she asked.

'The lodger, ma'am. Pimenov works at your factory.'

'Really? I thought a watchmaker must be living here.'

'He repairs watches privately, in his spare time. It's his hobby, ma'am.'

After a brief silence, during which only the ticking of the clocks and the scraping of pen on paper could be heard, Chalikov sighed and said in a disgruntled, sarcastic voice, 'There's no getting away from it, you can't make much money from being a gentleman or office clerk. You can wear decorations on your chest, you can have a title, but you'll still starve. If you ask me, if some ordinary man from the lower classes helps the poor, he's much more of a gentleman than some Chalikov who's bogged down in poverty and vice.'

To flatter Anna he produced a few more sentences that were derogatory to his own social position, and he was obviously trying to lower himself, since he considered he was her superior. Meanwhile she had finished the letter and sealed it. The letter would be thrown away, the money would not be spent on medicine – all this she knew and yet she still put twenty-five roubles on the table, adding two ten-rouble notes after further reflection. Mrs Chalikov's gaunt yellow hand flashed before her like a hen's claw, crumpling the money.

'You've been kind enough to give us money for medicine,' Chalikov said in a trembling voice. 'But please lend me a helping hand – and my children as well,' he added, sobbing. 'My poor, poor children! I don't fear for myself, but for my daughters. I fear the Hydra of corruption!'

As she tried to open her purse with its jammed lock, Anna grew flushed with embarrassment. She felt ashamed that people were standing there before her, looking at her hands, waiting, and most probably silently laughing at her. Just then someone entered the kitchen and stamped his feet to shake the snow off.

'The lodger's back,' Mrs Chalikov said.

Anna grew even more embarrassed. She did not want any of the factory workers to find her in that ridiculous situation. And then, at the worst possible moment, the lodger came into his room – just as she had finally managed to break the lock open and was handing Chalikov some banknotes, while that same Chalikov bellowed like a paralytic and moved his lips as if looking for somewhere to kiss her. She recognized the lodger as that workman who had once made an iron sheet clatter in front of her in the foundry and had explained things to her. Clearly, he had come straight from the works, as his face was smudged with soot. His hands were completely black and his unbelted shirt gleamed with greasy dirt. He was a broad-shouldered man, about thirty, of medium height, with black hair and he was obviously very strong. Anna immediately recognized that foreman whose wages were not less than thirty-five roubles a month. He was a harsh, loud-mouthed man who knocked workmen's teeth out – that was plain from the way he stood, from the pose he suddenly, instinctively, assumed when he saw a lady in his room, but chiefly from his habit of wearing his trousers outside his boots, from the pockets on the front of his shirt, from his sharp, beautifully trimmed beard. Although her late father Akim had been the owner's brother, he had been scared of foremen like this lodger and tried to keep in their good books.

'Excuse me, we seem to have set up house here while you were out,' Anna said.

The workman gave her a surprised look, smiled awkwardly, but did not say a word.

'Please speak a bit louder, ma'am,' Chalikov said softly. 'When he comes home of an evening Mr Pimenov's a bit hard of hearing.'

But Anna, pleased now that there was nothing more to do there, nodded and left quickly. Pimenov saw her out.

'Have you been working for us long?' she asked in a loud voice, without looking at him.

'Since I was nine. I got my job in your uncle's time.'

'That was ages ago! My uncle and father knew all the workers, but I know hardly any of them. I've seen you before, but I didn't know that your name is Pimenov.'

Anna felt that she should defend herself by pretending she hadn't been serious just before, when she gave the money away – that it was only a joke.

'Oh, this poverty!' she sighed. 'We do good deeds every single day, but it makes no sense. I think it's pointless trying to help people like Chalikov.'

'How right you are,' Pimenov agreed. 'Everything you give him will go on drink. And now that husband and wife will spend the whole night squabbling and trying to take the money away from each other,' he added, laughing.

'Yes, our acts of charity are useless, tiresome and ludicrous, I must admit. However, one can't just give up the struggle; something has to be done. Now, what can be done about those Chalikovs?'

She turned to Pimenov and stopped, waiting for his answer. He stopped too and slowly shrugged his shoulders without saying a word. Evidently he knew what should be done about the Chalikovs, but this was so crude and inhuman that he could not bring himself to mention it. For him, the Chalikovs were so boring and mediocre that a moment later he had forgotten all about them. As he looked into Anna's eyes he smiled with pleasure, like someone having a wonderful dream. Only now as she stood close to him could Anna tell from his face, particularly his eyes, how exhausted and sleepy he was.

'I should give *him* the fifteen hundred!' she thought, but the idea struck her as rather absurd, and insulting to Pimenov.

'You must be aching all over from that work, but it doesn't stop you seeing me out,' she said, going downstairs. 'Please go back.'

But he did not hear. When they came out into the street he ran on ahead, unbuttoned the sledge cover and said 'Happy Christmas!' to Anna as he helped her into her seat.

II

MORNING

'The bells stopped ringing *ages* ago! There'll be no one left in church by the time you get there! Heaven help us! Please get up!'

'Two horses running, running . . .' Anna said as she woke up. Masha, her red-haired maid, was standing before her with a candle. 'What's the matter? What do you want?'

'The service is over already!' Masha said despairingly. 'It's the third time I've tried to wake you! I don't care if you sleep till evening, but you yourself asked me to wake you.'

Anna raised herself on her elbow and looked out of the window. Outside it was still quite dark, apart from the lower edge of the window frame that was white with snow. The rich, deep ringing of bells could be heard, but it came from a parish church some distance away. The clock on the small table showed three minutes past six.

'All right, Masha . . . Just two minutes,' Anna pleaded, covering her head with the blanket.

She pictured the snow by the porch, the sledge, the dark sky, the crowded church and the smell of juniper, but despite the misgivings this filled her with she decided to get up right away and go to early service. The whole time she lay there in her warm bed, struggling against sleep – sleep is so sweet when one *has* to get up – and conjuring up visions of a huge garden on a hill, Gushchin's house, there was the nagging thought that she should get up immediately and go to church.

But when she did get up it was quite light and the clock showed half past nine. During the night a great deal of fresh snow had piled up, the trees were clothed in white and the air was unusually bright, clear and serene, so that when Anna looked through the window she wanted first to take a very deep breath. But as she was washing herself, a vestige of the joy she had felt as a child on Christmas Day stirred within her – and then she felt easier, free and pure at heart, as if her soul itself had been cleansed or dipped in white snow. In came Masha, in her best clothes and tightly corseted, and wished her happy Christmas, after which she spent a long time combing her hair and helping her to dress. The smell and feel of that beautiful, magnificent new dress, with its rustle, and the smell of fresh perfume all excited Anna.

'So, it's Christmas,' she gaily told Masha. 'Now let's do some fortune-telling.'

'Last year it came out that I would marry an old man. Three times it came out like that, it did.'

'Don't worry, God is merciful.'

'I'm not so sure, ma'am. As I see it, I'd be better off married to an old man than running around getting no-where,' Masha sighed sadly. 'I'm past twenty now and that's no joke.'

Everyone in the house knew that red-haired Masha was in love with Misha the butler and that this deep, but hopeless passion had lasted for three years now.

'Don't talk such nonsense,' Anna said consolingly. 'I'll soon be thirty, but I still intend marrying someone young.'

While the mistress of the house was dressing, Misha — in his new tail-coat and lacquered boots — paced the ballroom waiting for her to come out so that he could wish her happy Christmas.

He had his own peculiar manner of walking, and treading softly and delicately. If you watched his legs, arms and the angle of his head you might have thought that he wasn't just walking, but practising the first figure of the quadrille. Despite his fine, velvety moustache and his handsome, even rather roguish exterior, he was as staid, sober-minded and pious as an old man. He always prostrated himself when praying and he loved burning incense in his room. He respected and revered the rich and influential, but he despised the poor and any kind of humble petitioner with the whole might of his 'holier-than-thou' flunkey's soul. Under his starched shirt was a flannel vest which he wore winter and summer — he attached great importance to his health. His ears were stuffed with cotton-wool.

When Anna and Masha came across the ballroom, he leaned his head downwards, slightly to one side, and said in a pleasant, sugary voice, 'I have the honour, ma'am, to offer my compliments on the solemn occasion of Jesus Christ's nativity.'

Anna gave him five roubles and poor Masha was stunned. His festive appearance, his pose, his voice and what he said astounded her with their elegance and beauty. As she followed her mistress she had no thoughts, saw nothing, smiling first blissfully and then bitterly.

The upper storey was called 'the best rooms' or 'the apartment', whereas the lower floor, where Aunt Tatyana held sway, was called the 'tradesmen's', 'old people's' or simply the 'women's quarters'. In the best rooms they usually received upper-class, educated people, and in the downstairs section ordinary people and Auntie's personal friends. Beautiful, buxom, healthy, still young and fresh, and highly conscious of her magnificent dress, which, she felt, was radiating light in all directions, Anna went down to the lower floor.

There she was greeted with reproaches: an educated person like her had forgotten God, had missed morning service by oversleeping and had not come down to break her fast. All clasped their hands and assured her most sincerely that she was exceptionally pretty. She took them at their word and laughed, kissed them and gave them one, three or five roubles each, depending on the person. She liked it downstairs. Wherever she looked there were icon-cases, icons, icon-lamps, portraits of church dignitaries. It smelt of monks. Knives clattered in the kitchen and a rich, very savoury smell spread everywhere. The yellow stained floors shone and narrow rugs with bright blue stripes stretched like little paths from the doors to the corners where the icons were. The sun blazed through the windows.

Some old women – strangers – were sitting in the dining-room. In Barbara's room there were old women as well, together with a deaf and dumb girl who appeared very shy and who kept making a mumbling sound. Two skinny little girls who had been asked over from the orphanage for the holidays came up to kiss Anna's hand but stopped, dumb-founded by the richness of her dress. She noticed that one of the girls was a little cross-eyed, and although she was in a relaxed, holiday mood, her heart suddenly sank at the thought that the girl would be ignored by the young men and would never marry. Five huge peasants in new shirts — not factory workers but relatives of the kitchen servants — were sitting over the samovar in Agafya the cook's room. As soon as they saw Anna the peasants jumped up and stopped chewing, out of politeness, although all had a full mouth. Stefan her chef, in white hat and knife in hand, came out from the kitchen to wish them merry Christmas. House porters in felt boots arrived and offered their good wishes too. A water-carrier with icicles on his beard showed his face but dared not enter.

Anna walked through all the rooms, the whole assembly following her: Auntie, Barbara, Nikandrovna, Martha the seamstress, and 'downstairs Masha'. Slim and slender, taller than anyone else in the house, dressed all in black and smell-ing of cypress-wood and coffee, Barbara crossed herself and bowed before the icon in every room. Each time you looked at her you were somehow reminded that she had prepared her own shroud for the day she died, and that in the same trunk where she kept this shroud she had hidden her lottery tickets.

'Come on, Anna dear, show some Christmas spirit!' she said, opening the kitchen door. 'Forgive that miserable wretch! What a crowd!'

Panteley the coachman, who had been dismissed for drun-kenness in November, was on his knees in the middle of the kitchen. A kind man, he was liable to become violent when drunk. Then he just couldn't sleep and he marched round the factory blocks shouting menacingly 'I know everything!' From his bloated lips, puffy face and bloodshot eyes it was plain that he had been on the bottle non-stop since November.

'Please forgive me, Miss Anna!' he said hoarsely, banging his forehead on the floor and revealing a neck like a bull's.

'It was my aunt who dismissed you, so go and ask *her*.'

'Did you say "aunt"?' asked Auntie as she came puffing and panting into the kitchen. She was so fat one could have put a samovar and tray of cups on her chest. 'What's all this about your aunt? You're mistress here, so you see to it. I'd rather these ruffians cleared out of here altogether. Come on, get up, you great pig!' she shouted, losing patience. 'Out of my sight! I'll forgive you this one last time, but if it happens again don't expect any mercy.'

They went into the dining-room for coffee. People could be heard blowing their noses and there was a low, deep coughing and a sound of footsteps as if newly shod horses were being led into the ante-room near the ballroom. All was quiet for about half a minute, then suddenly the carol-singers shrieked so loud that everyone jumped. While they sang, the almshouse priest arrived with the deacon and lay-reader. As he put on his stole the priest slowly declared that 'it had snowed during the night when the bells were ringing for early morning service', that 'it hadn't been cold but towards morning the frost began to harden, confound it, and it was twenty below, in all likelihood'.

'Many people, however, maintain that winter is healthier than summer,' the deacon said, but he immediately assumed a serious expression and followed the priest in singing 'Thy Nativity, Oh, Christ Our Lord'.

Shortly after, the priest from the factory sick-bay arrived, then nurses from the community hospital and children from the orphanage. The singing went on almost non-stop. They sang, they ate, they left.

About twenty of the works staff came to offer their compliments of the season. They were all senior men – engineers, their assistants, pattern-makers, the accountant and so on. All looked eminently respectable in their new black frock-coats and they were all fine men, the select few, and each knew his worth. If any one of them were to lose his job that day, another factory would be only too pleased to take him on tomorrow. They seemed to take a great liking to Anna's aunt, since they were relaxed with her and even smoked, while the accountant put his arm around her ample waist as they all crowded over to the food. Perhaps they felt so free and easy because Barbara, who had wielded great power in the old man's day and had been custodian of the servants' morals, now had no authority at all in the house. Perhaps another reason was that many of them still remembered the time when Aunt Tatyana, who was kept on a tight rein by her brothers, had dressed like a simple peasant, in the same style as Agafya, and when even Miss Anna had run round the yard near the factory blocks and everyone had called her Annie.

The factory staff ate their food, talked and glanced at Miss Anna in bewilderment. How she had grown up, how pretty she had become! But this elegant girl, brought up by governesses and tutors, was a stranger to them, a mystery, and they could not help staying close to the aunt, who spoke to them as though they were on her level, constantly urged them to eat and drink and clinked glasses with them, having already drunk two glasses of rowanberry vodka. Anna had always feared that they might think she was vain, an upstart, a crow in peacock's feathers. And now, as the staff crowded around the food, she stayed in the dining-room, where she took part in the conversation. She asked Pimenov, whom she had met the day before, 'Why are there so many clocks in your room?'

'I repair them,' he replied. 'It's something I do in my spare time, during holidays, or when I can't sleep.'

'So, if my watch goes wrong I can ask you to repair it?' Anna asked, laughing.

'Of course, that would give me great pleasure,' Pimenov said, and he seemed deeply touched when, without knowing why, she unhooked her magnificent watch from her corsage and handed it to him. Silently he inspected it. 'Why, yes, with pleasure,' he repeated. 'I don't usually repair pocket watches nowadays. My eyes are bad and the doctor advised me not to do any close work. But for you I'll make an exception.'

'Doctors are liars,' the accountant said. Everyone burst

out laughing. 'Don't you believe what they say,' he continued, flattered by the laughter. 'Last year, during Lent, a cog-wheel flew out of a drum and hit old Kalmykov right on the head; you could see his brains. The doctor said he would die, but he's still alive and working, only he talks with a stutter after what happened.'

'Doctors *can* talk rubbish, I do agree, but not that much,' Auntie sighed. 'Peter Andreyevich, God rest his soul, lost his sight. Like you, he worked all day in the factory near a hot furnace and he went blind. Heat damages the eyes. Well, what's the use of talking?' She gave a start. 'Let's have a drink! Merry Christmas, my dears! I don't usually drink, but I'll have one with you, God forgive me! Cheers!'

After what had happened yesterday, Anna felt that Pimenov despised her as a 'do-gooder', but that, as a woman, she enchanted him. She glanced at him and it seemed he was behaving very nicely and was properly dressed for the occasion. True, his coat sleeves were rather short, the waist was too high and the trousers not broad, according to the latest style. On the other hand his tie was knotted with tasteful neglect and it wasn't as loud as the others'. And he clearly was a good-natured man, for he obediently ate everything that Auntie put on his plate. She remembered how black he had looked the day before, how much he had wanted to sleep, and for some reason the memory of it moved her.

When the staff were ready to leave, Anna offered Pimenov her hand and wanted to ask him to visit her some time, but her tongue would not obey her and she could not produce one word. In case his workmates thought she had taken a fancy to Pimenov, she offered them her hand as well.

Then the boys arrived from the school of which she was a governor. All of them had short hair and all were dressed in identical grey smocks. Their master, a tall young man, without a moustache and his face covered in red blotches, obviously felt nervous and made his pupils stand in rows. The boys began to sing in harmony, but their voices were harsh and unpleasant. Nazarych, the works manager, a bald, eagle-eyed believer in the Old Creed, had never got on with the schoolmasters, but he really hated and despised this teacher, who was fussily giving directions with his arm. Why this was so, he himself couldn't say. He treated him arrogantly and rudely, withheld his wages, interfered with the teaching. In an effort to get rid of him for good, he had appointed a distant relative of his own wife as school care-taker – a drunken peasant who disobeyed the schoolmaster in front of the boys.

Anna knew all about this, but she was unable to help, as she herself was scared of Nazarych. Now she wanted at least to be kind to the schoolmaster and tell him that she was very satisfied with him. But when the singing was over and he embarked on a highly embarrassed apology for some-thing, and after Auntie had spoken to him like a little boy and unceremoniously bundled him over to the table, she felt bored and awkward. After leaving instructions for the children to receive their presents she went upstairs to her own part of the house.

'There's really a great deal of cruelty about these festivities,' she said aloud to herself a little later as she looked through the window at the crowd of boys on their way from the house to the gates, shrinking from the cold and putting their furs and coats on as they went. 'On holidays all one wants is some rest, to be at home with the family, but those poor boys, that schoolmaster, the staff – for some reason they're obliged to go out into the freezing cold to wish you merry Christmas and convey their respects. They feel awkward . . .'

Misha, who was standing just by the ballroom doors, heard this. 'We didn't start it,' he said, 'and it won't finish with us. Of course, I'm not an educated man, Miss Anna, but as I see it the poor always have to pay their respects to those what's rich. They say God puts his mark on rogues. You'll only find poor folk in prisons, doss-houses, pubs, but respectable folk are always the rich ones, you see. Money comes to money, that's what they say about the rich.'

'Misha, you always talk such boring stuff that it's impossible to understand you,' Anna said and went to the far end of the ballroom.

It was only just twelve o'clock. The silence of those huge rooms, broken only now and then by the sound of singing that drifted up from the ground floor, made one feel like yawning. The bronzes, the albums, the paintings on the walls depicting an ocean scene with small ships, a meadow with cows, views of the Rhine, were really so dull, one's eyes swiftly glided over them without seeing a thing. The holiday mood had already begun to pall. Anna still considered herself as beautiful, kind and exceptional as before, but she felt these virtues were useless to anyone. It seemed that there had been no point at all in wearing that expensive dress. Whom did she want to please? And as usually happened on every holiday, she began to tire of the loneliness and was unsettled by the nagging thought that her beauty, health and wealth were nothing but an illusion, since she was a superfluous sort of person, unwanted, unloved by anyone. She walked through all her rooms, humming and looking through the windows. Stopping in the hall she could not help starting a conversation with Misha.

'I really don't know, Misha, who you think you are,' she sighed. 'God will surely punish you for this.'

'What do you mean, ma'am?'

'You know very well. Forgive me for interfering with your personal affairs, but I have the impression you're ruining your life out of sheer obstinacy. Don't you agree it's the right time for you to marry now, she's such a beautiful, deserving girl? You won't find a better. She's beautiful, clever, gentle, devoted . . . And as for her looks! If she were one of our circle, or in high society, everyone would love her for her wonderful red hair alone. Just look how her hair suits her complexion! God, you understand nothing and don't know yourself what you want,' Anna said bitterly, the tears welling up in her eyes. 'That poor girl. I feel so sorry for her! I know you're looking for someone with money, but I've already told you that I'll give Masha a dowry.'

Misha imagined that his future wife could only be someone tall, buxom, well-shaped and religious, with a walk like a peacock's and never without a long shawl on her shoulders. But Masha was thin, delicate, tightly corseted and with an unpretentious walk. Most important, she was too seductive and at times Misha did feel strongly attracted to her. However, according to him, that kind of thing was only conducive to loose behaviour, not marriage. He had hesitated a little when Anna promised a dowry. But then some poor student with a brown coat over his tunic had arrived with a letter for Anna and had been so enraptured with Masha that he couldn't control himself and had embraced her near the coat hooks downstairs. She had given a faint cry. Misha saw what happened from the staircase above and ever since had felt aversion for her. A poor student! Who knows, things might have turned out quite differently if some rich student or officer had embraced her instead . . .

'Why don't you marry her?' Anna asked. 'What more do you want?'

Misha did not answer and stood quite still staring at an armchair, eyebrows raised.

'Do you love someone else?'

Silence. In came red-haired Masha with some letters and visiting cards on a tray. She guessed that they were talking about her and blushed until the tears came.

'The postmen are here,' she muttered. 'And there's a clerk called Chalikov, he's waiting downstairs. Says you told him to come here today for something.'

'What impertinence!' Anna said furiously. 'I told him nothing of the sort! Tell him to clear off, I'm not at home!'

The door-bell rang: the priests from her own parish had arrived. They were always received in the best part of the house – and that was upstairs. They were followed by Nazarych the works manager and the factory doctor. Then Misha announced the inspector of secondary schools. The reception had begun.

Whenever she had a free moment, Anna would sit deep in an armchair in the drawing-room, close her eyes and conclude that her loneliness was something quite natural, since she had not married and never would. But this wasn't her fault. Fate itself had taken her from an ordinary working-class background (where, if her memory was to be trusted, she felt so comfortable and at home) and thrown her into these vast rooms where she never knew what to do with herself. Nor could she understand why so many people were dashing in and out. The present events struck her as of no consequence, fruitless, since they had never brought her a moment's happiness and they never could.

'If only I could fall in love,' she thought, stretching herself, and this thought alone warmed her heart. 'And if I could get rid of that factory,' she brooded, imagining all those ponderous blocks, those barracks, that school, being eased from her conscience. Then she remembered her father and thought that had he lived longer he would surely have married her to some ordinary man, like Pimenov, and that would have been that. It would have been a good thing, as the factory would have fallen into the right hands.

She pictured his curly hair, the bold profile, those fine, mocking lips, the strength – the terrible strength – of his shoulders, arms and chest, and how moved he had been when he inspected her watch earlier in the day. 'Why not?' she said. 'I can't see anything against it. Yes, I'd marry him.'

'Miss Anna!' Misha called as he noiselessly entered the drawing-room.

'What a fright you gave me!' she said, trembling all over. 'What do you want?'

'Miss Anna,' he repeated, putting his hand to his heart and raising his eyebrows. 'You are the lady of the house, my benefactress, and you alone can tell me whom to marry, as you're like a mother to me. But please tell them to stop teasing me, laughing at me downstairs. They don't give me a moment's peace!'

'And how do they tease you?'

'They keep calling me Masha's Misha!'

'Ugh, what rubbish!' Anna said, getting angry. 'What a stupid lot you all are! You included, Misha. I'm sick and tired of you and I don't want to see you!'

III

DINNER

Like the previous year, the last guests to come were state councillor Krylin and Lysevich, the well-known lawyer. When they arrived it was quite dark already. Krylin, in his sixties, had a wide mouth, grey mutton-chop whiskers and the face of a lynx. He wore the ribbon of St Anna on his uniform, and white trousers.

He held Anna's hand for a long time in both of his, staring into her face and moving his lips. Finally he said in a slow, deliberate voice pitched on one note, 'I respected your uncle . . . and your father, and they were well-disposed towards me. Now, as you can see, I consider it my pleasant duty to convey seasonal greetings to their respected heiress, despite my being ill and having to travel so far. And I'm delighted to see you looking so well.'

Lysevich the barrister, a tall, handsome fair-haired man, with slightly greying temples and beard, was celebrated for his exceptionally refined manners. He would dance into the room, make an apparently reluctant bow, twitch his shoulders as he spoke, all this being executed with the lazy grace of a spoilt horse grown idle from standing about. He was well-fed, extremely healthy and rich. Once he won as much as forty thousand roubles, but didn't breathe a word about it to his friends. He loved eating well, especially cheese, truffles, grated radish with hempseed oil, and he maintained he had eaten fried, uncleaned giblets in Paris. He spoke articulately, smoothly, never hesitating, and only rarely allowed himself a simpering pause or click of the fingers, as if indicating he was at a loss for the *mot juste*. He had long stopped believing anything he was called upon to say in court: perhaps he did believe what he said, but attached no importance to it: it was all such old hat, so trivial. He believed only in the esoteric, the unusual. Copy-book ethics, expressed in an original form, reduced him to tears. His two notebooks were crammed with unusual sayings culled from various authors, and whenever he felt in need of some expression, he would nervously rummage in both books, usually failing to find what he wanted. Once old Akim, in a moment of euphoria and wanting to go one better than his competitors, had engaged him as lawyer at the works, at a fixed salary of twelve thousand. But the only legal matters that cropped up there were a few minor cases that Lysevich delegated to his assistants.

Anna knew that there was no work for him at the factory, but could not bring herself to dismiss him – she did not have the courage, and, what was more, had grown used to him. He termed himself her 'legal adviser', calling his salary – which he sent for every first day of the month, on the dot – that 'mundane affair'. Anna knew that after her father died and the forest was sold for timber to make railway sleepers, Lysevich had made more than fifteen thousand from the sale and split it with Nazarych. When she found out about the swindle she wept bitterly but then accepted the fact.

After wishing her happy Christmas and kissing both her hands, Lysevich looked her up and down and frowned.

'There's no need for it,' he said with genuine distress. 'I said, my dear, that there's no need for it!'

'What are you talking about, Victor?'

'What I said was, you shouldn't put on weight. Your whole family has this unfortunate tendency. There's no need for it,' he pleaded again and kissed her hand. 'You're such a good person! You're so wonderful!' He turned to Krylin and said 'My dear sir, I can recommend the only woman in this world I ever loved seriously.'

'That doesn't surprise me. At your age, to know Anna and not to love her is impossible.'

'I adore her!' the lawyer continued with complete sincerity, but with his usual lazy gracefulness. 'I love her – not because I'm a man and she's a woman. When I'm with her I feel as if she is some third kind of sex, and myself a fourth,

74

and we seem to be whirling away into the realm of the most delicate hues, where we blend into one spectrum. Leconte de Lisle is best at defining such relationships. He has a wonderful passage, somewhere, it's really amazing.'

Lysevich rummaged first in one book, then the other. Not managing to find the passage, he grew quiet. They began discussing the weather, the opera, Duse's* imminent arrival. Anna remembered that Lysevich and (so she thought) Krylin had dined with her the previous Christmas. Now, as they prepared to leave, she urged them in the most genuinely pleading voice to stay for dinner, arguing that they had no more visits to make. After a moment's hesitation they agreed.

Besides the usual dinner, consisting of cabbage soup, roast sucking-pig, goose with apples and so on, a French or 'chef's special' dinner was prepared in the kitchen on major holidays, in case any of the upstairs guests felt like indulging themselves. When the clatter of crockery came from the dining-room, Lysevich began to show visible excitement. He rubbed his hands, twitched his shoulders, screwed up his eyes and talked with great feeling about the dinners the old men used to give and the superb turbot *matelote* the present chef could produce – more a divine revelation than a *matelote*! He was so looking forward to the dinner, mentally relishing and savouring it in advance. When Anna took his arm and led him into the dining-room and he had drunk his glass of vodka and popped a tiny slice of salmon into his mouth, he even purred with pleasure. He chewed noisily and disgustingly, making curious sounds through his nose, while his eyes became oily and greedy.

It was a sumptuous *hors-d'œuvre*. Among other things there were fresh white mushrooms in sour cream and *sauce provençale* made with fried oysters and crayfish tails well flavoured with sour pickles. The main meal consisted of delicately refined dishes with a festive flavour, and the wines were excellent. Misha served like someone in a trance. Whenever he placed a fresh dish on the table and removed

* Italian actress (1859–1924).

the lid from a glittering tureen, or poured out wine, he performed it with the solemnity of a professor of black magic. From his expression and the way he walked, he seemed to be executing the first figure of a quadrille, and the lawyer thought to himself several times 'What an idiot!'

After the third course Lysevich turned to Anna,

'A *fin de siècle* woman – I mean young and rich, of course – must be independent, clever, refined, intelligent, bold and rather corrupt. I say *rather* corrupt, just a little bit, since, as you'll agree, anything in excess becomes exhausting. And you, my dear, you must not vegetate, you must not live like all the others, but must relish life, and moderate dissipation is the spice of life. Bury yourself deep in flowers of over-powering fragrance, choke on musk, eat hashish, but above all, you must love, love . . . The first thing I would do, if I were in your place, would be to have seven men, one for each day of the week. One would be called Monday, the next Tuesday, the third Wednesday and so on, each would know his allotted day.'

What he said disturbed Anna. She did not eat a thing and drank only one glass of wine.

'Let me have my say!' she exclaimed. 'Personally, I don't recognize love without the family. I'm lonely, lonely as the moon in the sky above – a waning moon, what's more, and for all you say I'm convinced, I feel intuitively, that this waning can only be reversed by love in its usual meaning. This kind of love defines my responsibilities, my work, it illumines my view of life. I require spiritual peace and calm from love. I want to escape as far as possible from musk, your occultism and *fin de siècle* hocus-pocus. Briefly,' she added, growing embarrassed, 'I want a husband and children.'

'You want to get married? All right, that's also possible,' Lysevich agreed. 'You must try everything – marriage, jealousy, the sweetness of the first infidelity, children even . . . But do hurry up and *live*, my dear. Hurry! Time's passing, it won't wait.'

'Then I *shall* marry!' she said angrily, glancing at his

smooth, self-satisfied face. 'I shall marry in the most ordinary, the most vulgar way and I'll be radiant with happiness.
And I'll marry some simple working man, a mechanic or a
draughtsman, if you can imagine that.'

'That wouldn't be a bad idea either. A princess falls for a
swineherd – being a princess she can do that. And you too
will be allowed to do the same, as you're no ordinary person.
If you want to love a Negro or Arab, my dear, don't be
shy, go and order a Negro. Don't deny yourself a thing.
You should be as bold as your own desires, don't lag behind
them.'

'Why do you find me so hard to understand?' Anna said
in amazement, her eyes glistening with tears. 'Please try and
understand. I have an enormous business on my hands, I'm
responsible for two thousand workers before God. People
who work for me go blind and deaf. Life terrifies me, just
terrifies me! While I'm suffering like this you can be so
heartless as to talk about some Negro or other and smile!'
Anna thumped her fist on the table. 'To continue living as I
do now, to marry someone as idle, feckless as myself would
be criminal. I can't go on living like this,' she said furiously,
'I just can't!'

'How pretty she is!' Lysevich said, enraptured. 'Good
God, how pretty! But why are you so angry, my dear? I
admit I could be wrong, but do you think it will make
things any better for the workers if, for the sake of ideals,
which I happen to respect deeply, you're miserable all the
time and renounce all joy in life? Not one little bit. There
has to be depravity, dissipation!' he said determinedly. 'You
must be corrupt, it's your duty! Have a good think about
that, my dear.'

Anna was glad that she had spoken her mind and she
cheered up. She was pleased to have spoken so eloquently
and now she was convinced that if Pimenov, for example,
were to fall in love with her she would be delighted to
marry him.

Misha poured some champagne.

'You irritate me, Victor,' she said, clinking glasses with

the lawyer. 'It annoys me that you can offer advice when you have no knowledge of life at all. You seem to think that mechanics or draughtsmen are ignorant peasants. But they're terribly clever, they're really remarkable!'

'I knew your father and uncle . . . and I respected them,' Krylin said with slow deliberation. He was sitting as rigid as a statue and had been eating non-stop the whole time. 'They were people of the highest intellect and . . . the loftiest moral qualities.'

'All right, we know all about those qualities,' the lawyer muttered and asked permission to smoke.

When dinner was over, Krylin was led off to sleep. Lyse-vich finished his cigar and followed Anna into her study, walking unsteadily after all the food he had eaten. He had no love for cosy nooks with photographs, fans on the walls, the inevitable pink or light-blue lamp in the middle of the ceiling, considering them the expression of a dull, unoriginal kind of personality. Furthermore, memories of certain previous affairs, of which he was now ashamed, were bound up with that type of lamp. But he did like Anna's study with its bare walls and tasteless furniture. It was soft and comfortable sitting there on the sofa, looking at Anna, who usually sat on the carpet in front of the hearth, her knees clasped in her hands as she pensively stared into the fire. At that moment he felt that her peasant, Old Believer's blood was throbbing in her veins now.

After dinner, when coffee and liqueurs were served, he would always liven up and tell her various bits of literary news. He used the florid, inspired style of someone carried away by his own oratory as she listened and – as always – concluded that she would pay him not twenty thousand but three times as much for the entertainment. And she would forgive him for everything she found unlikeable in him. At times he told her the plots of short stories, even novels, and on those occasions two or three hours would pass like minutes without them noticing. Now he began in a some-what listless, feeble voice, his eyes closed.

'It's a long time since I read anything, my dear,' he said

when she asked him to tell her some story. 'However, I sometimes read Jules Verne.'

'And I thought you had something new to tell me.'

'Hm . . . new,' Lysevich murmured sleepily and sank even further into the corner of the sofa. 'None of modern literature is for you or me, dear lady. Of course, it is what it is and can't be anything else. Not to accept it would be the same as rejecting the natural order of things, and I do accept it, but . . .'

Lysevich seemed to have fallen asleep, but soon his voice was heard again: 'The whole of modern literature is like the autumn wind in the chimney, moaning and groaning: "Oh, you're so unhappy! Oh, your life is a prison. Oh, how dark and damp for you there! Oh, you are doomed, there's no escape!" That's all very nice, but I would prefer a literature that teaches you how to escape from prison. The only contemporary writer I read now and then is Maupassant.' Lysevich opened his eyes. 'A good writer, an excellent writer!' Lysevich slid forward a little on the sofa. 'A remarkable artist! A terrifying, monstrous, supernatural artist!' Lysevich got up from the sofa and raised his right arm. 'Maupassant!' he exclaimed rapturously. 'Read Maupassant, my dear! One page of his will give you more than all the world's riches. Every line is a new horizon! The most subtle, tender movements of the soul alternate with violent, tempestuous sensations, as if a forty-thousand-fold atmospheric pressure had been brought to bear on it, turning it into an insignificant particle of some indeterminate pinkish matter which might taste sharp and sensuous if you could put it on the tongue. Such frenzied transitions, motifs, melodies! You are resting on a bed of lilies and roses when suddenly a terrifying, beautiful, irresistible thought descends on you out of the blue, like a locomotive enveloping you in hot steam and deafening you with its whistle. Read, read Maupassant! My dear, I insist!'

Lysevich waved his arms and walked up and down in great agitation. 'No, it's not possible,' he said, as if in desperation. 'His last work exhausted, intoxicated me! But I'm afraid you'll be indifferent to it. In order to be carried away vou have to savour it, slowly squeeze the juice from each line. drink. Yes, you must drink it!'

After a long preamble full of many phrases like 'demoniac sensuality', 'network of the most delicate nerves', 'simoom', 'crystal' and so on, he finally began to tell her the novel's plot. He no longer indulged in flowery language and he went into great detail, quoting entire descriptive passages and conversations. He was enchanted by the characters and assumed different poses as he described them, altering his voice or facial expression, like a true actor. In his delight he would laugh out loud, first in a low-pitched voice, then very shrilly, clasping his hands or clutching his head as if he expected it to burst any minute. Although she had read the book, she listened enchanted, finding the lawyer's rendering far more beautiful and complex than the novel itself. He directed her attention to various fine points and emphasized exquisitely turned expressions and profound thoughts. But she could only see real life itself there, and herself, as if she were one of the characters in the book. She cheered up, laughed out loud and clasped her hands like him, thinking it was impossible to go on with the life she had been leading, that there was no need to lead a wretched existence when one could live beautifully. She remembered what she had said and thought during dinner and she was proud of it. When the figure of Pimenov suddenly loomed large in her mind, she felt gay and wanted him to love her.

When he had finished his exposition, Lysevich sank back exhausted on the sofa.

'What a wonderful, beautiful person you are!' he began a little later, in a feeble, ailing voice. 'I'm happy when I'm near you, my dear. But why am I forty-two and not thirty? Your tastes and mine don't coincide. You should be dissipated, but I've long outlived that phase and I desire the most refined kind of love, as insubstantial as a sunbeam. I mean to say, I'm no damned good to a woman of your age.'

He said that he liked Turgenev, the bard of virginal love, youth and the melancholy Russian countryside. But his fondness for this 'virginal love' was not something directly experienced, but only something he had heard speak of, abstract, beyond the bounds of reality. Now he was trying to convince himself that his love for Anna was platonic, idealistic, although he didn't know the meaning of the words. He felt comfortable, warm and at ease, though, and Anna seemed enchanting in her eccentricity. He thought that this pleasant feeling of well-being generated by his surroundings was identical with that so-called 'platonic love'.

He pressed his cheek to her hand and asked in the kind of voice usually resorted to in order to win over young children, 'Why have I been punished, my dear?'

'How? When?'

'I didn't receive my Christmas bonus.'

Anna had never heard of lawyers receiving Christmas bonuses and now she felt awkward, not knowing how much to give him. But give she must, as he was expecting it, even as he looked at her with loving eyes.

'Nazarych must have forgotten,' she said. 'But it's not too late to rectify matters.'

Suddenly she remembered yesterday's fifteen hundred roubles that were lying on her bedroom dressing-table. When she brought down that loathsome money and handed it to the lawyer, who stuffed it into a side pocket, with effortless grace, it was all so charming and natural. That unexpected reminder of the bonus, the fifteen hundred roubles – all this seemed so right for Lysevich.

'*Merci,*' he said, kissing her finger.

Krylin entered with a blissful, sleepy look, and without his ribbons. He and Lysevich sat for a little longer, drank a glass of tea each and prepared to leave. Anna was in something of a quandary: she had completely forgotten where Krylin worked and she wondered if she should give him money as well. If so, should she give it him there and then, or send it in an envelope?

'Where does he work?' she whispered to Lysevich.

'Damned if I know,' the lawyer muttered, yawning.

Anna concluded that if Krylin had visited her uncle and father to pay his respects, it would not have been for nothing. Obviously he had acted for them in performing good deeds, having been employed by some charitable institution. As she said goodbye, she thrust three hundred roubles into his hand. He seemed amazed at this and stood looking at her for a short while in silence, with lustreless eyes. But then he seemed to cotton on.

'But, Miss Glagolev, I can't give you a receipt before the New Year.'

Lysevich had grown quite limp and he staggered as Misha helped him into his fur coat. As he went downstairs he looked completely enervated and it was plain that he would fall asleep the moment he was in his sledge.

'My dear sir,' he asked Krylin languidly, stopping halfway down, 'have you ever had the feeling that some invisible power was stretching you out, making you longer and longer until you finally turned into the finest wire? Subjectively speaking it's a special, voluptuous sensation that you can't compare with anything else.'

Anna could see them both hand Misha a banknote.

'Now don't forget me! Goodbye!' she shouted after them and ran into her bedroom.

Quickly she threw off that dress which she was now tired of, put on her house-coat. Like a child she made her feet clatter as she ran downstairs. She desperately wanted some fun and games.

IV

EVENING

Auntie, in a loose cotton-print dress, Barbara and two old women were having supper in the dining-room. On the table in front of them was a large chunk of salt-beef, a ham, and various other salted delicacies. Steam rose to the ceiling from the very fat, tasty-looking salt-beef. Downstairs they did not drink wine, but there was a large assortment of spirits and fruit liqueurs. Agafya the cook, a plump, fair-haired, well-fed woman, was standing at the door with her arms crossed, talking to the old women, while 'downstairs Masha' – a brunette with a crimson ribbon in her hair – took the dishes round and served. The old women had been gorging themselves since morning, and an hour before supper had eaten a sweet, rich pie with their tea, so that now they were forcing themselves to eat, as if it were their duty.

'Oh, dear me!' Auntie sighed when Anna suddenly dashed into the dining-room and sat on the chair next to her. 'You nearly frightened the life out of me!'

The whole household was pleased when Anna was in good spirits and started playing the fool, which never failed to remind them that the old men were dead, that the old women no longer held power in that house and that they could all do as they liked without fear of being mercilessly made to answer for it. Only the two old women whom Anna didn't know squinted at her in amazement: she was singing – and singing at table was a sin.

'Our mistress is as pretty as a picture,' Agafya droned in a sugary voice. 'Our precious jewel! So many came to see our princess today, Lord be praised! Generals, and officers, and gentlemen . . . I kept looking through the window, trying to count them all I was, but I couldn't keep up, so I stopped.'

'I'd rather those rogues had stayed at home,' Auntie said. She gazed sadly at her niece and added, 'All they've done is waste the poor girl's time.'

Anna was starving, having eaten nothing since the morning. They poured her a very bitter tasting fruit cordial, which she drank; and she ate some salt-beef with mustard and found it exceptionally tasty. Then 'downstairs Masha' served turkey, soused apples and gooseberries. This she liked too. What was unpleasant was the heat pouring out of the tiled stove in waves, which made the room stuffy, and everyone's cheeks were burning. After supper they took the cloth away and put dishes of mint cakes, nuts and raisins on the table.

'Come on, sit down with us!' Auntie told the cook.

Agafya sighed and sat down at the table. Masha stood a cordial glass in front of her too and Anna had the impression that as much heat was coming from Agafya's white neck as from the stove. Everyone said how difficult it was to marry these days, and that at one time men had at least been tempted by money; now it was hard to tell what they wanted. At one time only hunchbacks and cripples had been left on the shelf; nowadays even the rich and beautiful were ignored. Auntie began by saying that this immoral situation arose from people not fearing God, but then she suddenly remembered that her brother Ivan and Barbara had both led devout lives and both believed in God. For all that they had had children from illicit unions and packed them off to a home. Then she suddenly pulled herself up and changed the subject to someone who had once courted her, a factory worker, and how she had loved him. But her brothers had forced her to marry a widowed icon-painter, who died two years later, thank God. 'Downstairs Masha' also took a seat at the table and told them, with a very mysterious look, that a black-moustached stranger in a black coat with a lambskin collar had started appearing in their yard every morning for the past week. He would come into the yard, look at the windows of the big house, and then go on to the factory blocks. He was a fine figure of a man, quite handsome, in fact . . .

All this talk gave Anna a sudden urge to get married – so strong it was quite painful. She felt that she would give half her life and all her wealth just to know that there was a man upstairs closer to her than anyone in the world, who loved her deeply and who yearned for her. The thought of such an enchanting intimacy, so impossible to put into words, excited her. And the healthy instincts of a young woman flattered her with the false message that the true poetry of life had not yet arrived, but lay ahead, and she believed it. She leant back in her chair so that her hair hung loose and she started laughing, which made the others follow suit. For a long time the dining-room was filled with inconsequential laughter.

Someone then announced that 'Beetle' had come to spend the night. With Pasha or Spiridovna as her real names, this small, pious lady of about fifty, in her black dress and white shawl, was sharp-eyed, sharp-nosed and sharp-chinned. She had cunning, spiteful eyes and seemed to look right through people. Her lips were pursed. Because she was so spiteful and hateful she was known as 'Beetle' in merchants' houses.

After she came into the dining-room she went straight over to the icons without so much as a glance at anyone and sang in an alto voice 'Thy Nativity', then 'Virgin this Day' and 'Christ Is Born', after which she turned around and gave everyone a piercing look.

'Happy Christmas!' she said, kissing Anna on the shoulder. 'It was an awful job, really awful, getting here, my ladies of charity.' She kissed Auntie on the shoulder. 'I set off this morning, but on my way I stopped at some kind people's house for a little rest. "Please stay," they said. It was evening before I noticed it.'

As she didn't eat meat she was served caviare and salmon. She scowled at everyone as she ate, and she drank three glasses of vodka. When she had finished she said a little prayer and bowed low to Anna. They started playing Kings, as they had done the previous year and the year before that. Every single servant from the two floors crowded at the door to watch the game. Anna thought that she twice glimpsed Misha, with that condescending smile of his, in the crowd of common peasant men and women. First to be king was 'Beetle'. Anna, a soldier, had to pay her a forfeit. Then Auntie became king and Anna was a peasant or 'yokel', which delighted everyone, while Agafya became a prince and was embarrassed at feeling so pleased. Another card game started at the far end of the table: both Mashas, Barbara and Martha the seamstress (whom they specially woke up to play Kings and who looked sleepy and irritable).

During the game the conversation turned to men, to how difficult it was to find a good man nowadays, whether a spinster was better off than a widow.

'You're a pretty, healthy, strong lass,' Beetle told Anna. 'Only I just don't understand who you're saving yourself for, my girl.'

'What can I do if no one will have me?'

'Perhaps you made a vow never to marry,' Beetle continued as if she had not heard. 'All right, that's fine, don't marry . . .' she repeated, eyeing her cards attentively, viciously. 'Stay as you are . . . yes . . . But spinsters, bless their hearts, come in all shapes and sizes,' she sighed, dealing a king. 'Oh, all shapes and sizes, my dear! There's some what live like nuns, pure as angels they are. But if one of them happens to sin, the poor girl goes through such torments you just couldn't bring yourself to tell her off. And there's others as wear black and make their own shrouds, while they love rich old men on the sly. Yes, my little songbirds, there's witches who'll put spells on an old man and keep him under their thumbs. Oh, yes, my dears, they'll call the tune, do what they like with him and as soon as they've pinched his money and lottery tickets they'll bewitch him, so he dies.'

All Barbara did was sigh in reply to these remarks and look at the icon. Her face was filled with Christian humility.

'There's a girl I know, my fierce enemy,' Beetle went on, surveying everyone triumphantly. 'She's always sighing away and looking at the icons, the she-devil. When she had an old man under her thumb and you went to see her, she'd give you a little something to eat and order you to bow down to the ground while she read out loud "A Virgin brought forth". On holidays she'd give you a morsel to eat, but on ordinary days she'd tell you off. So, now I'm off to have a good laugh at her, my little pets!'

Barbara looked at the icons again and crossed herself.

'No one will have me, Spiridovna,' Anna said, to change the subject. 'What can I do?'

'It's your own fault, dear. The only thing is to wait for a gentleman, someone educated. You should marry your own kind, a businessman.'

'We don't want a businessman, God help us,' Auntie said in alarm. 'A gentleman'll squander all your money, but he won't be too hard on you, you silly woman! But a businessman'll be so strict with you that you'll never feel at home in your own house. You'll be wanting to snuggle up close to him, but he'll be after your money. If you sit down at table with him, the oaf'll blame you for eating all *his* food – and in your own house! Go and marry a gentleman!'

Everyone spoke at once, noisily interrupting each other, while Auntie banged the nutcrackers on the table.

'You don't need a businessman,' she said, angry and red-faced. 'If you bring one into this house I'll go into a workhouse!'

'Shush! Be quiet!' Beetle shouted. When everyone was silent she screwed up one eye and said 'Do you know what, Anna, my precious? There's no point in your marrying like ordinary folk do. You're rich, free, your own mistress. But I don't think it's right for you to stay an old maid, my child. I'll go and find you some useless fool whom you'll marry for show – and then off on the town! Oh, you'll shove five or ten thousand under your husband's nose and let him go back where he belongs and then you'll be mistress in your own house. And then you'll be able to love who you like and no one can say a word about it. You'll be able to love your educated gentlemen all right then. Oh, you'll be living in clover!' Beetle clicked her fingers and whistled. 'Go and have a good time, dear!'

'But that would be sinning!' Auntie said.

'So, it's a sin then,' Beetle said grinning. 'She's educated, she understands. Of course it's a sin cutting someone's throat or bewitching an old man, but loving your boyfriend is no sin. What is it, after all? No sin in it at all! All that was thought up by pious old women to hoodwink simple folk. I'm always saying that a sin is a sin, but I don't know why.'

Beetle drank some fruit liqueur and cleared her throat. 'Go and have a good time,' she said, evidently talking to herself this time. 'For thirty years I've been thinking about sin and was always scared of it, but now I seem to have missed out. I've let my chance slip. Oh, what a fool I am!' she sighed. 'A woman's life is short and she should treasure every day. You're beautiful, Anna, and very rich into the bargain, but when your thirty-fifth or fortieth birthday comes along, that'll be the end of you. Now don't listen to what people say, dear, go and enjoy yourself until you're forty – there'll be plenty of time for praying, for making amends and sewing shrouds. Let your hair down! Well, what do you say? Do you want to give pleasure to some man?'

'I do,' Anna laughed. 'But I couldn't care less now, I'd marry an ordinary working man.'

'Yes, and that would be a good thing too. Oh, then you could take your pick!' Beetle frowned and shook her head. 'By heaven you could!'

'That's what I keep telling her,' Auntie said. 'If you can't wait for a gentleman, then don't go and marry a business-man, but someone more ordinary. At least we'd have a man in the house. And there's no shortage of good men, is there? Just take some of our own factory workers, all sober and respectable.'

'And how!' Beetle agreed. 'All wonderful lads. What if I arranged a match for Anna with Vasily Lebedinsky, Auntie?'

'Well, Vasily's got long legs,' Auntie said seriously. 'He's very dull, nothing much to look at.'

The crowd at the door laughed.

'Well, Pimenov then. Would you like to marry Pimenov?'

'Yes, marry me to Pimenov.'

'Do you mean it?'

'Yes, go ahead and arrange it,' Anna said determinedly and thumped the table. 'I'll marry him, word of honour!'

'You really will?'

Anna suddenly felt ashamed that her cheeks were burning and that everyone was looking at her. She mixed up the cards on the table and tore out of the room. After she had dashed upstairs, reached the upper floor and sat by the grand piano in the drawing-room, she heard a rumbling from down below, like the roar of the sea. They must be talking about her and Pimenov, and perhaps Beetle was taking advantage of her absence to insult Barbara – and of course she wouldn't be too particular about her language.

Only one lamp was lit on the whole upper floor – in the ballroom – and its dim light found its way through the doorway into the dark drawing-room. It was about ten, no later. Anna played a waltz, then a second, then a third, without stopping. She peered into the dark corner behind the piano, smiled, imagined she was calling out to someone, and then she had an idea: why not go at once to town and visit just anyone – Lysevich, for example – and tell him what was going on in her heart? She wanted to talk non-stop, to laugh, play the fool, but that dark corner behind the piano was gloomily silent; and all around her, in every room on that floor, it was quiet and deserted.

She loved sentimental songs, but as her voice was rough and untrained, she could only play accompaniments and she sang barely audibly, in gentle breaths. She sang one song after the other in a whisper, and all of them were mainly about love, parting, lost hope. She imagined herself stretching out her hands: 'Pimenov, take this burden from me!' she would tearfully plead. And then, as if her sins had been forgiven, she would feel joyful and relieved. A free and perhaps happy life would follow. In an agony of expectation she bent over the keys and longed for the change in her life to come right away, that very minute. She was terrified to think that her present way of life would continue for some time to come. Then she began to play again and she sang barely audibly, while all around it was quiet. No longer could she hear the roar from downstairs; they must all have gone to bed. It had struck ten ages ago. A long, lonely, tedious night was approaching.

Anna paced through all the rooms, lay down on the study sofa and read some letters delivered that evening. There were twelve wishing her happy Christmas and three anonymous ones, unsigned. In one of these an ordinary workman complained, in dreadful, barely decipherable handwriting, that, in the factory shop, workers were sold only rancid vegetable oil that smelt of kerosene. In another, someone politely denounced Nazarych for accepting a thousand-rouble bribe when buying iron at an auction. In another she was abused for her inhumanity.

The mood of festive excitement was fading now and in an attempt to maintain it Anna sat at the piano and quietly played a new waltz. Then she remembered how cleverly and frankly she had reasoned and expressed her thoughts over dinner. She looked round at the dark windows, at the paintings on the walls, at the weak light coming from the ballroom and suddenly, quite unexpectedly, she burst into tears. She was upset because she was so alone, because she had no one to talk to and to whom she could turn for advice. She tried to cheer herself up by picturing Pimenov in her mind, but she was unsuccessful.

The clock struck twelve. In came Misha, wearing a jacket now and no longer in tail-coat; silently he lit two candles. Then he left and a minute later returned with a cup of tea on a tray.

'What's funny?' she asked, seeing the smile on his face.

'I was downstairs and heard you joking about Pimenov,' he said, covering his laughing face with one hand. 'You should have invited him to dinner along with Mr Lysevich and Mr Krylin, he would have died of fright.' Misha's shoulders shook with laughter. 'He probably doesn't even know how to hold a fork.'

The servant's laughter, what he said, his jacket and his little whiskers, all left Anna with an impression of dirtiness. She closed her eyes so as not to have to look at him, and she could not help imagining Pimenov dining with Lysevich and Krylin. And then Pimenov's subservient, stupid appearance struck her as pathetic, helpless, and filled her with revulsion. Only now did she understand clearly – and for the first time that day – that all she had thought and said about Pimenov, about marrying an ordinary workman, was senseless, absurd and opinionated. In an effort to convince herself that the opposite was the case, and to overcome her disgust, she wanted to remember exactly what she had said during dinner, but was unable to. The feeling of shame at her own thoughts and behaviour, the fear that she might have said something stupid, revulsion at her own lack of nerve – all these things troubled her deeply. She took a candle and dashed downstairs as if someone were chasing her; she woke Spiridovna and assured her that she had been joking. Then she went to her bedroom. Red-headed Masha, who had been drowsing in an armchair near the bed, jumped up to arrange the pillows. Her face was weary and sleepy, and her magnificent hair had fallen to one side.

'That clerk Chalikov was here again this evening,' she said, yawning. 'But I didn't dare tell you. He was dead drunk. Says he'll come back tomorrow.'

'What does he want from me?' Anna said angrily, flinging her comb on the floor. 'I don't want to see him, I don't!'

She concluded that there was nothing in her life besides this Chalikov now. He would never stop hounding her – a daily reminder of how boring and absurd her life was.

Without undressing, she lay down and burst out sobbing from shame and boredom. Most annoying and ridiculous of all, she thought, was the fact that earlier in the day her thoughts about Pimenov had been decent, noble, honourable. But at the same time she felt that Lysevich and even Krylin were closer to her than Pimenov and all the factory workers put together. Now she thought that if it were only possible to reproduce that long day she had just gone through in a painting, then everything that was nasty and cheap – the dinner, for example, what the lawyer had said, the game of Kings – would have been the truth, whereas her dreams and the conversation about Pimenov would have stood out as something false and artificial.

And she thought that now it was too late to dream of happiness, that it was impossible to return to that kind of life where she had slept in her mother's bed, to devise some new, special life-style.

Red-headed Masha was kneeling in front of the bed

looking at her sadly and in astonishment. Then she too burst into tears and pressed her face to Anna's hand. There was no need for words to express why she felt so distressed.

'We're a pair of fools, you and I,' Anna said, both crying and laughing. 'We're fools! Oh, what fools!'

My Life

A Provincial's Story

I

'I'm only keeping you on out of respect for your esteemed father,' the manager told me. 'Otherwise I'd have sent you flying long ago.'

I replied, 'You flatter me too much, sir, in supposing I'm capable of flight.'

Then I heard him say 'Take this gentleman away from here, he's getting on my nerves.'

Two days later I was dismissed, which meant I'd had nine different jobs since the time I'd reached adulthood – to the great chagrin of my father, the town architect. I had worked in various government departments, but all nine jobs had been exactly the same and involved sitting on my backside, copying, listening to idiotic, cheap remarks and waiting for the sack.

When I arrived at Father's, he was deep in his armchair and his eyes were closed. His gaunt, wasted face, with that bluish-grey shadow where he shaved (he looked like an elderly Catholic organist), expressed humility and resignation. Without acknowledging my greeting, or opening his eyes, he told me, 'If my beloved wife, your mother, were alive today, the kind of life you lead would be a constant torment for her. I see the workings of Divine Providence in her untimely death. I'm asking you, you miserable wretch,' he went on, opening his eyes, 'to tell me what I should do with you.'

When I was younger, my relatives and friends had known what to do with me: some advised me to volunteer for military service, some told me to get a job in a chemist's shop, while others said I should work in a telegraph office.

But now that I had turned twenty-five (I was even going a little grey at the temples) and had been in the army, had worked in a chemist's shop and in a telegraph office, it seemed that I had exhausted all earthly possibilities, and so they stopped advising me and merely sighed or shook their heads.

'Who do you think you are?' Father continued. 'At your age young men already have a sound position in life, but just take a look at yourself, you common riff-raff, living off your father!'

As usual, he went on about the young people of today being doomed by their atheism, materialism and inflated opinions of themselves, and about the need to ban amateur theatricals, as they distracted young people from their religion and their duties.

'Please hear me out,' I said morosely, fearing the worst from this conversation. 'What you call "position in society" is nothing but the privileges bestowed by capital and education. But the poor and uneducated earn their living by manual labour and I see no reason why I should be any exception.'

'When you talk about manual labour you sound so stupid and trite,' Father said irritably. 'Can't you get this into your thick head, you dim-wit, that there's something besides brute strength inside you. You have the divine spirit, the sacred fire which sets you miles apart from an ass or a reptile and makes you akin to the sublime! The finest people needed thousands of years to produce that fire. General Poloznev, your great-grandfather, fought at Borodino. Your grandfather was a poet, public orator, marshal of the gentry. Your uncle's a teacher. And lastly, I, your father, am an architect! So all the Poloznevs have preserved this divine fire, only for you to put it out!'

'Please be fair,' I said. 'Millions of people do manual work.'

'Well, let them! They're fit for nothing else! Anyone can do manual work, even a downright idiot or criminal. It's the distinguishing mark of slaves and barbarians, whereas the sacred fire is granted only to the few!'

There was no point in talking any more. Father worshipped himself and could only be convinced by what he himself said. What's more, I knew very well that his pompous attitude to manual labour was not founded on thoughts of sacred flames so much as on a secret fear that I might become a labourer and thus make myself the talk of the town. However, the main thing was that all my contemporaries had graduated long ago and were doing well, and that the son of the manager of the State Bank was already quite an important civil servant, whereas I, an only son, was a nobody! It was useless continuing this disagreeable conversation, but I sat there feebly protesting in the hope that he would understand what I meant. After all, the problem was simple and clear enough – how was I to earn my living? But simplicity went unnoticed as Father trotted out those sickly phrases about Borodino, the sacred fire, my grandfather – a forgotten poet who wrote bad, meretricious verse at some time. I felt insulted – being called dim-wit and brainless fool was highly insulting. But how I wanted to be understood! In spite of everything I loved my father and sister. My childhood habit of asking them for advice had become so deeply rooted in me that I would never shake it off. Whether I was right or wrong, I was always afraid of upsetting them, afraid that Father was so excited now that his skinny neck had turned red and that he might have a stroke.

'Sitting in a stuffy room,' I said, 'copying, competing with a typewriter, is shameful and insulting for a man of my age. What does all *that* have to do with sacred flames?'

'But it's still brain work,' Father said. 'However, that's enough for now, we must stop this conversation. In any case, I'm warning you: if you don't go back to the office and if you persist in these contemptible inclinations of yours, then my daughter and I will cast you from our hearts. I'll disinherit you, I swear to God I will!'

In all sincerity and to demonstrate the unquestionable

purity of the motives by which I wished to be guided all my life I replied, 'The question of my inheritance is of no importance to me. I renounce it in advance.'

Quite contrary to what I was expecting, these words hurt Father deeply. He turned crimson.

'Don't you dare talk to me like that, you fool!' he shouted in a thin, shrill voice. 'You ignorant lout!'

Swiftly and deftly, in his usual practised way, he slapped me twice in the face. 'You're forgetting yourself!'

When Father beat me as a child I had to stand to attention, hands to my sides and look him in the face. And now, whenever he beat me, I would panic completely, stand to attention and try to look him in the face, just as though I were a small child again. Father was old and very thin, but those slender muscles must have been as tough as leather straps, as he really hurt me.

I staggered back into the hall, where he grabbed his umbrella and struck me several times on the head and shoulders. Just then my sister opened the drawing-room door to see what the noise was about, but immediately turned away with a look of horror and pity, without a word in my defence.

I remained unshakeable in my determination not to return to the office, and in my intention to start a new life as a working man. All I had to do was choose a job, and this didn't seem particularly difficult, since I thought that I was terribly strong, had great stamina and was therefore equal to the most arduous work. A workman's life lay ahead of me, with all its monotony, hunger, stench and grim surroundings. And there was the constant worry of having enough to live on. Returning from work on Great Dvoryansky Street, I might still envy Dolzhikov the engineer, who worked with his brain. Who knows? But now the thought of these future misfortunes cheered me up. At one time I used to dream of intellectual work, imagining myself as a teacher, doctor or writer, but my dreams never came true. My liking for intellectual pleasures such as the theatre and reading had grown into a passion, but I cannot say whether I had any flair for brain work. At school I had an utter aversion to Greek and I had to be taken out of the fourth form; for a long time I was coached by private tutors who tried to get me into the fifth. Then I worked in different government departments, spending most of the day doing absolutely nothing: this, I was told, constituted brain work. My school and office work called for neither mental effort, nor talent, nor any particular ability or creative energy. It was just mechanical. I consider that type of brain work beneath manual labour. I despise it and do not think that it could justify an idle life of leisure for one minute, since it's only a sham, another form of idleness. Probably I never knew what real brain work was.

Evening set in. We lived in Great Dvoryansky Street, the town's main thoroughfare, where our *beau monde* strolled in the evenings for want of a decent municipal park. This delightful street was a partial substitute for a park, since poplars (particularly sweet-smelling after rain) grew along both sides; acacias, tall lilac bushes, wild cherries and apple trees hung out over fences and railings. The May twilight, the soft green leaves and shadows, the scent of lilac, the droning beetles, the silence, the warmth – spring returns every year, but how fresh, how marvellous everything seemed nonetheless! I would stand by the gate watching the promenaders. I had grown up with most of them and got up to mischief with them when we were children. But they would most likely be startled at the sight of me now, as I was poorly, unfashionably dressed. People called my very narrow trousers and large, clumsy boots 'macaroni on floats'. Moreover, I had a bad name in that town because I had no social status and frequently played billiards in low pubs. Perhaps another reason was that I'd twice been hauled off to the police station, although I'd done absolutely nothing.

Someone was playing the piano in Mr Dolzhikov's flat in the large house opposite. It was growing dark and stars twinkled in the sky. Along came Father with my sister on his arm, wearing that old top-hat with its broad, upturned brim and acknowledging the bows of passers-by as he slowly walked past.

'Just look!' he was saying to my sister, pointing at the sky with the same umbrella he had struck me with. 'Just look at that sky! Even the smallest star is a world of its own! How insignificant is man compared with the universe!'

His tone suggested that he liked being insignificant and found it exceedingly flattering. What a bungler he was! Unfortunately, he was our only architect and not one decent house had been built in the town for the past fifteen or twenty years that I could remember. When he was commissioned to design a house, he usually drew the ballroom and drawing-room first. Just as boarding-school girls, long ago, could dance only if they began from where the stove was, so his creative ideas could only develop by starting from the ballroom and drawing-room. He would add a dining-room, nursery, study – all of them linked by doors. Inevitably, they turned into corridors, each room having two or even three doors too many. He must have had a vague, extremely confused and stunted creative imagination. Always sensing that something was missing, he would resort to different kinds of extensions, lumping one on top of the other. I can still see those narrow entrance-halls, narrow little passages and small, crooked staircases leading on to mezzanines where you could not stand up straight, with three enormous steps instead of a floor, like shelves in a bath-house. And the kitchen was invariably underneath the main house, with vaulted ceilings and brick floors. The façades had a stubborn, harsh look; their lines were stiff, timid, and the roofs were low, squashed-looking. It seemed that the squat, dumpy chimneys just had to be capped with wire cowls and squeaky black weather-vanes. The houses that Father built were almost identical – somehow they vaguely put me in mind of his top-hat and the forbidding, rigid lines of the back of his neck. As time passed the town grew used to Father's ineptitude: it took root and became established as the ruling style.

Father also introduced this style into my sister's life. To

start with, he called her Cleopatra, just as he had called me Misail. When she was a little girl he would scare her by talking about the stars, about the sages of antiquity and our ancestors, explaining the concepts of life and duty in great detail to her. And now that she was twenty-six, he was still at it. Only *he* was allowed to take her arm when they went for a walk and he somehow imagined that sooner or later a respectable young man would turn up and want to marry her out of respect for his moral virtues. She worshipped Father, was afraid of him and thought him exceptionally clever.

It grew quite dark and the street gradually became deserted. The music died away in the house opposite; gates opened wide and a troika jauntily careered off down the street, its bells softly jingling. The engineer and his daughter had gone for a ride. It was time for bed!

I had my own room in the house, but I lived in a little hut joined on to a brick shed probably built as a harness-room at one time, as large spikes were driven into the walls. But now it was no longer needed for storage and for thirty years Father had been stacking only newspapers there. For some obscure reason he had them bound every six months and would not let anyone touch them. Living in that hut I saw much less of Father and his guests and I felt that if I didn't have a proper room and didn't go into the house for dinner every day, that would make Father's remarks about my being a burden seem less hurtful.

My sister was waiting for me. Without Father's knowledge, she had brought me supper – a small piece of cold veal and a slice of bread. In our house people were always going on about 'counting the copecks' or 'taking care of the roubles', and so on. Subjected to all this banal talk, my sister's only concern was how to save money – and as a result we ate badly. After she put the plate on the table she sat down on the bed and burst into tears.

'Misail,' she said, 'what are you doing to us?'

She did not cover her face; tears trickled on to her breast and arms and she looked most despondent. Then she slumped on to the pillow and gave free rein to her tears, shaking all over and sobbing.

'That's another job you've left,' she said. 'Oh, it's absolutely terrible!'

'*Please* try and understand, my dear sister,' I said, and her tears filled me with despair.

And as though on purpose, my lamp ran out of paraffin – it was smoking and about to go out. The old spikes on the walls had a sombre look and their shadows flickered.

'Please spare a thought for us!' my sister said, getting up. 'Father is dreadfully upset, I'm not well and nearly going out of my mind. What will become of you?' she sobbed, holding her hands out. 'I beg you, I implore you, for our dear mother's sake, go back to your job!'

'I can't, Cleopatra,' I said, almost giving in. 'I can't!'

'Why not?' my sister continued. 'Why not? If you couldn't get on with your boss you should have found another job. Why don't you go and work on the railway, for instance? I've just been speaking to Anyuta Blagovo and she tells me they're bound to take you on. She's even promised to put in a word for you. For heaven's sake, Misail, think about it! Think about it, I beg you!'

After a little more discussion I gave in. I told her I'd never given much thought to working on the railway and that I'd try it.

She smiled joyfully through her tears, squeezed my hand – and then she started crying again, unable to stop. I went to get some paraffin from the kitchen.

II

No one in that town had greater enthusiasm for amateur theatricals, concerts and *tableaux vivants* for charity than the Azhogins, who owned a house on Great Dvoryansky Street. They provided the premises for every performance, looked after the organization and took responsibility for all expenses. This rich, landowning family had about eight thousand acres in the district with a splendid manor-house,

but they had no love for the country and lived in town all
year round.

The family consisted of the mother, a tall, thin, refined
woman, with short hair, a short blouse and plain skirt in the
English style; and three daughters who, instead of being
called by their Christian names were simply known as
'Eldest', 'Middle' and 'Youngest'. All three of them had
ugly, sharp chins, were shortsighted and round-shouldered.
They dressed just like their mother and had an unpleasant
lisp. But in spite of this they insisted on taking part in every
performance and were always doing charitable work
through their acting, reading or singing. They were very
earnest, never smiled and even acted – completely lifelessly
– in musical comedies with a business-like look, as though
they were book-keepers at work.

I loved our shows, in particular the frequent, somewhat
chaotic, noisy rehearsals, after which we were always
given supper. I had no part in selecting the plays or casting
– my work was back-stage. I painted scenery, copied out
parts, prompted, helped with the make-up. I was also
entrusted with various sound-effects, such as thunder, night-
ingales' songs, and so on. As I had no status in society or
decent clothes I kept away from everyone at rehearsals,
hiding in the darkness of the wings and maintaining a
bashful silence.

I painted the scenery – in the Azhogins' brick shed or
out in the yard. I was helped by a house-painter or, as he
liked to call himself, 'decorating contractor' named Andrey
Ivanov. He was about fifty, tall, very thin and pale, with a
sunken chest, sunken temples and dark blue patches under
his eyes which made him look rather frightening. He
suffered from some wasting disease and every spring and
autumn people said he was dying, but after a spell in bed he
would get up again and declare in a surprised voice 'So, I'm
still here, ain't I!'

In the town he was called Radish – people said it was his
real name. He loved the theatre as much as I did and the
moment he heard rumours of a new show he would drop

whatever he was doing and go off to the Azhogins' to paint scenery.

The day after that show-down with my sister I worked from morning to night at the Azhogins'. The rehearsal was due to start at seven p.m., and an hour beforehand all the company assembled in the ballroom; the three sisters, Eldest, Middle and Youngest, walked up and down the stage reading from notebooks. In his long, reddish-brown coat and with a scarf around his neck, Radish stood with his head against the wall, reverently watching the stage. Mrs Azhogin went up to each of the guests to say something pleasant. She had a way of staring you in the face and speaking softly, as if telling a secret.

'It must be hard work painting scenery,' she said softly, coming over to me. 'I was talking to Mrs Mufke about superstitions just now when I saw you come in. Good heavens, I've struggled against superstition all my life! To try and convince the servants how stupid their fears are I always light three candles in my room and start any important business matters only on the thirteenth of the month.'

Miss Dolzhikov, the engineer's daughter, arrived. She was a pretty, buxom blonde, dressed in 'Paris fashion' as they described it in the town. She didn't do any acting, but they put a chair for her on the stage during rehearsals and the shows didn't start until she was sitting in the front row, looking radiant and amazing everyone with her dresses. As she came from the Capital, she was allowed to pass remarks during rehearsals, which she did with a pleasant, condescending smile, and she obviously thought that our shows were childish games. It was said that she had studied singing at the St Petersburg Conservatoire and had even sung for a winter season in a private opera house. She attracted me very much and at rehearsals or performances I could hardly take my eyes off her.

I had already picked up the notebook for prompting when suddenly my sister appeared. Without taking off her hat and coat she came over to me and said 'Come with me, please.'

I went. Anyuta Blagovo was standing in the doorway back-stage. She also wore a hat, with a dark veil. She was the daughter of the deputy judge who had been serving in our town for some time, almost since the day the local court was first set up. Being tall and well built, she was considered indispensable for *tableaux vivants*, and when she represented some fairy, or 'Fame', her face would burn with shame. But she never took part in the plays, just dropping in at rehearsals on some business or other and never entering the hall. And she had obviously looked in only for a moment now.

'Father's been talking about you,' she said dryly, without looking at me and blushing. 'Dolzhikov's promised you a job on the railway. Go and see him tomorrow, he'll be at home.'

I bowed and thanked her for her trouble.

'You can leave that,' she said, pointing to the notebook.

She and my sister went up to Mrs Azhogin and they whispered for a minute or two, looking at me now and again. They were consulting one another about something.

'Indeed,' Mrs Azhogin said quietly as she came over to me and stared me in the face, 'indeed, if this is keeping you from more serious work' (she took the notebook from me) 'you can hand it over to someone else. Don't worry, my dear friend. Off with you now – and good luck.'

I said goodbye and left, feeling rather put out. As I went down the stairs I saw my sister and Anyuta Blagovo hurriedly leaving. They were talking excitedly, most probably about my railway job. My sister never used to come to rehearsals and was probably feeling guilty, afraid that Father might find out that she had been at the Azhogins' without his permission.

Next day, at about half past twelve, I went to see Dolzhikov. A man-servant showed me into a very fine room which the engineer used as drawing-room and office. Here everything was soft, elegant and even rather strange for someone like me, unused to such surroundings. There were expensive carpets, huge armchairs, bronzes, pictures, gilt and plush frames. The photographs all over the walls were of very beautiful women with clever, fine faces, in natural poses. From the drawing-room a door led straight on to a balcony overlooking the garden, where I could see lilac, a table laid for lunch, a great number of bottles and a bunch of roses. It smelt of spring, expensive cigars – the true smell of happiness – and everything seemed to be telling me that this man had really lived, worked hard and attained such happiness as is possible in this world. The engineer's daughter was sitting at the writing-table reading the paper.

'Have you come to see Father?' she asked. 'He's having a shower and he'll be down in a moment. Please take a seat.'

I sat down.

'You live opposite, don't you?' she asked after a brief silence.

'Yes.'

'Every day I watch you out of the window, from nothing better to do. I hope it doesn't bother you,' she went on, glancing at the newspaper, 'and I often see you or your sister. She always has such a kind, concentrated expression.'

Dolzhikov came in. He was drying his neck on a towel.

'Papa, this is Monsieur Poloznev,' she said.

'Yes, yes, so Blagovo told me,' he said, turning briskly towards me without offering his hand. 'Now listen, what do you want from me? What job do you think I have for you?'

In a loud voice, as if telling me off, he continued, 'You're a strange lot! Twenty men come here every day, thinking it's an office I'm running here! I have a *railway* to run, gentlemen, and it's damned hard work. I need mechanics, metal workers, navvies, carpenters, well-sinkers, but all you lot can do is sit on your behinds and scribble! You're just writers!'

He exuded that same air of prosperity as his carpets and armchairs. Stout, rosy-cheeked, broad-chested, well-washed, he looked just like a china figure of a coachman in his cotton-print shirt and baggy trousers. He had a rounded, curly beard, a hooked nose, and his eyes were dark, clear, innocent. He didn't have one grey hair on his head.

'What can you do?' he went on. 'Nothing! I'm an engineer and I'm financially secure. But before I was put in charge of this railway I spent years sweating my guts out. I was an engine-driver, then I worked in Belgium for two years as a common greaser. So what work do you think I can give you, young man?'

'Yes, you're right, of course,' I muttered. I was terribly taken aback and could not bear those clear, innocent eyes of his.

'But you can at least work a telegraph, can't you?' he asked after a moment's thought.

'Yes, I've worked in a telegraph office.'

'Hm . . . well, we'll see. Go to Dubechnya for the time being. I do have someone there, but he's a bloody dead loss.'

'And what will my duties be?' I asked.

'We'll see. Now, off you go for the time being and I'll see to it. Only don't start boozing while you're working for me or come asking for any favours, or you'll be out on your neck!'

He walked away without even a nod. I bowed to him and his daughter, who was reading the paper, and left. I felt so terribly depressed that when my sister asked what kind of reception I'd had at the engineer's I just could not speak one word.

Next morning I rose very early, at sunrise, to go to Dubechnya. Great Dvoryansky Street was absolutely deserted – everyone was still in bed – and my footsteps had a hollow, solitary ring. The dew-covered poplars filled the air with their gentle fragrance. I felt sad and reluctant to leave the town. I loved my birthplace, it seemed so beautiful and warm! I loved the greenery, the quiet sunny mornings, the sound of church bells. But the people I had to live with bored me, were like strangers and at times they disgusted me. I neither liked nor understood them. I could not understand what these sixty-five thousand people were living for or how they made ends meet. I knew that Kimry earned its living from boots, that Tula made samovars and rifles, that

Odessa was a port. But I had no idea what our town was or what it produced. The people of Great Dvoryansky Street, and two other better-class streets, lived off their capital and civil servants' salaries that were paid by the government. But how the remaining eight streets that ran parallel for two miles and disappeared behind the hill coped was always an insoluble mystery to me. It embarrasses me to describe how they lived. No public gardens, no theatre, no decent orchestra. Only young Jewish men went into the town and club libraries, so magazines and new books lay uncut for months. Rich, educated people slept in stuffy, cramped bedrooms on wooden beds crawling with bugs, children were kept in disgustingly dirty rooms called nurseries and even old and respected servants slept on the kitchen floor, covered in rags. On fast days the houses reeked of borshch and on others of sturgeon fried in sunflower oil. They ate nasty food and drank unwholesome water. At the town hall, the governor's, the bishop's – all over the place – they had been talking for years about the town not having good, cheap water and maintained that two hundred thousand should be borrowed from the government to provide a proper supply. The three dozen or so very rich people in town, who had been known to gamble away whole estates at cards, also drank the bad water and were forever talking excitedly about the loan: this was something I just could not understand. It struck me that it would have been simpler for them to lay out the money from their own pockets.

I did not know one honest man in the whole town. My father took bribes, imagining that he was given them out of respect for his moral virtues. If schoolboys wanted to get into a higher class, they boarded with their teachers, who charged them the earth. At recruiting-time the military commander's wife took bribes from the young men, even allowing them to buy her a few drinks, and once she was too drunk to get up off her knees in church. The doctors also took bribes at recruiting-time, while the town medical officer and vet levied a tax on butchers' shops and inns. The local college traded in certificates granting exemption to certain classes; the senior clergy took bribes from the lower and from churchwardens. Anyone making an application at the municipal offices, the citizens' bureau, the health clinic and any other kind of institution was followed as he left by shouts of 'Don't forget to say *thank you*,' which meant going back and handing over thirty or forty copecks. And those who didn't accept bribes – officials from the law department, for example – were arrogant, shook hands with two fingers, and were callous and narrow-minded. They played cards a great deal, drank a lot, and married the rich girls. There was no doubt that they had a harmful, corrupting influence on their surroundings. Only a few young girls gave any hint of moral purity. Most of them had honourable aspirations, were decent and pure of heart. But they had no knowledge of life and believed that bribes were given out of respect for moral virtue. After marrying they let themselves go, aged quickly and were hopelessly swallowed up in the mire of that vulgar, Philistine existence.

III

They were building a railway in our district. On Saturday evenings gangs of louts roamed around the town. They were called navvies and the people were scared of them. I often saw one of these brutes, bloody-faced and capless, hauled off to the police station, while material evidence in the form of a samovar or underwear still wet from the washing-line, was carried behind. The navvies usually congregated around pubs and markets. They ate, drank, and swore and pursued every woman of easy virtue who happened to be passing with piercing whistles. To amuse this starving riff-raff our shopkeepers gave dogs and cats vodka to drink, or tied a paraffin can to a dog's tail and then whistled, making it tear down the street. Squealing in terror from the can clattering after it, the dog would think some dreadful monster was in hot pursuit and ran way out of town, far into the fields, until it dropped exhausted. And there were some dogs in the town that never stopped trembling, their tails permanently between their legs. People said the joke was too much for them and they had gone mad.

The station was being constructed about three miles from town. The engineers were said to have asked for a bribe of fifty thousand roubles if they brought the line right up to the town. But the council was not prepared to pay more than forty and they fell out over the ten thousand. And now the citizens were sorry, because they had to build a road to the station which, according to estimates, would cost a great deal more. Sleepers and rails had already been laid along the whole line and service trains ran, carrying building materials and workmen. The only delay was with the bridges, which Dolzhikov was building, and one or two unfinished stations.

Dubechnya, as the first station was called, was about eleven miles away. I walked there. As the morning sun caught them, the cornfields shone bright green. The countryside was flat and cheerful round about here, and in the distance the station, hillocks and remote farmsteads were clearly outlined. How good it was to be out in the open country! And how I longed to be saturated by this awareness of freedom – if only for one morning – so that I could forget what was happening in town, forget how hungry and poor I was. Nothing was so off-putting as those sharp pangs of hunger, when loftier notions became strangely intermingled with thoughts of buckwheat porridge, mutton chops and fried fish. There I was standing in the fields looking up at a skylark hovering motionless in the air, hysterically pouring out its song, while all I could think was 'Some bread and butter would be nice!' Or I would sit by the roadside with my eyes closed, to rest and to listen to the wonderful sounds of May – when suddenly I'd recall the smell of hot potatoes. In general, for someone so tall and strongly built as myself, I wasn't getting enough to eat and therefore my overriding sensation during the day was one of hunger. Perhaps it was because of this that I understood so well why many people work just for their daily bread and can talk only of food.

At Dubechnya the inside of the station was being plastered
and an upper wooden storey added to the pumping-house.
It was hot, there was a smell of slaked lime and the workmen
idly wandered around piles of wooden shavings and rubble.
A pointsman was sleeping near his hut and the sun beat
right into his face. There wasn't a single tree. The telegraph
wires, with hawks perched on them here and there, hummed
faintly. Not knowing what to do I wandered among the
heaps of rubbish and remembered the engineer's reply when
I asked what my duties would be: '. . . we'll see'. But what
was there to see in this wilderness? The plasterers talked
about a foreman and a certain Fedot Vasilyev. It was all
foreign to me and I became more and more depressed – a
physical depression when you are conscious of your arms,
legs and massive body, but when you have no idea what to
do with them or where to put them.

After wandering about for at least two hours I noticed
some telegraph poles stretching away from the station to
the right of the track, stopping by a white stone wall about
a mile off. The workmen said that the office was over there
and at last I understood that that was where I had to report.

It was a very old, long-abandoned country estate. The
spongy stone wall, severely weathered, had collapsed in
places. The blind wall of one of the outbuildings – which
had a rusty roof patched with shiny bits of tin – faced the
open country. Through the gates I could see a spacious yard
thick with weeds and an old manor-house with sun-blinds
in the window and a steep roof red with rust. On each side
of the house stood the outbuildings, which were identical.
One had its windows boarded up, while the other's were
open. A line of washing hung nearby and some calves were
wandering about. The last telegraph pole stood in the yard
with a wire leading from it to a window in the outbuilding
with the outward-facing blank wall. The door was open
and I went in. A man with dark curly hair and a canvas
jacket was sitting at a table by the telegraph apparatus. He
gave me a stern, sullen look, but immediately smiled and
said, 'Hallo, Better-than-Nothing.'

It was Ivan Cheprakov, an old friend from school who had been expelled from Form Two for smoking. During the autumn we used to catch goldfinches, greenfinches and grosbeaks and sell them in the market early in the morning, while our parents were still asleep. We would lie in wait for flocks of migrant starlings, shooting at them with pellets and then gathering up the wounded. Some of them died in the most terrible torment – to this day I can remember them squeaking at night in the cage in my room. The ones that recuperated were sold and we swore blindly that they were males. In the market once I had only one starling left which I had been trying to sell and finally let it go for a mere copeck. 'Still, *it's better than nothing!*' I said, trying to console myself as I put the copeck in my pocket. From that time street urchins and the boys from school nicknamed me 'Better-than-Nothing'. Urchins and shop-keepers still teased me with this name, although no one except me could remember its origin.

Cheprakov wasn't strongly built. He was narrow-chested, round-shouldered and long-legged. His tie was like a piece of string, he had no waistcoat, and his down-at-heel boots were in a worse state than mine. He rarely blinked and always had a look of urgency about him, as though about to grab something.

'Now, wait a jiff,' he said, fidgeting. 'And listen! Now, what was I saying?'

We started talking. I found out that the estate where I now was had been the Cheprakovs' property until recently, and only last autumn had passed into the hands of Dolzhikov, who thought it more profitable to put his money into land than keep it in cash. Already he had bought three sizeable estates in the district on mortgage. At the sale Cheprakov's mother had reserved the right to live in one of the outbuildings for two years and had talked them into giving her son a job in the office.

'It would have surprised me if he hadn't bought it!' Cheprakov said, referring to the engineer. 'He makes so much out of the contractors alone! He fleeces everybody!'

Then he took me off to dinner, having decided, after a great deal of fuss, that I would live with him in the outbuilding and have my meals at his mother's.

'She's very tight-fisted with me,' he said. 'But she won't charge you very much.'

It was very cramped in the small rooms where his mother lived. All of them, even the hall and lobby, were crammed with furniture brought from the big house after the sale of the estate. It was all mahogany and very old-fashioned. Mrs Cheprakov, a very plump, middle-aged woman with slanting Chinese eyes, was sitting in a large armchair at the window knitting a stocking.

She greeted me with great ceremony.

'Mother, this is Poloznev,' Cheprakov said, introducing me. 'He'll be working here.'

'Are you a *gentleman*?' she asked in a strange, unpleasant voice. I thought I could hear fat gurgling in her throat.

'Yes,' I replied.

'Please sit down.'

It was a poor meal. All we had was sour curd pie and milk soup. Mrs Cheprakov, our hostess, kept winking strangely, first with one eye, then the other. Although she spoke and ate, there was something deathly about her whole body and she even seemed to smell like a corpse. There was scarcely a flicker of life in her, only the dim consciousness that she was a lady, and a landowner, who had once owned serfs, and that she had been a general's wife, whom the servants had to call madam. When these pathetic remnants of life briefly flared up she would tell her son, 'Jean, you're not holding your knife properly.'

Or she would breathe deeply and tell me, with all the affectedness of a hostess anxious to entertain her guest, 'As you know, we've sold the estate. It's a pity, of course, we'd grown so used to it. But Dolzhikov has promised to make Jean station-master at Dubechnya, so we shan't be leaving. We'll live in the station, which is really the same as being on the estate. Such a nice man, that engineer! He's very handsome, isn't he?'

Not long before, the Cheprakovs had been living in style, but after the general died everything changed. Mrs Cheprakov started quarrelling with the neighbours and taking people to court. She stopped paying her managers and workmen. She was in perpetual fear of being robbed and in about ten years Dubechnya had become unrecognizable.

Behind the main house was an old garden that had run wild, and it was choked with weeds and bushes. I walked up and down the terrace, which was still firm and beautiful. Through a french window I could see a room with a parquet floor – most probably the drawing-room. The only furniture was an old-fashioned piano and engravings in broad mahogany frames on the walls. All that was left of the flower-beds were peonies and poppies holding their white and bright red heads above the grass. Young maples and elms, gnawed at by cows, grew over the paths, stretching out and crowding one another. The garden was thickly overgrown and seemed impenetrable, but this was only near the house, where there were still poplars, pines and ancient limes, all of the same age and survivors of former avenues. Beyond them, however, the garden had been cleared for mowing hay, and here it was not so damp, one's mouth and eyes were not attacked by cobwebs, and now and then a gentle breeze stirred. The deeper you went into that garden the more it opened out. Here there were wild cherry and plum trees, wide-spreading apple trees disfigured by props and canker. There were such lofty pear trees that it was hard to believe they really were pear trees. This part of the garden was rented to women traders from the town and it was guarded against thieves and starlings by an idiot peasant who lived in a cottage.

As it gradually thinned out the garden became a real meadow sloping down to a river overgrown with green rushes and osiers. Near the mill-dam was a deep pond full of fish. A small mill with thatched roof angrily hummed away and frogs croaked furiously. Occasionally the mirror-like surface of the water was broken by ripples, water-lilies trembled as lively fish brushed past them. On the far side of the stream was the hamlet of Dubechnya. The calm blue millpond drew one to it, promising cool and rest. And now all this – the millpond, the mill and the pleasant river banks – belonged to the engineer!

And so I started my new job. I received and dispatched telegrams, wrote out expense sheets, made fair copies of order forms, claims and reports that were sent to our office by illiterate foremen and workmen. Most of the day I did nothing but pace the room waiting for telegrams. Or I would make a boy sit there and go out into the garden for a walk until he came running to tell me that the telegraph machine was clicking. I had dinner at Mrs Cheprakov's. They hardly ever served meat and we usually had nothing but milk dishes; on fast days such as Wednesday and Friday, they brought out the 'Lenten' pink plates. Mrs Cheprakov was in the habit of always winking and I felt ill at ease whenever I was with her.

As there wasn't enough work in the outbuilding, even for one person, Cheprakov slept or went down with his rifle to the millpond to shoot ducks. In the evenings he would get drunk in the village or at the station, and before going to bed would look at himself in the mirror and shout, 'Hello, Ivan Cheprakov!'

When drunk he looked very pale, and he kept rubbing his hands and producing a neighing laugh. He would strip and run around the field stark naked for the fun of it. He used to eat flies and said that they had a rather sour taste.

IV

One day, after dinner, he came running breathlessly into the outbuilding and said, 'You'd better get moving, your sister's arrived.'

I went out. A cab from the town was standing at the entrance to the main house. My sister had come with Anyuta Blagovo and a gentleman in military tunic. As I went closer I recognized him as Anyuta's brother, an army doctor.

'We've come for a picnic!' he said. 'I hope it's all right.'

My sister and Anyuta wanted to ask how I was getting on, but neither spoke and simply stared at me. They could see I didn't like it there and my sister's eyes filled with tears, while Anyuta Blagovo blushed. We went into the garden with the doctor leading the way and exclaiming rapturously, 'What air! My goodness, what air!'

He still looked like a student, he spoke and walked like one, and his grey eyes had the lively, natural, open look of a good student. Next to his tall, beautiful sister he seemed frail and thin. His beard was thin too, as was his pleasant tenor voice. He had been serving somewhere with his regiment and was now home on leave. He said that he was going to St Petersburg in the autumn to sit for his M.D. A family man with a wife and three children, he had married young, when he was a second-year student, and people in the town said he had an unhappy life at home and that he wasn't living with his wife.

'What's the time?' my sister asked anxiously. 'We'll have to be back early. Daddy said I could come and see my brother, but only if I'm back by six, without fail.'

'Oh, blow your father!' the doctor sighed.

I put the samovar on and we drank our tea on a rug in front of the terrace of the big house. The doctor knelt as he drank out of a saucer, saying that it was sheer bliss. Then Cheprakov fetched a key, opened the french window, and we all went into the house. It was gloomy, mysterious and smelt of fungus. Our footsteps had a hollow ring as if there was a cellar under the floor. The doctor stood at the piano and touched the keys, which replied with a weak, tremulous, rather blurred but melodious chord. He tested his voice and sang a song, frowning and impatiently stamping his foot when he touched a dead key. My sister had forgotten about going home, and excitedly paced the room saying, 'I feel so gay, so very, very gay!'

There was a note of surprise in her voice and it was as if she did not think that she too could be happy. It was the first time I had seen her looking so cheerful. She even looked prettier. In profile she wasn't very pretty, with protruding nose and mouth, so that she always seemed to be blowing. But she had beautiful, dark eyes, a pale, very delicate complexion and a kind, sad look that was most touching. When she spoke she seemed attractive, beautiful even. Both of us took after our mother – we were broad-shouldered, strong, and with great staying-power – but her pallor was that of a sick person. She was always coughing and sometimes I detected in her eyes the look of a person who was seriously ill but who was somehow trying to hide it. There was something child-like, naive in her gaiety now, as if the child's sense of joy that had been crushed and stifled by our strict upbringing had suddenly awakened in her and was struggling to express itself.

But when evening came and the horses were brought round my sister became quiet and seemed to shrink. She sat down in the carriage like a prisoner in the dock.

When they had driven off and everything became quiet, it struck me that Anyuta Blagovo had not spoken one word to me the whole time.

'An amazing girl!' I thought. 'Wonderful!'

St Peter's Fast arrived and every day we had only Lenten food. Idleness and the uncertainty of my position had brought on a physical depression. Feeling dissatisfied with myself, sluggish and hungry, I lounged around the estate, just waiting until I was in the right mood to leave.

One day, late in the afternoon, when Radish was with us in the outbuilding, Dolzhikov unexpectedly came in, very sunburnt and grey with dust. He had spent three days on his section of the line, had just travelled to Dubechnya on a railway engine and had walked over from the station to see us. While he was waiting for a cab to come from town and collect him, he made a tour of the estate with his manager, giving orders in a loud voice. Then he sat in our building for a whole hour writing letters. While he was there some telegrams came through and he tapped out the answers himself. The three of us stood to attention, not saying a word.

'What a mess!' he said, looking disgustedly at the records. 'In a fortnight's time I'm transferring the office to the station and I just don't know what I'm going to do with you.'

'I'm trying very hard, sir,' Cheprakov said.

'I can see how you're trying. All you can do is draw your wages,' he continued. 'Just because you have people to pull strings for you, you think it's easy to get a quick leg-up. Well, *no one* gets that from me. No one ever bothered about *me*. Before I was in charge of the railway I was an engine-driver. I worked in Belgium as an ordinary greaser. Hey, you, Panteley,' he said, turning to Radish, 'what are you doing here? Getting drunk with this lot, eh?'

For some reason he called all simple labourers Panteley, while he despised people like myself and Cheprakov, calling us scum and drunken pigs behind our backs. On the whole he was hard on his junior clerks, fined them and coolly gave them the sack without any explanation.

At last his carriage arrived. By way of farewell he promised to sack the lot of us in a fortnight and called his manager a blockhead. Then he sprawled back in his carriage and bowled off to town.

'Andrey,' I asked Radish, 'can I work for you?'

'Oh, all right.'

And we went off to town together. When the station and manor-house were far behind I asked 'Andrey, why did you come to Dubechnya just now?'

'Firstly, my lads are working on the line, and secondly I went to pay the general's widow the interest I owe her. Last year I borrowed fifty roubles and now I'm paying her a rouble a month.'

The painter stopped and caught hold of one of my coat buttons. 'My dear Misail,' he went on, 'the way I see it is this. An ordinary working man or gent who lends money – even at the very lowest rates – is a villain. The truth cannot dwell in him.'

Thin, pale and terrifying, Radish closed his eyes, shook his head and spoke out, in the solemn voice of a sage, 'Grass doth perish, iron rusts and lies devour the soul. God save us sinners!'

V

Radish was an impractical person, with no head for business. He took on more work than he could handle, tended to lose his nerve when settling up, and as a result was almost always losing money. He did painting, glazing, wallpapering and even roofing jobs, and I can remember him running around for three days looking for roofers – just because of some miserable little job. He was an excellent workman and sometimes earned as much as ten roubles a day. But for his wish to be boss at all costs, to call himself a contractor, he would have been quite prosperous.

He was paid by the job, while he paid me and the other lads by the day – between seventy copecks and a rouble. When the weather was hot and dry we did different outside jobs, mainly roof painting. I was not used to this kind of work and my feet burned – I felt I was walking over red-hot flag-stones – and when I put my felt boots on my feet were even hotter. But this was only at the beginning; later on I got used to it and everything went as smooth as clock-work.

Now I was living among people who had to do physical work, for whom it was unavoidable and who slaved like cart-horses, often without being aware of the moral meaning of work and never using the word 'work' in conversation even. Next to them I felt rather like a cart-horse myself. I became ever more aware that what I was doing just had to be done, there was no avoiding it, and this made life easier and freed me from all doubts.

At first I found everything new and absorbing, as if I had been reborn. I could sleep on the ground or go barefoot, which was extremely pleasant. I could stand in a crowd of ordinary people without attracting any bad feeling, and when a cabman's horse fell down in the street I would rush to help pull it up without worrying if my clothes got dirty.

Most important, I was earning my own living and wasn't a burden to anyone.

Painting roofs, particularly when we used our own paint, was considered highly profitable, and so even such good workmen as Radish didn't turn their noses up at this rough, tedious work. With skinny, purple legs, he looked like a stork in his short trousers as he walked over the roofs, and I would hear him sigh deeply as he wielded his brush 'Woe, woe unto us sinners!'

He walked over roofs as easily as over the ground. Despite being as pale and sickly as a corpse, he was extraordinarily agile, painting the cupolas and domes of churches just like a young man, without using any scaffolding – only ladders and ropes. It was rather frightening seeing him there, poised aloft, far above the ground, stretching himself to his full height and pronouncing solemnly, on behalf of some person unknown, 'Grass doth perish, iron rusts and lies devour the soul!'

At times he would ponder something and answer his own thoughts: 'Anything's possible! Anything!'

When I went home from work, everyone sitting on benches near their gates – shop-assistants, errand-boys and their masters – followed me with sneers and abuse. At first this worried me and seemed quite monstrous.

'Better-than-Nothing!' I heard from all sides. 'Got yer paint, botcher!'

No one was so unkind to me as those very people who only recently had themselves been ordinary labourers and earned their living by unskilled labour. When I passed the row of shops, water was 'accidentally' thrown over me near the ironmonger's and once someone even threw a stick at me. A grey-haired old fish merchant once barred my path, eyed me malevolently and said, 'I'm not sorry for you, you fool! It's your father I'm sorry for!'

For some reason my friends were embarrassed if they met me. Some looked on me as a crank or a clown, others were sorry for me, while others did not know how to approach me and I found it difficult to make them out. One day I met

Anyuta Blagovo in a side-street near Great Dvoryansky Street. I was on my way to work, carrying two long brushes and a bucket of paint. She flared up when she recognized me.

'Please don't bow to me in the street,' she said, in a nervous, stern, trembling voice, without offering to shake hands, and suddenly tears glistened in her eyes. 'If you really must do this kind of thing, then go ahead, but please try and avoid meeting me in public.'

I had left Great Dvoryansky Street and was living in the suburb of Makarikha with my old nanny Karpovna, a kindly but morose old woman who lived in perpetual fear that something dreadful was about to happen. She was frightened by any kind of dream and even saw evil omens in the bees and wasps that flew into her room. In her opinion my becoming a workman was an evil portent.

'It's all up with you!' she said mournfully, shaking her head. 'You're finished!'

Prokofy the butcher, her adopted son, lived with her in that little house. He was a hulking, clumsy fellow of about thirty, with reddish hair and wiry moustache. Whenever we met in the hall he would not speak and would politely give way to me – if he happened to be drunk he would accord me a full military salute. When he dined in the evenings I could hear him grunting and sighing through the wooden plank partition as he polished off one glass of vodka after the other.

'Ma!' he would call in a low voice.

'What is it?' Karpovna would reply. (She loved her adopted son dearly.) 'What is it, sonny?'

'I'm going to do you a favour, ma. I'll keep you in your old age, in this vale of tears, and when you die I'll pay all the funeral expenses. I mean it.'

I would be up before dawn every morning and I went early to bed. We house-painters had good appetites and slept soundly, but for some reason my heart would beat violently at night. I never quarrelled with my workmates. All day long there was an endless torrent of abuse, obscene oaths, and sentiments such as 'Damn your eyes!' or 'Blast your guts!' were typical. However, we were all good friends. The lads suspected I was some kind of religious fanatic and poked good-humoured fun at me, saying that even my own father had disowned me. Then they would tell me that they seldom showed up at church and that many of them hadn't been to confession for ten years. They tried to justify this slackness by saying that painters were the black sheep of humanity.

The other men respected me and looked up to me. They were obviously pleased that I didn't smoke or drink, that I led a quiet, steady life. But they were rather shocked when I didn't help them steal drying oil or join them when they went to ask customers for tips. Stealing employers' oil and paint was common practice among painters and decorators and was not considered a crime. Remarkably, even someone as virtuous as Radish always took some whiting and oil after work, and even respectable old men with their own houses in Makarikha weren't above asking for tips. I would feel angry and ashamed when the lads, at the start or finish of some job, would all go cringing before some little pip-squeak, humbly thanking him for the ten copecks he gave them.

They behaved like sly courtiers to customers and almost every day I was reminded of Shakespeare's Polonius.

'Oh, it looks like rain,' a customer would remark, glancing at the sky.

'Yes, sir, no doubt about it,' the painters would agree.

'On the other hand, those aren't rain clouds. Perhaps it's not going to rain.'

'Oh, no, sir, that's for sure!'

Behind customers' backs their attitude was usually ironical – when they saw a gentleman, for example, sitting on his balcony with a newspaper they would remark, 'Can sit reading his paper all right, but I dare say he's got nothing to eat.'

I never visited my family. When I returned from work I would often find brief, worried notes from my sister, about Father. One day he'd been unusually pensive over dinner and had eaten nothing. Or he'd fallen down. Or he'd locked himself in his room and had not emerged for a long time. News like this worried me and kept me awake. I even used to walk past our house in Great Dvoryansky Street at night, looking into the dark windows and trying to find out if things were all right at home. On Sundays my sister would visit me, but she did this furtively, pretending she had come to see Nanny, not me. If she came into my room she would invariably look very pale, with tear-stained eyes, and she would immediately start crying.

'Father will never get over it!' she said. 'If something should happen to him, God forbid, it will be on your conscience for the rest of your life. It's dreadful, Misail! I beg you, turn over a new leaf, for Mother's sake!'

'My dear sister,' I said, 'how can I turn over a new leaf when I'm convinced that I'm acting according to my conscience? Try and understand that!'

'I know you're obeying your conscience, but why can't you do it differently, without upsetting everyone?'

'Oh, goodness gracious!' the old woman would sigh from behind the door. 'It's all up with you! There's trouble brewing, my dears, there's trouble brewing!'

VI

One Sunday Dr Blagovo paid me an unexpected visit. He was wearing a tunic over his silk shirt and high, patent-leather boots.

'I've come to see you!' he began, pressing my hand like a student. 'Every day I hear things about you and I've been meaning to come and have a heart-to-heart with you, as they say. It's deadly boring in this town. They all seem dead and there's no one you can have a conversation with. God, it's hot!' he went on, taking his tunic off, leaving just his silk shirt. 'My dear chap, please let's talk!'

I myself felt bored and for a long time had been wanting some other company than house-painters. I was genuinely delighted to see him.

'Let me begin,' he said, sitting on my bed, 'by saying how deeply I feel for you and how deeply I respect the kind of life you're leading. You're misunderstood in this town, but there's no one capable of understanding you here. As you know only too well, with one or two exceptions, they're all a lot of pig-faced freaks. Right away, at the picnic, I guessed the kind of person you were. You are a noble, honest person with high principles. I respect you and it's a great honour to shake you by the hand!' he continued rapturously. 'To change your life as drastically and abruptly as you did, you first had to experience a complex emotional crisis. To continue as you are, always true to your convictions, you must try and put your heart and soul into it, day after day, never flagging. And now for a start, tell me if you agree that if you exercised your will-power, effort, all your potential, on something else – on eventually becoming a great scholar or artist – would your life be richer, deeper, more productive, in every respect?'

We kept talking and when we came to the subject of manual labour, I expressed the following opinion: 'The strong should not enslave the weak, the minority must not be parasites on the majority, or leeches, forever sucking their life-blood. By that I mean – and without exception – everyone, strong or weak, rich or poor, should play his part in the struggle for existence. In this respect there's no better leveller than physical work, with *everyone* being forced to do some.'

'So you think that absolutely everyone must do physical work?' asked the doctor.

'Yes.'

'All right, but supposing everyone, including the cream of humanity – the thinkers and great scholars – played his part in the struggle for existence and wasted his time breaking stones or painting roofs. Wouldn't that be a serious threat to progress?'

'But where's the danger?' I asked. 'Surely progress is all about good deeds and obeying the moral law. If you don't enslave anyone, if you aren't a burden to anyone, what more progress do you need?'

'Look here!' Blagovo said, suddenly flying into a rage and leaping to his feet. 'Really! If a snail in its shell passes its time trying to perfect itself, messing around with moral laws – would you call that progress?'

'Why *messing around*?' I said, taking offence. 'If you stop compelling your neighbour to feed, clothe you, to transport you from place to place, to protect you from your enemies, isn't that progress, in the context of a life founded on slavery? In my opinion, that's progress and perhaps the only kind possible for man, the only kind that is really necessary.'

'There's no limit to the progress that man can make, and this applies all over the world. Any talk of "possible" progress, limited by our needs or short-term considerations, is strange, if you don't mind my saying so.'

'If progress has no limits, as you put it, then its aims are bound to be vague,' I said. 'Imagine living without knowing what for!'

'All right! But this "not knowing" isn't as boring as your "knowing". I climb a ladder called progress, civilization, culture. I keep climbing, not knowing precisely where I'm going, but in fact this wonderful ladder alone makes life worth living. But you know why you are living – so that some people stop enslaving others, so that the artist and the man who mixes his colours both have the same food to eat. But this vulgar, sordid, grey side of life – aren't you revolted, living for that alone? If some insects enslave others, then to hell with them! Let them gobble each other up! But it's not them we should be talking about; they will die and rot anyway, however hard you try to save them from slavery. The Great Unknown which awaits all mankind in the remote future – *that's* what we should be thinking about.'

Blagovo argued heatedly, but I could see that something else was worrying him. 'I don't think your sister's coming,' he said, looking at his watch. 'When she was with us yesterday she said she'd come out here to see you. You keep on and on about slavery . . .' he continued. 'But that's a particular case, isn't it, and mankind solves such problems gradually, as it goes along.'

We talked about gradual development. I said, 'The question whether to do good or evil is decided by each person by himself, without waiting for mankind to solve the problem gradually. What's more, gradual development cuts two ways. Side by side with the gradual development of humane ideas we can observe the gradual growth of quite different ideas. Serfdom has been abolished, but capitalism flourishes. Notions of freedom are all the rage now, the majority still feeds, clothes and defends the minority, just as in the times of the Tartars, while it starves, goes naked and unprotected itself. This state of affairs fits in beautifully with any trend or current of opinion you like, since the art of enslavement is also being gradually refined. We don't flog our servants in the stables any more, but we develop refined forms of slavery — at least, we are very good at finding justification for it in isolated instances. Ideas are all right, but if now, at the end of the nineteenth century, it became possible for us to lumber working men with all our more unpleasant bodily functions, then lumber them we would. And then of course we would try and justify ourselves by saying that if the élite — the thinkers and great scholars — wasted their priceless time on these functions, then progress would be seriously jeopardized.'

Just then my sister arrived. Seeing the doctor, she fidgeted nervously, grew flustered and immediately said it was time to go home to Father.

'Now, Cleopatra,' Blagovo uged her, pressing both hands to his heart. 'What can possibly happen to Daddy if you stay just half an hour with me and your brother?'

He was quite open with us and was able to infect others with his high spirits. After a moment's deliberation my sister burst out laughing and suddenly cheered up, as she had done on the picnic. We went out into the fields, lay down on the grass and continued our conversation, looking at the town, where every window facing west seemed to have turned bright gold from the setting sun.

Every time my sister subsequently came to see me, Bla-govo would turn up, and they greeted each other as if they had met accidentally in my room. As I argued with the doctor, my sister would listen, and her face would take on an ecstatic, deeply affected, inquisitive look. I had the impression that another world was gradually opening up before her, one that she had never even dreamt of and whose meaning she was now trying to fathom. Without the doctor there she was quiet and sad, and if she sometimes cried when she sat on my bed she never told me the reason.

In August Radish ordered us to leave for the railway line. Two days before we had received the command to 'get going' out of that town. Father came to see me. He sat down and wiped his red face without hurrying or looking at me. Then he took a local *Herald* out of his pocket and proceeded to read slowly, emphasizing every word, about how someone – the same age as me – the son of the manager of the State Bank, had been appointed departmental director in a provincial revenue office.

'Just look at yourself now!' he said, folding the paper. 'Beggar! Tramp! Ruffian! Even the working classes and peasants are educated, so they can take their place in life. And you, a Poloznev, for all your distinguished, noble ancestors, are heading straight for the rubbish dump. But I didn't come here to talk to *you*. I've already given you up as a bad job,' he went on in a subdued voice as he stood up. 'I've come to find out where your sister is, you scoundrel. She left the house after dinner, it's getting on for eight and she's still not back. She's started going out fairly often now without telling me. She hasn't the same respect for me – there I can see your evil, rotten influence. Where is she?'

He was holding that umbrella I knew so well and I was at my wits' end. Expecting a beating, I stood to attention. But he saw me glance at the umbrella and this probably put him off.

'Do what you like!' he said. 'You won't have my blessing!'

'Oh dear, oh dear!' Nanny muttered behind the door.

'You poor, stupid wretch. I feel deep down that there's trouble brewing. I can feel it!'

I started work on the railway line. For the whole of August it rained non-stop and it was damp and cold. They could not get the crops in from the fields, and on the big farms, where they used harvesting-machines, the wheat was lying in heaps instead of sheaves – I can remember those miserable heaps growing darker with every day that passed, the wheat germinating in them. It was hard to do any sort of work. The heavy rain ruined everything we tried to do. We weren't allowed to live or sleep in the station buildings, so we took shelter in filthy, damp dug-outs where the navvies had lived during the summer, and I could not sleep at night for the cold and the wood-lice crawling across my face and arms. When we were working near the bridges, a whole gang of navvies turned up in the evenings just to give the painters a thrashing – this was a form of sport for them. They beat us, stole our brushes and – to provoke us to a fight – they smeared the railway huts with green paint. To cap it all, Radish started paying us extremely irregularly. All the painting in this section was handed over to some contractor who passed it on to someone else, who handed it on to Radish for a twenty-per-cent commission. We weren't paid much for the work – and there was that incessant rain. Time was wasted, we were unable to work, but Radish was obliged to pay the men daily. The hungry painters came near to beating him up, called him a swindler, bloodsucker, Judas, while the poor man sighed, held up his hands to heaven in desperation and went time and again to Mrs Cheprakov for money.

VII

A rainy, muddy, dark autumn set in. There was no work around and I would sit at home for days on end without anything to do. Or I would take on different jobs not connected with painting – shifting earth for foundations and getting twenty copecks a day for it. Dr Blagovo had gone to St Petersburg, my sister did not come any more, Radish was at home ill in bed, expecting to die any day.

And the general mood was autumnal. Perhaps it was because I was a working man now that I saw only the seamy side of town life and therefore I could not avoid making discoveries nearly every day that drove me to despair. My fellow citizens, of whom I already had a low opinion, or who appeared to be perfectly decent, now turned out to be contemptible, cruel people, capable of the meanest trick. They swindled simple working men like us, cheated us out of our money, made us wait hours on end in freezing entrance-halls or kitchens, insulted us and treated us very roughly. During the autumn I papered the reading-room and two other rooms at the club. I was paid seven copecks a roll, but I was told to sign for twelve, and when I refused, a handsome gentleman with gold-rimmed spectacles (most probably one of the senior members) told me, 'Just one more word from you and I'll bash your face in, you swine!'

And when a waiter whispered to him that I was the son of Poloznev the architect, he blushed with embarrassment, but immediately recovered and said 'To hell with him!'

At the local shops we workmen were fobbed off with rotten meat, stale flour and weak tea. In church we were shoved around by the police; in hospital we were robbed by junior staff and nurses, and if we didn't have the money to bribe them with, they took revenge by giving us our food on filthy plates. The most junior post office clerk thought he had the right to address us as if we were animals, yelling roughly and insolently: 'Hey, you there, wait! Where do you think you're going?' Even house dogs were hostile and attacked us particularly viciously. However, what startled me more than anything in my new job was the complete lack of fair play — precisely what the common people mean when they say that someone has become a 'lost soul'. Hardly a day passed without some kind of swindle. The merchants who sold us mixing oils, the main contractors, workmen, even customers — they all tried it on. Of course, there was no question of our having any rights, and we always had to beg for the money we had earned as we stood cap in hand at the back door.

I was papering one of the rooms next to the club reading-room. One evening as I was about to leave, Mr Dolzhikov's daughter came in carrying a pile of books. I bowed.

'Oh, hello!' she said, immediately recognizing me and holding out her hand. 'So glad to see you.'

She smiled and gave my smock, bucket of paste, the rolls of paper scattered over the floor an inquisitive, puzzled look. I was embarrassed and she felt the same.

'Please forgive me for staring at you,' she said. 'People have told me so much about you, especially Dr Blagovo. He's simply crazy about you. And I've met your sister. She's a charming, likeable girl, but I was unable to convince her that there's nothing terrible about the simple life you're leading. On the contrary, you're the most fascinating man in town now.'

She glanced once again at the bucket of paste and the wallpaper and went on 'I've asked Dr Blagovo to help us to get to know each other better, but he's obviously forgotten or was too busy. At any rate, we already know each other and I'd be extremely obliged if you dropped in to see me some time. I'm really longing to have a talk with you! I'm a straightforward sort of person,' she continued, holding out her hand to me, 'and I hope you won't feel shy at my place. Father's away in St Petersburg.'

Her dress rustled as she entered the reading-room. It took me a long time to get to sleep after I was home.

During that gloomy autumn some kind soul, who obviously wanted to make my life a little easier, sent me tea, lemons, cakes and roast grouse from time to time. Karpovna said that a soldier always brought the food, but she didn't know who the sender was. The soldier would ask if I was well, if I had a hot meal every day and if I had warm clothes. When the frosts set in, the soldier came over as before, while I was out, with a soft woollen scarf. It had a delicate, very faint smell of perfume and I guessed who my good fairy was. The perfume was lily-of-the-valley, Anyuta Blagovo's favourite.

Towards winter there was more work about and everything cheered up. Radish recovered once more and together we worked in the cemetery chapel, cleaning the iconostasis and scraping it with palette knives before the gilding. It was clean, relaxing work – money for jam, as the lads put it. In one day we could get through a lot of work and besides that the time flew past imperceptibly. There was no swearing, laughter or noisy conversation. The very place encouraged us to be quiet and well-behaved and inspired us with calm, serious thoughts. Immersed in our work, we would stand or sit, as motionless as statues. There was the deathly silence befitting a cemetery and if someone dropped his tool or if the icon-lamp sputtered there was a sharp, resonant, echoing sound, which made us all look round. After a long silence we would hear a humming, just like a swarm of bees – they were reading burial prayers at the porch for an infant, in unhurried, hushed voices. Or the artist who was painting a dove surrounded by stars on a cupola would start softly whistling, then suddenly stop, remembering where he was. Or Radish would answer his own thoughts and sigh 'Anything's possible! Anything!' Or bells would toll slowly and mournfully above our heads and the painters would say that they must be burying some rich man.

I spent the days in that silence, in the church twilight, and on long evenings played billards or sat in the theatre gallery wearing the new woollen suit that I had bought with my wages. The performances and concerts had already started at the Azhogins'. Radish painted the scenery by himself now. He told me the plots of the plays and *tableaux vivants* which he had managed to see at the Azhogins', and I listened enviously. I had a strong urge to go to rehearsals, but I could not bring myself to go to the Azhogins'.

Dr Blagovo arrived a week before Christmas. Once again we argued and in the evenings we played billiards. During the games he would take off his jacket, unbutton his shirt at the front, and for some reason he was always trying to look like some inveterate rake. He did not drink very much, but became very rowdy when he did have a drop, managing to part with twenty roubles in an evening in a low pub like the Volga.

Once again my sister began visiting me. Both she and the doctor seemed surprised every time they happened to meet, but it was obvious from her joyful, guilty face that these meetings were not accidental. One evening the doctor asked me, when we were playing billiards, 'Listen, why don't you call on Masha Dolzhikov? You don't know how clever and charming she is, such a simple, kind soul.'

I told him about the reception I had got from her father in the spring.

'But it's stupid to talk like that!' the doctor laughed. 'There's a world of difference between the father and her! Now, my dear boy, don't offend her, try and call on her some time. What if we both went along tomorrow evening, together? Would you like that?'

He persuaded me. The following evening I put on my new woollen suit and set off, full of apprehension, to see Miss Dolzhikov. The footman didn't seem so snooty and intimidating as before, nor did the furniture look so luxurious as on that morning when I came to ask for a job. Miss Dolzhikov was expecting me and welcomed me like an old friend, shaking my hand firmly and warmly. She was wearing a grey, full-sleeved dress and her hair was done in the style that was called 'dogs' ears' a year later, when it became fashionable in town: it was combed back from the temple, over the ears, which made her face seem broader, and on this occasion she struck me as very like her father, who had a broad red face and an expression rather like a coachman's. She looked beautiful and elegant, but not young – about thirty perhaps, although she was in fact no more than twenty-five.

'That dear doctor, I'm so grateful to him!' she said, asking me to sit down. 'You wouldn't have come to see me if it hadn't been for him. I'm bored to death! Father's gone away and left me alone, and I don't know what to do with myself in this town.'

Then she began questioning me as to where I was working, what my wages were, where I lived.

'Do you earn enough to live on?' she asked.

'Yes.'

'You lucky man!' she sighed. 'I think all the evil in life comes from idleness, boredom, from nothing to exercise your mind on, and that's inevitable when you're used to living off others. Please don't get the idea that I'm just trying to impress. I mean this sincerely. It's not very interesting or pleasant being rich. They say "Make to yourselves friends of the mammon of unrighteousness" because there's no such thing as honest wealth and there never can be.'

She gave the furniture a cold, serious look as if she wanted to make an inventory. Then she went on, 'Comfort and luxury have a magical power. They gradually drag even strong-willed people down. Father and I once lived modestly and simply, but now take a look. It's just unheard of. We get through twenty thousand a year,' she said, shrugging her shoulders. 'In the provinces!'

'Comforts and luxuries should be viewed as the inevitable privilege of capital and education,' I said, 'and it strikes me that the comforts of life can be combined with any type of work, even the hardest and dirtiest. Your father is rich, but he himself says that he once had to work as an engine-driver and ordinary greaser.'

She smiled and sceptically shook her head. 'Papa sometimes eats bread soaked in kvass too,' she said. 'It's just a whim of his!'

At that moment the door-bell rang and she stood up.

'Educated and rich people should work like everyone else,' she went on, 'and everyone should be able to share in the creature comforts. There shouldn't be any privileges. Well, that's enough of the theorizing. Tell me something to cheer me up. Tell me about the house-painters. What are they like? Funny?'

The doctor came in. I started telling them all about the painters, but I was short of conversational practice. This had an inhibiting effect and I talked in the earnest dull voice of an ethnographer. The doctor told some stories too, about workmen's lives. He staggered, wept, knelt and even lay down on the floor to imitate a drunkard. It was an excellent piece of mimickry and Masha watched him and laughed until the tears came. Then he played the piano and sang in his pleasant, slight tenor voice while Masha stood nearby choosing the songs and correcting him when he made a mistake.

'I've heard that you sing as well,' I said.

'Yes, she sings "as well"!' the doctor said, horrified. 'She's wonderful, a true artist. And you say she sings "as well". Really, that's a bit much!'

'I used to study it once quite seriously,' she answered, 'but I've given it up now.'

Sitting on a low stool, she told us about her life in St Petersburg and imitated some well-known singers, mimicking their voices and styles. She made a sketch of the doctor in her album and then me. Although she was poor at drawing, she produced good likenesses of us both. She laughed, grew mischievous, pulled faces most charmingly. This suited her better than all her talk of ill-gotten gains. I felt that she had not really meant what she had just said about wealth and comfort, that it was all a kind of masquerade. She was an excellent comic actress. I pictured her next to the young ladies from the town, and even the beautiful, majestic Anyuta Blagovo didn't bear comparison with her. The difference was enormous – like that between a fine, cultivated rose and a wild one.

The three of us had supper together. The doctor and Masha drank red wine, champagne and then coffee with brandy. They clinked glasses and drank to friendship, intellect, progress, freedom. They didn't get drunk, only went red in the face, and they kept laughing at nothing until the tears flowed. As I didn't want to appear a wet blanket, I drank some red wine too.

'Extremely clever, richly gifted people,' Masha said, 'know how to live and they go their own way. But average people, like myself, for example, know nothing and can't do anything on their own. All that's left for them is to take note of important social trends and swim along with them.'

'But you can't take note of what doesn't exist, can you?' the doctor asked.

'Doesn't exist? We only say that because we can't actually see it.'

'Really? Social trends are an invention of modern literature. We don't have any such trends.'

And an argument started.

'We don't have any profound social currents and we never did,' the doctor said in a loud voice. 'There's just no limit to what this modern literature has invented. It's even thought up these intellectual tillers of the soil, but search any village around here – all you'll find is country bumpkins in their jackets or black frock-coats who can't even write a three-letter word without making four mistakes. In this land of ours cultural life hasn't even begun. There's that same savagery, that same out-and-out boorishness, that same mediocrity that existed five hundred years ago. These trends and currents are a load of piffling, pitiful trash – they're all bound up with lousy little interests! How can you possibly see anything worthwhile in them? If you think you've spotted some important social trend and follow it and devote your life to the latest rage – say freeing insects from slavery, or abstaining from beef rissoles – then I must congratulate you, madam. We must study and study. But as for significant social trends, we're not mature enough for them yet and, to be honest, we understand nothing about them.'

'You don't understand, but I do,' Masha said. 'Heavens, you're so dreadfully boring this evening!'

'Our job is to study, to try and accumulate as much knowledge as we can, since important social trends are to be found together with knowledge. The future happiness of mankind will proceed from knowledge alone. I drink to learning!'

'One thing is certain: we must reorganize our lives somehow,' Masha said after a pause for thought. 'Up to now life hasn't been worth living. Let's not talk about it.'

When we left her the cathedral clock was already striking two.

'Did you like her?' the doctor asked. 'She's wonderful, isn't she?'

On Christmas Day we dined at Masha's and we visited her almost every day during the holidays. We were the only visitors and she was right when she said that she knew no one in town besides myself and the doctor. We spent most of the time in long conversations. Sometimes the doctor brought a book or magazine, from which he read aloud to us. He was in fact the first educated man whom I had met. I'm not qualified to judge how much he knew, but he always let others into what he knew, as he wanted them to benefit from it. When it came to medicine, he was quite unlike any of our town doctors and what he said struck me as novel, something special. I felt that he could have become a real scholar had he wished. And he was perhaps the only man who had any serious influence on me at this time. After our frequent meetings and reading the books he gave me, I felt more and more the need for knowledge that might breathe life into my cheerless labours. Now it seemed strange that I hadn't known before that the whole world consisted of sixty elements, for example, or what oils or paint were made from, and that somehow I had got by without knowing these things. My friendship with the doctor uplifted me morally too. We often argued, and although I usually stuck to my opinions, it was thanks to him that I gradually became aware I just didn't understand everything, and I tried to devise the most stringent moral guidelines, so that my conscience would not be clouded or muddled.

For all that, the doctor, the most educated, the best man in the whole town, was far from perfect. In his manners, in his readiness to argue, in his pleasant tenor voice – even in his friendliness – there was something rather crude and bumptious. Whenever he took his coat off and walked around in his silk shirt, or when he tipped a waiter at a restaurant, I always had the impression that there was something of the barbarian in him, despite his being a cultured man.

One morning, towards Epiphany, he returned to St Petersburg. After dinner my sister came to see me. Without taking off her fur coat or hat she sat silently, very pale, staring at something. She had the shivers and I could see she was fighting against it.

'You must have caught a cold,' I said.

Her eyes filled with tears. She stood up and went over to Karpovna without a word to me, as if I had offended her. Shortly afterwards I heard her bitterly complaining voice: 'Nanny, what have I been living for up to now? What for? Tell me, I've wasted my youth, haven't I? The best years of my life have been spent keeping accounts, pouring tea, counting copecks, entertaining guests, in the conviction that there was nothing better! Please understand, Nanny, I have spiritual needs like anyone else and I want to lead a full life. But all they've done is turn me into a kind of housekeeper! Don't you think that's dreadful?'

She flung the keys through the doorway and they fell clattering to the floor in my room. They were the keys to the sideboard, kitchen cupboard, cellar and china cabinet – keys that Mother had once carried.

'Oh dear, oh dear me!' the old woman said in horror. 'Saints above!'

As she left, my sister came into my room to pick up the keys.

'Forgive me,' she said. 'Something strange has been happening to me recently.'

VIII

One day, in the late evening, I came home from Masha's to find a young police officer in a new uniform sitting at my table looking through a book.

'At last!' he said, standing up and stretching himself. 'This is the third time I've been. The Governor has ordered you to report to him at precisely nine o'clock tomorrow morning. Without fail.'

After taking a signed statement from me that I would do exactly what the Governor had ordered, he left. The police officer's late visit, plus the unexpected invitation to the Governor's, utterly depressed me. Since early childhood I have always been scared of gendarmes, policemen and court officials, and now I was worried stiff that I might really have committed some crime. I just could not sleep. Nanny and Prokofy were upset too and they couldn't sleep either. And Nanny had ear-ache as well. She kept groaning, and several times she started crying from the pain. Hearing that I was awake, Prokofy gingerly entered my room with a lamp and sat down at the table.

'You should drink some pepper-brandy,' he said after a moment's thought. 'A drink won't never do you harm in this vale of tears. And if Nanny had a drop of that stuff in her ear it would do her the world of good.'

After two o'clock he prepared to leave for the slaughter-house to fetch some meat. I knew that I wouldn't sleep before morning, so I went with him to kill the time until nine o'clock. We took a lamp with us. Prokofy's assistant Nikolka, a thirteen-year-old boy with blue patches on his face from frostbite – a real bandit from the look of him – urged on his horse in a husky voice as he followed us in a sledge.

'Like as not you'll be punished at the Governor's,' Prokofy told me on the way. 'Governors, archimandrites, officers, doctors – every calling has its own proper way of doing things. But you don't fall into line at all, you won't get away with that.'

The slaughter-house was beyond the cemetery and up to now I'd only seen it from the distance. It consisted of three gloomy sheds surrounded by a grey fence, and they gave off a suffocating stench when the wind blew from their direction on hot summer days. But it was so dark as we went into the yard we couldn't see them. I kept meeting horses and sledges – either empty or laden with meat. Men were walking around with lamps, cursing and swearing obscenely. Prokofy and Nikolka swore just as badly, and the incessant sound of abuse, coughing and the neighing of horses filled the air.

There was a smell of carcases and dung. It was thawing and snow mingled with the mud – in the darkness I felt I was walking over pools of blood.

When our sledge was fully laden we went off to the butcher's stall in the market. Day was breaking. Cooks with baskets and elderly women in cloaks passed by, one after the other. Cleaver in hand and wearing a blood-stained white apron, Prokofy swore terribly, crossed himself in the direction of the church and shouted all over the market that he was selling his meat at cost price, at a loss even. He gave short weight and short change. Despite seeing this, the cooks were so deafened by his shouting that they offered no protest, apart from calling him swindler and crook. Raising and bringing down that fearful cleaver with a fierce 'Ugh!' every time, he assumed picturesque poses. I was scared that he really might chop off someone's head or hand.

I spent the whole morning at the butcher's and when I finally went to the Governor's my fur coat smelt of meat and blood. I felt that someone had ordered me to go and attack a bear with a spear. I remember that steep staircase with its striped carpet and the young clerk in coat-and-tails with bright buttons silently pointing towards a door with both hands and then dashing off to announce me. I entered the hall, which was luxurious but cold, and tastelessly furnished. The narrow wall mirrors and bright yellow curtains were particular eyesores. I could see that governors might come and go, but the furnishings stayed the same forever. The young clerk again pointed at the door with both hands and I went over to a large green table, behind which stood a general with the Order of Vladimir round his neck.

'Mr Poloznev, I asked you to report to me,' he began, holding some letter and opening his mouth wide, like the letter 'O'. 'I asked you to come here so that I can inform you of the following. Your dear respected father has applied both orally and in writing to the Provincial Marshal of the Nobility, requesting him to summon you and make quite clear to you the absolute incompatibility of your behaviour with the title of gentleman, to which class you have the honour to belong. His Excellency Alexander Pavlovich, rightly assuming that your behaviour might lead others into temptation, and finding that mere persuasion on his part might be insufficient and that it was a clear-cut case for serious intervention on the part of the authorities, has conveyed his opinion of you in this letter. That opinion I happen to share.'

He said all this softly, respectfully, standing upright as though I were his superior. And there was nothing at all severe in the way he looked at me. His face was flabby, worn, and covered with wrinkles, with bags under the eyes. He dyed his hair and it was impossible to guess his age by looking at him – he could have been forty or sixty.

'I hope,' he went on, 'that you appreciate the tact of honourable Alexander Pavlovich in approaching me privately and not through official channels. I also invited you unofficially and I'm not talking to you as Governor but as a sincere admirer of your father. So, I'm asking you. Either mend your ways and return to those responsibilities befitting your rank. Failing that, to keep yourself out of trouble, go and live somewhere else, where you're not known and where you can do what you like. Otherwise I shall be compelled to take extreme measures.'

He stood surveying me in silence for about thirty seconds, his mouth wide open. 'Are you a vegetarian?' he asked.

'No, sir, I eat meat.'

He sat down and reached for some document. I bowed and left.

It wasn't worth going to work before dinner and I went back home to sleep, but I was unable to because of the unpleasant feelings aroused by the slaughter-house and the conversation with the Governor. I waited until evening and then went off to Masha's in a gloomy, troubled frame of mind. I told her that I had been to the Governor's and she looked at me in disbelief. Then she suddenly broke into the kind of loud cheerful, uninhibited laugh that only good-natured people with a sense of humour can produce.

'If only I could tell them in St Petersburg!' she said, leaning towards the table and nearly collapsing with laughter. 'If only I could tell them in St Petersburg!'

IX

Now we met quite often, about twice a day. Almost every afternoon she came to the cemetery, where she read the inscriptions on crosses and tombstones while waiting for me. Sometimes she would come into the church and stand by me, watching me work. The silence, the painters' and gilders' simple work, Radish's good sense, the fact that outwardly I was no different from the other men and worked just as they did, in waistcoat and old shoes, and the fact that they spoke to me as if I were one of them – all this was new to her and she found it moving. Once when she was there an artist who was high up painting a dove shouted down to me, 'Misail, give me some whiting.'

I carried it up to him, and afterwards, when I was climbing down the rickety scaffolding, she looked at me, moved to tears, and smiling.

'What a dear you are!' she said.

Ever since I was a child I remembered how a green parrot had escaped from its cage in one of the rich men's houses in the town and how it had wandered round the town for a whole month, lazily flying from garden to garden, lonely and homeless. Masha put me in mind of that bird.

'At the moment I've absolutely nowhere to go besides the cemetery,' she told me laughing. 'I'm bored to death in this town. At the Azhogins they do nothing but read, sing and babble away; I just can't stand them lately. Your sister keeps to herself, Mademoiselle Blagovo hates me for some reason, and I don't like the theatre. So where can I go?'

When I visited her I smelt of paint and turpentine and my

hands were black. She liked this and wanted me to wear only my ordinary working clothes when I called on her. But they made me feel awkward in her drawing-room – it was as if I were in uniform, and therefore I always wore my new woollen suit when I went there. She didn't like this.

'You must admit, you haven't quite got used to your new role,' she told me once. 'You feel awkward and embarrassed in your workman's clothes. Tell me, is it because you've lost confidence in yourself, because you're dissatisfied? This work you've chosen – all this splashing paint around – does that really satisfy you?' she asked, laughing. 'I know that painting makes things prettier, makes them last longer, but surely these things belong to the rich people in town and are really luxuries. Besides, as you yourself said more than once, everyone should earn bread by his labours, whereas you earn money, not bread. Why don't you stick to the literal meaning of what you say? If it's *bread* that you have to earn, then you must plough, sow, reap, thresh, or do something directly connected with agriculture – keeping cows, for example, digging, building log-huts . . .'

She opened a pretty little cupboard near her writing-table and said, 'I've been telling you all this because I want to let you into my secret. *Voilà*. This is my agricultural library. Here are books on arable land, vegetable gardens, orchards, cattle-yards and bee-keeping. I love reading them, and I know all the theory already, in great detail. It's my dream, my cherished wish to go to Dubechnya as soon as March is here. It's wonderful there, fantastic! Don't you agree? For the first year I'll just look around to get the hang of things, but the following year I'll really start work, without sparing myself, as they say. Daddy's promised me Dubechnya and I can do anything I want there.'

Blushing, laughing and excited to the point of tears, she daydreamed aloud about her life at Dubechnya, about how interesting it would be. And I envied her. March wasn't far away, the days were drawing out, thawing snow dripped from the roofs at midday in the bright sun and the smell of spring was in the air. I too longed for the country.

When she said that she was moving to Dubechnya I immediately saw myself left alone in the town, and I felt jealous of her book cupboard and her farming.

I didn't know a thing about farming and I had no love for it. I almost told her that farming was a form of slavery, but I remembered my father having said something of the sort more than once, so I remained silent.

Lent began. Victor Dolzhikov, the engineer, whose existence I had just about forgotten, arrived from St Petersburg quite unexpectedly, without even sending a telegram beforehand. When I arrived – in the evening, as usual – there he was, pacing the drawing-room and talking. He had just had a bath, and with his hair cut short he looked about ten years younger. His daughter was kneeling by his trunks, taking out boxes, scent-bottles and books and handing them to Pavel, one of the male servants. When I saw the engineer I couldn't help taking a step backwards, but he stretched both hands out to me and revealed his firm, white, coachman's teeth as he smiled and said, 'So it's him! Here he is! Delighted to see you, Mr Painter! Masha's told me everything; she's been praising you to the skies. I understand you and heartily approve of what you're doing.'

He took me by the arm and continued 'Being an honest workman is a sight more clear-headed and decent than using up reams of paper and wearing a ribbon in your hat. I used to work in Belgium myself, with these hands you see here, then I was an engine-driver for two years.'

He wore a short jacket and comfortable house-slippers, and he walked with a slight roll, as if he were suffering from gout; he kept rubbing his hands. He hummed, purred softly and squeezed himself from the sheer pleasure of being home again and having taken his beloved shower.

'There's no denying it,' he told me over supper, 'there's no denying it. You are all nice, charming people, but as soon as you try to do any physical work or look after the peasants you end up religious fanatics. Why is it? Now, don't deny it, you belong to some religious sect, don't you? You don't drink vodka, eh? What's that if it isn't belonging to some sect?'

Just to please him I drank some vodka, and some wine too. We tried different cheeses, sausages, pâtés, pickles and various savouries which the engineer had brought with him, and the wines that had arrived while he was abroad. The wines were excellent. Somehow he managed to bring in his wines and cigars duty-free. Someone sent him caviare and smoked sturgeon for nothing; he paid no rent for the flat since the landlord supplied paraffin to the railway. The general impression he and his daughter gave me was that all the best things in life were theirs for the asking and they received them free of charge.

I went on visiting them, but not so enthusiastically as before. The engineer cramped my style and I always felt uncomfortable when he was around. I could not stand those clear, innocent eyes, and his offensive remarks were very tiresome. I was irked by the thought too that only recently I had been under the command of that well-fed, red-faced man and that he had been dreadfully rude to me. True, he put his arm round my waist now, gave me friendly slaps on the shoulder and approved of my way of life, but I sensed that he still despised me for being a mediocrity and he only put up with me for his daughter's sake. I could no longer laugh or say what I wanted, so I became stand-offish, and I was always expecting him to address me as a servant, like Pavel. How my petty provincial pride suffered! I, one of the working masses, a house-painter, visited the rich almost every day, people who lived in a different world, whom the whole town looked on as foreigners. Every day I drank expensive wines at their houses and ate exotic food – my conscience would not come to terms with that! On my way to their place I tried to look gloomy and avoided passers-by and scowled at them as if I really did belong to some religious sect. But when I left the engineer's I was ashamed I had wined and dined so well.

Most of all, I was scared of falling in love. Whether I was walking down the street, working, talking to my workmates, all I could think of was going to see Masha in the evening, and I would imagine her voice, her laughter, her walk. Before each visit I would stand for a long time in front of Nanny's crooked looking-glass, tying my tie. My woollen suit repelled me. I was going through hell and at the same time I despised myself for taking such trivial things so seriously. When she called out from another room to say that she was not dressed yet and asked me to wait, I could hear her putting on her clothes. This disturbed me and I felt as though the floor were sinking under me. Whenever I saw a woman in the street, even far off, I could not help making comparisons, and then all our women and girls seemed vulgar, ridiculously dressed and without poise. These comparisons aroused the pride in me. Masha was the best of the lot! And at night I dreamed of both of us.

Once, at supper, both of us, together with the engineer, polished off a whole lobster. Back home I remembered the engineer twice calling me 'My dear young man!' over supper and I realized that they were spoiling me like a huge, wretched stray dog; that they were only amusing themselves with me; and that they would drive me away like a dog when they were bored with me. I was ashamed and hurt – so hurt, I was close to tears, as if someone had insulted me. I looked up at the sky and vowed to put an end to it all.

Next day I didn't go to the Dolzhikovs. Late that evening (it was quite dark and raining) I strolled along Great Dvoryansky Street looking at the windows. At the Azhogins' everyone was in bed – only one light burnt in one of the windows right at the end of the house – that was old Mrs Azhogin embroidering by the light of three candles and imagining she was carrying on the battle against superstition. Our house was dark, but over the road, at the Dolzhikovs', the windows were bright, though I couldn't see inside for the flowers and curtains. I continued to walk up and down the street and was drenched by the cold, March rain. I heard Father returning from the club; he knocked on the gate and a minute later a light appeared at one of the windows and I saw my sister hurrying with a lamp and smoothing her thick hair with one hand as she went. Then Father paced the drawing-room, talking and rubbing his hands together, while my sister sat motionless in an armchair thinking and not listening to him.

But then they left the room and the light went out. I looked round at the engineer's house – it was as dark as a well there now. In the gloom and the rain I felt desperately lonely, left to the mercy of fate. I felt that in comparison with my loneliness, my present sufferings, with what lay in store for me, how trivial everything was that I had ever done or wished for, thought or spoken of. Alas, the actions and thoughts of living beings are not nearly as important as their sorrows! Without knowing exactly what I was doing, I tugged as hard as I could at the bell on the Dolzhikovs' gate – and broke it. I ran off in terror down the street like a naughty child, convinced they would come out at once and recognize me. When I stopped to catch my breath at the end of the street all I could hear was falling rain and a nightwatchman, far away, banging on his iron sheet.

For a whole week I stayed away from the Dolzhikovs'. I sold my woollen suit. There was no painting work about and once again I was half-starving, earning ten to twelve copecks a day where I could by doing heavy, nasty work. Wallowing up to my knees in cold mud and using all my strength, I tried to suppress any memories, as if taking revenge on myself for all those cheeses and tinned delicacies the engineer had treated me to. But no sooner did I climb into bed, hungry and wet, than my sinful imagination began to conjure up wonderful, seductive pictures and to my amazement I realized that I was in love, passionately so, and I would drop into a sound, healthy sleep, feeling that all the penal servitude was only making my body stronger.

One evening it snowed – quite out of season – and the wind blew from the north as if winter had returned. When I was home from work I found Masha sitting in my room. She wore her fur coat, with her hands in a muff.

'Why don't you come any more?' she asked, raising her clever, bright eyes. I was overcome with joy and stood stiffly in front of her, just as I had done before Father when he was about to hit me. She looked into my face and I could see by her eyes that she understood why I was overcome.

'Why don't you come any more?' she repeated. 'Well, as you don't want to, I've come to you instead.'

She stood up and came close to me.

'Don't leave me,' she said, her eyes filling with tears. 'I'm lonely, so terribly lonely!'

She began to cry and hid her face in her muff. 'I'm lonely. Life is so dreadful, really dreadful, and besides you I've no one in the whole wide world. Don't leave me!'

She searched for a handkerchief to dry her eyes and gave me a smile. We said nothing for some time, then I embraced her and kissed her, scratching my cheek on her hat-pin until it bled. And we started talking as if we had been close to one another for a long, long time.

X

Two days later she sent me to Dubechnya, and words could not describe how delighted I was. As I walked to the station and later, as I sat in the train, I laughed for no reason and people thought I was drunk. It was snowing and there was frost in the mornings, but the roads were turning brown, and cawing rooks circled above them.

The first thing I wanted was to arrange accommodation for Masha and myself in the outbuilding, opposite Mrs Cheprakov's. But it turned out to have long been the home of pigeons and ducks and it would have been impossible to clean it out without destroying a large number of nests. Whether we liked it or not, we had to move into the bleak rooms with Venetian blinds in the big house. This house was called The Palace by the peasants. It had more than twenty rooms, but the only furniture was a piano and a child's armchair in the attic. Even if Masha had brought all her furniture from the town, we could not have destroyed that bleak, empty cold atmosphere. I chose three small rooms with windows looking on to the garden, and I was busy from dawn to dusk cleaning them, putting in new window-panes, hanging wallpaper and filling in cracks and holes in the floor. It was easy, pleasant work. Now and then I ran down to the river to see if the ice was breaking up and I kept imagining that the starlings had returned. At night, as I thought of Masha, I felt overjoyed and entranced as I listened to the scurrying rats and the wind sighing and knocking above the ceiling. It sounded as if some old house-goblin was coughing up in the attic.

The snow was deep. At the end of March there was another heavy fall, but it thawed quickly, as if by magic. The spring floods surged past and by the beginning of April the starlings were already chattering and yellow butterflies flitted around the garden. It was marvellous weather. Every day, just before evening, I went off to town to meet Masha. And how enjoyable it was walking barefoot along a road that was drying, but still soft! Halfway I would sit down and look at the town, not daring to go nearer. The sight of it disturbed me. I kept wondering how my friends would react once they heard of my love. What would Father say? The thought that my life had become so complicated that I could no longer keep it under control worried me more than anything. Life was carrying me away like a balloon – God knows where. I no longer thought about making ends meet or earning a living. I honestly can't remember what I was thinking about.

When Masha arrived in her carriage, I would sit next to her and we would drive off to Dubechnya, happy and free. At other times, after waiting for the sun to set, I would go home, disconsolate and bored, wondering why she hadn't come. Then suddenly a delightful apparition would greet me at the gate or in the garden – Masha! Later it turned out that she had come by train and had walked from the station. And what a wonderful occasion this used to be! She wore a modest woollen dress and scarf and held a simple umbrella. At the same time, she was tightly corseted and slim, and she wore expensive foreign boots. This was a talented actress playing the part of a small-town housewife. We would inspect the place and try to decide what rooms we would

take and plan the paths, kitchen-garden and beehives.
Already we had ducks and geese that we loved because they
were ours. We had clover, oats, timothy grass, buckwheat
and vegetable seeds – all ready for sowing. We spent a long
time examining these things and wondering what the har-
vest would be like. Everything that Masha told me seemed
exceptionally clever and fine. This was the happiest time of
my life.

Soon after Easter we were married in our parish church
at Kurilovka, the village about two miles from Dubechnya.
Masha wanted everything simple. At her wish the ushers
were lads from the village, and one parish clerk did all the
singing. We returned from church in a small, shaky trap,
which she drove. The only guest from town was my sister,
to whom Masha had sent a note a couple of days before the
wedding; she wore a white dress and gloves. During the
ceremony she cried softly for joy, being deeply touched,
and her expression was motherly, infinitely kind. Our happiness had intoxicated her and she smiled continually, as if
inhaling heady fumes. Watching her during the service I
realized that for her there was nothing finer in the whole
world than earthly love. This was what she had always
secretly longed for, timidly yet passionately. She kissed and
embraced Masha. Not knowing how to express her joy she
told her, 'He's a good man, so good!'

Before leaving she changed into her ordinary clothes and
led me into the garden to talk to me in private.

'Father's very upset you didn't write,' she said. 'You
should have asked for his blessing. But he's actually very
pleased with you. He says that this wedding will raise your
social status and that, under Masha's influence, you'll take
things more seriously. We only talk about you in the evenings, and yesterday he even called you "our Misail". This
gave me so much joy. It seems he has a plan of some kind
and I think that he wants to show you how magnanimous
he can be, by being the first to talk of a reconciliation. Most
likely he'll soon be coming to see you here.'

Several times she quickly made the sign of the cross over

me and said, 'Well, God bless you. Be happy. Anyuta Blagovo is a very clever girl. She says that your marriage is a
fresh ordeal sent by God. Yes, family life is not all bliss,
there's suffering too. You can't avoid it.'

Masha and I walked about two miles with her as we saw
her off. On our way back we walked quietly and slowly,
as if taking a rest. Masha held my arm; I felt easy at heart
and I didn't want to talk about love any more. After the
wedding we had grown even closer, had become kindred
spirits, and it seemed nothing could keep us apart.

'Your sister is a nice person,' Masha said, 'but she looks as
if she's been suffering never-ending torments. Your father
must be a horrible man.'

I began telling her how my sister and I had been brought
up and how our childhood had really been a meaningless
ordeal. When she learnt that my father had struck me only
recently she shuddered and pressed close to me.

'Don't say any more,' she said. 'It's terrible.'

And now she did not leave me. We lived in three rooms
in the big house and in the evenings we bolted the door to
the empty part of the house, as if some stranger we feared
was living there. I would rise at the crack of dawn and
immediately get down to work. I used to mend carts, lay
paths in the garden, dig the flower-beds, paint the roof of
the house. When the time for sowing oats came I tried
double-ploughing, harrowing. All this I did conscientiously,
and did not lag behind our farm labourer. I would become
exhausted; the rain and the sharp, cold wind made my face
and legs burn, and at nights I dreamed of ploughed land.
Working in the fields held no delights for me. I knew
nothing about farming and I disliked it – probably because
my ancestors had never been tillers of the soil and pure
town blood ran in my veins. I loved nature dearly, the fields
and meadows and the vegetable gardens. But the wet,
ragged peasant turning the earth with his plough and craning
his neck as he urged on his wretched horse was for me the
embodiment of crude, savage, monstrous strength. As I
watched his clumsy movements I could never stop myself

thinking of that long-past, legendary life, when man did not know the use of fire. Awesome bulls roaming around the peasant's herd, horses stampeding through the village with pounding hooves – they scared the wits out of me. Any creature that was in the least large, strong and angry, whether a horned ram, a gander or a watch-dog, seemed to symbolize that wild, crude strength. This prejudice was particularly strong in bad weather, when heavy clouds hung over the black plough-lands. But most of all, whenever I ploughed or sowed and two or three peasants stood watching me, I did not feel that my work was in any sense indispensable or that I was obliged to do it: I seemed to be merely amusing myself. I preferred working in the yard and I liked nothing better than painting roofs.

I used to walk through the garden and the meadow to our mill. This was rented to Stefan, a handsome, dark-skinned, tough-looking peasant from Kurilovka, with a thick black beard. He did not like working the mill, thinking it boring and unprofitable, and he only lived there to escape from home. He was a saddle-maker and always had a pleasant smell of tar and leather about him. Not very talkative, he was lethargic and sluggish. He was always humming, always sitting on the river bank or in his doorway. Sometimes his wife and mother-in-law – both pale-faced, languid and meek creatures – would come over from Kurilovka to see him. They would bow low and call him 'Mr' or 'Sir'. He would not reply with a single movement or word, but sat by himself on the river bank softly humming. An hour or so would pass in silence. Then, after whispering to each other, the mother-in-law and wife would stand up and look at him for some time, waiting for him to turn round. Then they would make low curtsies and say 'Goodbye, Mr Stefan!' in their sugary, sing-song voices. And then they would leave. Taking the bundle of rolls or the shirt they had left for him, Stefan would sigh and wink in their direction.

'Women!' he would say.

The two stones at the mill worked day and night. I helped

Stefan and I enjoyed it. Whenever he went away I willingly took over.

XI

After the fine, warm weather there was a wet spell. Throughout May it rained and it was cold. The sound of the mill-wheels and the rain made one feel sleepy and lazy; so did the shaking floor and smell of flour. My wife appeared twice a day in her short fur jacket and rubber boots, and she would invariably say the same thing: 'Call this summer! It's worse than October!'

We would drink tea together, cook porridge, or silently sit for hours on end waiting for the rain to stop. Once, when Stefan had gone to the fair, Masha spent the whole night at the mill. When we got up, there was no telling what the time was, as the whole sky was dark with rain clouds. But sleepy cocks crowed in Dubechnya and corn-crakes cried in the meadow: it was still very, very early. I went down to the millpond with my wife and hauled out the fish-trap that Stefan had thrown in the previous evening while we were there. One large perch was floundering about and a crayfish angrily stretched its claws upwards.

'Let them go,' Masha said. 'Let them be happy too . . .'

Because we had got up very early and then done nothing, the day seemed extremely long, the longest day in my life. Just before evening Stefan returned and I went back home to the big house.

'Your father came today,' Masha told me.

'Where is he, then?'

'He's gone. I sent him away.'

Seeing me standing there in silence, she realized that I was sorry for Father.

'One must be consistent. I didn't let him in and I sent a message telling him not to trouble himself about coming again.'

A minute later I was through the gates and on my way to sort things out with Father. It was muddy, slippery and cold. For the first time since the wedding I felt sad, and the thought that I was not living as I should flashed through my brain, which was exhausted by the long, grey day. I felt worn-out, and gradually I succumbed to faint-heartedness and inertia: I had no desire to move or to think. After a few steps I gave up and went home.

Dolzhikov was standing in the middle of the yard, in a leather coat with hood.

'Where's the furniture?' he shouted. 'There used to be beautiful empire-style things, paintings, vases, but they've collared the lot! To hell with her, I bought the estate *with* the furniture!'

Close by, Moisey, the general's wife's handyman, stood crumpling his cap. He was about twenty-five, thin, pock-marked and with small, cheeky eyes. One cheek was larger than the other, as if he'd been lying on it.

'But, sir, you did buy it without the furniture,' he said sheepishly. 'I do remember that.'

'Shut up!' the engineer shouted, turning crimson and shaking all over. His voice echoed right round the garden.

XII

Whenever I worked in the garden or in the yard, Moisey would stand nearby, hands behind his back, idly and cheekily looking at me with those tiny eyes of his. This irritated me so much that I would leave what I was doing and go away.

Stefan revealed that this Moisey had been Mrs Cheprakov's lover. I noticed that when people came for money they would first turn to Moisey, and once I saw a peasant, black all over (he was probably a charcoal-burner), prostrating himself in front of him. Sometimes after an exchange of whispers he would hand out the money himself, without telling the mistress, from which I deduced that he did business transactions of his own, on the quiet.

He used to go shooting right under the windows in the garden, filched food from our larders and took horses without our permission. We were furious, and Dubechnya didn't seem to be ours at all. Masha would turn pale.

'Do we have to live with this scum for another eighteen months?' she would ask.

Mrs Cheprakov's son Ivan was a guard on our railway. During the winter he had grown terribly thin and weak. Just one glass of vodka was enough to make him drunk and he felt the cold if he was out of the sun. He loathed and was ashamed of having to wear a guard's uniform. But it was a profitable job, he thought, since he was able to steal candles and sell them. My new position aroused mixed feelings in him – amazement, envy and the vague hope that he too might be lucky. He followed Masha with admiring eyes, asked what I had for dinner these days. His gaunt, ugly face would take on a sickly, sad expression and he twiddled his fingers as though he could actually touch my good fortune.

'Now, listen, Better-than-Nothing,' he said fussily, constantly relighting his cigarette. He always made a terrible mess wherever he stood, since he wasted dozens of matches on one cigarette. 'Listen, things have reached rock-bottom with me. The worst of it is, every tinpot little subaltern thinks he's entitled to shout "Hey, you, guard! You over there!" I've just about had enough of hearing all sorts of things in trains, and now I can see that this life stinks! My mother's ruined me! A doctor told me once in a train that if the parents have no morals, then the children turn out drunks or criminals. That's what!'

Once he came staggering into the yard, his eyes wandering aimlessly, his breathing heavy. He laughed, cried and went on as if he was delirious. All I could make out in that gibberish was 'Mother! Where's my mother?', which he said weeping, like a child that has lost its mother in a crowd. I led him into the garden and laid him down under a tree. All day and night Masha and I took it in turns to sit with him. He was in a bad state and Masha looked into his pale, wet face with revulsion.

'Are we really going to have this scum living in our yard

another eighteen months? That's horrible, horrible!' she said.

And how much distress the peasants caused us! How many deep disappointments we suffered from the very beginning, in the spring, when we yearned for happiness! My wife was building a school for them. I drew up a plan for a school for sixty boys. The local authorities approved it but advised us to build it at Kurilovka, that large village about two miles away. As it happened, the school at Kurilovka, which was attended by children from four villages, including Dubechnya, was old and cramped and one had to be careful walking over the rotten floor-boards. At the end of March Masha was appointed trustee of the Kurilovka school, as she had wished, and at the beginning of April we arranged three meetings where we tried to convince the peasants that their school was cramped and old, and someone from the local council and the inspector of state schools came. They too tried to make the peasants see sense. After each meeting they surrounded us and asked for a barrel of vodka. We felt hot amongst all that crowd and were very soon exhausted. So we went home, feeling dissatisfied and rather embarras-. sed. In the end the peasants picked a site for the school and had to fetch all the building materials from the town on their own horses. The first Sunday after the spring wheat had been sown, carts left Kurilovka and Dubechnya to fetch bricks for the foundations. The men left as soon as it was light and came back late in the evening – drunk, and complaining what a rotten job it was.

As if to spite us, the cold rainy weather lasted the whole of May. The roads were thick with mud. After returning from town the carts usually entered our yard, and what a dreadful sight this was! A pot-bellied horse would appear at the gates, straddling its forelegs. Before coming into the yard it appeared to bow; then a wet, slimy-looking thirty-foot beam would slide in on a low cart. Wrapped up against the rain, his coat flaps tucked inside his belt, a peasant would stride along beside it, not looking where he was going, and walking straight through the puddles. Another cart laden with planks would appear, then a third carrying a beam, then a fourth. Gradually the space in front of the house would become choked with horses, beams and planks. With heads covered and clothes tucked up, the peasants – both the men and women – would look malevolently at our windows, make a dreadful racket and demand that the lady of the house come out. The swearing was appalling. Moisey would stand to one side and seemed to be revelling in the ignominy of our position.

'We don't want to do any more shifting!' the peasants would shout. 'We're worn out! Let her go and fetch the stuff herself!'

Pale-faced and scared out of her wits at the thought that they might try and break into the house, Masha would send out the money for half a barrel. After that the noise would die down, and, one after the other, the long beams would trundle out of the yard again.

Whenever I went to the building-site my wife grew worried.

'The peasants are in a nasty temper,' she would say. 'They might do something to you. Wait a moment, I'm coming with you.'

We would drive to Kurilovka together and there the carpenters would ask us for a tip. The timber frame was ready; it was time for laying the foundations, but the bricklayers didn't turn up. The carpenters grumbled at the delay. When the bricklayers finally did turn up, they found that there was no sand – for some reason we'd forgotten this would be needed. The peasants took advantage of our desperate situation and asked for thirty copecks a load, although it wasn't more than a few hundred yards from the site to the river, where the sand was taken from. And we needed more than five hundred loads. There was no end to the misunderstandings, swearing and cadging, which exasperated my wife. The foreman-bricklayer – an old man of seventy, by the name of Titus Petrov – would take her by the arm and say, 'Look 'ere! Just you bring me that sand and I'll have ten men 'ere in two ticks and the job'll be done in a couple of days. You see to it!'

The sand was brought; two days, four days, a week went by and still there was a gaping hole where the foundations were to be laid.

'It's enough to drive you insane!' my wife said, terribly agitated. 'What dreadful, really dreadful people!'

While all these arguments were going on, Victor Dolzhikov came to see us. He brought some hampers of wine and savouries, took his time over his meal, then lay down on the terrace to sleep, snoring so loudly that the workmen shook their heads and said, 'Now wotcher think of that!'

Masha was never pleased when he came. She didn't trust him, but took his advice nonetheless. When he'd had his after-dinner nap, he would get up in a bad mood and say nasty things about the way we ran the house. Or he would say he was sorry that he'd bought Dubechnya, on which he'd lost so much money. At these moments poor Masha looked quite desperate. While she complained, he would yawn and say that the peasants needed a good thrashing. He called our marriage and life together a farce, a piece of irresponsible self-indulgence.

'It's not the first time she's done something like this,' he told me, referring to Masha. 'Once she imagined she was an opera-singer and ran away from me. I looked for her for two months and spent a thousand roubles on telegrams alone, my dear chap.'

He no longer called me 'sectarian' or 'Mr Painter' and he no longer approved of my living as a workman.

'You're a strange one, you are!' he said. 'You're not normal! I'm not one for prophesying, but you'll come to a bad end, you will!'

Masha slept badly at night and was always sitting at our bedroom window, deep in thought.

There was no more laughter at supper, no more of those endearingly funny faces. I felt wretched and when it rained every drop seemed to burrow its way into my heart. I was ready to fall on my knees before Masha and apologize for the weather. Whenever the peasants had a row in the yard, I felt that I was to blame for this as well. I would sit in one place for hours on end, just thinking what a wonderful person Masha was. I loved her passionately and everything she did or said captivated me. She had a liking for quiet, studious work and loved reading and studying for hours on end. Although she knew farming only from books, she amazed all of us with her knowledge. All the advice she gave us was always practical and was always put to good use. Besides this, she had such a fine character, such good taste and good humour – the good humour possessed usually only by very well-bred people.

For a woman like this, with a healthy, practical mind, the chaos in which we were living, with all its petty worries and squabbling, was a real ordeal. This was quite clear to me and I too could not sleep at night, as my brain was still active. Deeply affected by everything, I would toss and turn, not knowing what to do.

I used to gallop off to town to fetch books, papers, sweets and flowers for Masha. I would go fishing with Stefan and stood in the rain for hours on end, up to my neck in cold water trying to bring variety to our table with a burbot. I would swallow my pride and request the peasants not to make a noise, treat them to vodka, bribe them and make various promises. There was no end to the silly things I did!

Finally the rain stopped and the earth dried out. I would rise at four in the morning and go out into the garden – here there were flowers sparkling with dew, the sounds of birds and insects – and not a cloud in the sky. The garden, the meadows, and the river were all beautiful – and then I would remember the peasants, carts, the engineer! Masha and I would drive out into the fields in a racing-trap to look at the oats. She held the reins, with shoulders held high and the wind playing with her hair, while I sat behind.

'Keep to the right!' she would shout to passers-by.

'You're just like a coachman!' I once told her.

'That's quite possible! After all, my grandfather' (the engineer's father) 'was a coachman. Didn't you know?' she asked, turning round. And immediately she began to imitate the way coachmen sing and shout.

'That's great!' I thought as I listened. 'That's great!'

And then I remembered the peasants, carts, the engineer . . .

XIII

Dr Blagovo arrived on a bicycle and my sister became a frequent visitor. Once again we talked about physical labour, progress and that mysterious Unknown awaiting mankind in the remote future. The doctor didn't like farming, since it interfered with our discussions. Ploughing, reaping, grazing calves, he maintained, were not the right work for free men. In time people would delegate all these crude forms of the struggle for survival to animals and machines, while they would devote all their time to scientific research. My sister kept begging us to let her go home early, and if she stayed late or spent the night with us, there was terrible trouble.

'God, what a child you are!' Masha reproached her. 'It's really rather stupid!'

'Yes, it is,' my sister agreed. 'I admit it. But what can I do if I can't control myself? I always think I'm behaving badly.'

During haymaking my whole body ached, since I wasn't used to the work. If I sat on the terrace in the evening chatting I would suddenly fall asleep and everyone would roar with laughter, wake me up and sit me down at the supper table. Even so, I would still be overcome by drowsiness and as if half-dreaming, I would see lights, faces, plates. I would hear voices without understanding what they said – after that early-morning start I had immediately picked up my scythe, or I'd gone off to the building-site and been working there all day long.

On holidays, when I stayed at home, I noticed that my wife and sister were hiding something from me and even seemed to be avoiding me. My wife was as tender with me as before, but she was harbouring some thoughts of her own that she did not wish to reveal to me. There was no doubt that she was getting increasingly annoyed with the peasants and the life here had become much more difficult for her. But she no longer complained to me. Nowadays she preferred talking to the doctor than to me and I couldn't understand why.

It was the custom in our province, at haymaking and harvest-time, for the workers to come to the big house in the evenings for their vodka-treat. Even the young girls would drink a glass. But we did not observe this custom. The reapers and peasant women would stand in our yard until late evening, waiting for some vodka, and then they left swearing. Masha would frown sternly the whole time and say nothing, or else she would whisper irritably to the doctor, 'Savages! Barbarians!'

In the country, newcomers are usually met with an unfriendly, almost hostile reception, like new boys at school. And this was what we got. At first they took us for stupid, simple-minded people who had bought the estate because we did not know what to do with our money. They just laughed at us. Peasants let their cattle graze in our wood, even in the garden; they drove our cows and horses to the village and then came asking for money to repair the damage they had done. The whole village would flock into our yard, noisily maintaining that, when we were cutting the hay, we had trespassed on some fields at some Bysheyevka or Semyonikha or other that did not belong to us. But as we were not yet sure of our exact boundaries we took their word for it and paid the fine. Subsequently it turned out that we had been in the right after all. They stripped lime bark off the trees in our wood. One profiteer from Dubechnya, a peasant trading in vodka without a licence, bribed our workers, and the whole bunch of them played the most dirty tricks on us. They replaced our new cartwheels with old, they made off with the horse-collars we used for ploughing and sold them back to us, and so on. But worst of all was what happened at the Kurilovka building-site. The women there stole planks, bricks, tiles and iron at night. The village elder would search their places with witnesses and each one would be fined two roubles at a village meeting. Subsequently the money from the fines was spent on drinks for everyone in the village.

Whenever Masha found out about these things she would angrily tell the doctor or my sister, 'What animals! It's appalling, shocking!'

And more than once I heard her regretting that she had ever taken on the task of building a school.

'Please understand,' the doctor would try and convince her, 'if you build a school and generally do good deeds, it's not for the peasants, but in the interests of culture, it's for the future. And the worse the peasants are, the more reason there is for building a school. Please understand that!'

But there was no conviction in his voice and it struck me that he detested the peasants as much as Masha.

Masha often went to the mill with my sister and they would both laugh and say that they were going to look at Stefan because he was so handsome. As it turned out, Stefan was taciturn and slow on the uptake only with men; with women he was free and easy and could never stop talking. Once, when I went down to the river for a swim I happened to overhear them. Masha and Cleopatra, in white dresses, were sitting on the river bank in the broad shade of a willow, while Stefan stood nearby with his hands behind his back.

'D'ye think them peasants is human beings?' he asked. 'No, they're not. Begging your pardons, they're wild animals, crooks. What kind of life does a peasant lead? Drinking and eating the cheapest stuff he can get and bawling his head off in the pub. And he can't talk proper, can't be'ave, no manners. He's an ignorant oaf! He wallows in muck, so's his wife, so's his children. He sleeps in his clothes, picks spuds out of the soup with 'is fingers, drinks kvass with black beetles an' all – don't ever trouble hisself to blow 'em away!'

'But he's so dreadfully poor!' my sister interrupted.

'What d'ye mean poor! He's just not well-off; there's all

kinds of not being well-off, lady. If someone's in jail, or blind, or hasn't got no legs, you wouldn't wish that on anyone. But if he's free, has 'is wits about him, has eyes and hands, faith in God, what more does he need? It's just pampering hisself, lady. It's ignorance but it ain't poverty. Supposing you honest folk with your fine education tried to help him, out of pity. Why he's so low he'll spend all the money on drink. Even worse, he'll open a pub 'isself and use your money to cheat his own people with. You mentioned poverty. But does a rich peasant live any better? Begging your pardons, he lives like a pig too. He's a bully, a loud-mouth, a blockhead, broader than he's long, with a fat red mug. I'd like to take a swing and bash the bastard's face in. That old Larion from Dubechnya, he's got money, but I'll bet he's as good at stripping the trees in your forest as the poor ones. And he's got a foul mouth, and his children. And as soon as 'e's had a drop too much he'll flop face first into a puddle and fall asleep. They're not worth a light, lady. It's hell living in the same village as them. I'm sick and tired of the village and I thank the Lord above I've enough to eat. I've got clothes, I've served my time in the dragoons, was a village elder for three years and now I'm a free man. I live where I like. I don't want to live in the village and no one can force me. Folk tells me I've a wife, that it's my duty to live in a cottage with my wife. But why? I wasn't taken on as a servant.'

'Tell me, Stefan, did you marry for love?' Masha asked.

'What love can there be in a village?' Stefan replied, smiling. 'If you'd really like to know, lady, it's my second marriage. I'm not from Kurilovka, but Zalegoshch. I settled in Kurilovka when I got married. I mean to say, my father didn't want to divide the land between us – and there was five of us brothers. So I says my goodbyes and off I goes to a strange village, to my wife's family. But my first wife died young.'

'From what?'

'From being stupid. She used to cry, keep on and on for no reason at all and so she wasted away. She kept drinking herbs to make herself look prettier and it must have damaged her insides. My second wife, the one from Kurilovka — what's special about her? She's a village woman, a peasant, that's all. I felt drawn towards her when the match was being made, and thought she was young, all nice and pure-looking, and it was a clean-living family. Her mother was a Khlyst,* drank coffee. Most important, she lived cleanly. So I got married then, and the very next day, when we was sitting down to eat, I asked my mother-in-law for a spoon. She gave me one, but I saw her wiping it with her finger. Well, now, I thought to myself, that's how clean you are! I lived with them for a year and then I left. Per'aps I should have married a town girl,' he went on after a pause. 'They say a wife is a helpmate to her husband. What do I need a helpmate for? I can help myself. And I'd like you to speak nice and sensibly to me, not all that posh talk. Nice and proper, with feeling. What's life without a good natter!'

Stefan suddenly fell silent and immediately I heard his dull, monotonous humming. That meant he had spotted me.

Masha often went to the mill and she enjoyed talking to Stefan. She liked his company, because he seemed so genuine, so convincing when he cursed those peasants. Whenever she returned from the mill the village idiot who kept watch over the orchard would shout, 'Hey, girl! Hello, girlie!' And he would bark at her like a dog.

She would stop and look at him closely, as if she had found an answer to her thoughts in that idiot's barking. Most probably it had the same fascination as Stefan's swearing. Some unpleasant news was always waiting for her at home — for example, the village geese had flattened the cabbage in our garden, or Larion had stolen the reins. Smiling and shrugging her shoulders, she would say, 'But what do you expect from such people!?'

She would become highly indignant and things really were beginning to boil up inside her. But I grew used to the peasants and felt drawn more and more to them. They were

* Religious sect practising flagellation.

mostly very nervy, irritable, downtrodden people. They were people whose imagination had been crushed, they were ignorant, with a limited, dull range of interests and were forever thinking about grey soil, grey days, black bread. They were people who tried to be cunning but, like birds, thought that they could get away with hiding only their heads behind a tree. They couldn't count. Twenty roubles would not tempt them to come and help you in the hay-making, but for the same sum they would turn up for half a barrel of vodka, although it could have bought them four. And there was in fact filth, drunkenness, stupidity and cheating. But for all this, I had the feeling that, on the whole, peasant life had firm, sound foundations. Yes, the peasant did resemble some great clumsy beast as he followed his wooden plough; he did stupefy himself with vodka. But when one took a closer look, he seemed to possess something vital and highly important, something that Masha, for example, and the doctor lacked. What I'm talking about is his belief that truth is the chief thing on earth and that he and the whole nation can be saved only by the truth. Therefore he loves justice more than anything in the world. I used to tell my wife that she couldn't see the glass for the stains on the window-pane. She would either not reply or would hum like Stefan. Whenever that kind, clever woman turned pale with indignation and spoke to the doctor with trembling voice about drunkenness and cheating, she amazed me with the shortness of her memory. How could she forget that her father, the engineer, also drank – drank a great deal – and that the money with which he had bought Dubechnya came from a whole series of brazen, shameless swindles? How could she forget that?

XIV

My sister lived a life of her own too, which she took great pains to hide from me. She and Masha had frequent whispering sessions. Whenever I went up to her she would shrink back and her eyes would take on a guilty, pleading look.

Clearly something she feared or was ashamed of was preying on her mind. To avoid meeting me in the garden or being left alone with me she kept close to Masha the whole time. It was only rarely – during dinner – that I had the chance to speak to her.

One evening I was quietly walking through the garden on my way home from the building-site. It had already begun to grow dark. Without noticing me or hearing my footsteps there was my sister, as quiet as a ghost, near an old wide-spreading apple tree. She was dressed in black and was hurrying backwards and forwards in a straight line, always looking at the ground. An apple fell from a tree. She started at the noise, stopped and pressed her hands to her temples. At that moment I went over to her.

A feeling of tender love rushed to my heart as I tearfully held her shoulders and kissed her. For some reason our mother, our childhood, came to mind. 'What's the matter?' I asked. 'You're miserable. I've noticed that for a long time now. Tell me, what's wrong?'

'I'm frightened . . .' she said, trembling.

'What's the matter?' I asked again. 'For God's sake, you can be frank with me!'

'I will be frank, I'll tell you the whole truth. It's so hard, it's agony hiding things from you! Misail, I'm in love,' she went on in a whisper. 'I'm in love, in love . . . I'm happy, but why am I so frightened?'

We heard footsteps and Dr Blagovo, in a silk shirt and top-boots, appeared among the trees. Obviously they had a rendezvous, here by the apple tree. The moment she saw him she dashed impulsively over to him with a pained cry, as if he were being taken away from her.

'Vladimir! Vladimir!'

She pressed close to him and hungrily gazed into his eyes. Only then did I notice how thin and pale she had grown recently. This was especially noticeable from that long-familiar lace collar, which now hung more loosely than ever around her long, thin neck. The doctor was taken aback, but quickly recovered, stroked her hair and said,

'Now, now, it's all right. Why are you so nervous? I'm here now, you see.'

We said nothing and sheepishly eyed one another. Then the three of us went off and I heard the doctor telling me, 'Cultural life hasn't begun yet in this country. The old console themselves – even if nothing is happening at the moment things were happening in the forties and sixties, they say. But these are old men, and you and I are young, our brains aren't afflicted yet with senile decay, therefore we cannot comfort ourselves with such illusions. Russia began in the year A.D. 862, but civilized Russia, as I understand it, hasn't started yet.'

But I didn't attempt to follow these ideas of his. It was all rather strange. I didn't want to believe that my sister was in love, that here she was walking along arm-in-arm with a stranger, giving him fond looks. My own sister, that neurotic, downtrodden, enslaved creature, loved a married man with children! Something made me feel sorry, but I couldn't pinpoint it. I found the doctor's company somewhat disagreeable, and I had no idea what would become of this love of theirs.

XV

Masha and I drove to Kurilovka for the opening of the school.

'Autumn, autumn, autumn,' Masha said softly as she looked around. 'Summer has passed. The birds have gone, only the willows are green.'

Yes, summer was over. Bright, warm days had set in, but the mornings were chilly, shepherds were wearing their sheepskin coats now and the dew stayed all day on the asters in the garden. We kept hearing plaintive sounds and we couldn't tell if they were shutters groaning on rusty hinges or if the cranes were flying. It made one feel so good, so full of life!

'Summer has passed,' Masha said. 'Now you and I can take stock. We've worked a lot, thought a lot, and we are all the better for it and should feel proud of ourselves. We've improved our own lives, but has our success had any visible effect on the lives around us? Has it been of use to *anyone*? No. Ignorance, personal filthiness, drunkenness, a shockingly high infant mortality-rate – everything's just as it ever was. All your ploughing and sowing, my spending money and reading books – this hasn't made anyone's life better. We've worked, indulged in lofty thinking for ourselves alone – that's for sure.'

This kind of argument baffled me and I didn't know what to think.

'We've been sincere from start to finish,' I said, 'and sincere people have right on their side.'

'I don't deny it. We were right in our thinking but wrong in the way we set about things. It was mostly our methods that were wrong, weren't they? You want to be useful to people, but the mere fact of buying an estate rules out any possibility of helping them from the start. What's more, if you work, dress and eat like a peasant, you lend your authority and approval to their heavy clumsy clothes, their dreadful huts and stupid beards. On the other hand, let's suppose you work for a very long time – all your life – so that in the end you achieve some practical results. But what do these amount to? What good are they against elemental forces, such as wholesale ignorance, hunger, cold, degeneracy? They're a mere drop in the ocean! To counter those things you need a different line of attack, one that is powerful, bold, speedy! If you really do want to be useful, then you must abandon your narrow sphere of activity and act directly on the masses! Above all you need noisy, vigorous propaganda. Why is art – music, for example – really so alive, so popular, so powerful? Because the musician or singer influences thousands at the same time. Dear, wonderful art!' she went on, dreamily gazing at the sky. 'Art gives you wings and carries you far, far away! For those who are tired of filth, petty trifling concerns, for those who are confused, outraged, indignant, there is peace and satisfaction only in beauty.'

When we drove towards Kurilovka the weather was bright and joyful. In the farmyards, here and there, they were threshing and there was a smell of rye-straw. Behind some wattle fences was a bright red mountain-ash, and wherever one looked every tree was golden or red. The church bells were ringing and icons were being carried to the school. I could hear them singing 'Holy Virgin, Intercessor'. And how clear the air was, how high the pigeons were flying!

The service was held in a classroom. Then the peasants from Kurilovka presented Masha with an icon and those from Dubechnya brought her a large pretzel and a gilt salt-cellar. Masha began to sob.

'If we've said something out of turn or been a nuisance, please forgive us,' an old man said as he bowed to us both.

On the way home Masha kept looking around at the school. The green roof that I had painted glistened in the sun and we could see it for a long time afterwards. Masha was now glancing at it in farewell.

XVI

That evening she set off for town. Recently she had been going to town often and spending the night there. When she was away I couldn't work, my head drooped and I felt weak. Our great yard seemed like some bleak, revolting waste-land, and there were angry noises in the garden. Without Masha the house, the trees, the horses were no longer 'ours', as far as I was concerned.

I never left the house, but sat at Masha's table, near the cupboard full of farming books – those old favourites that were needed no longer and which looked at me with such embarrassment. For hours on end, while it struck seven, eight, nine, while the sooty black autumn night crept up to the windows, I would examine her old glove or the pen she always used, or her little scissors. I did nothing and I understood quite clearly that everything I'd done before –ploughing, reaping, felling trees – had only been done because that was her wish. If she had sent me to clean out a deep well, where I would have had to stand waist-deep in water, I would have climbed in without asking myself if it needed cleaning or not. But now, when she was away, Dubechnya struck me as sheer chaos with its ruins, banging shutters, untidiness, and stealing twenty-four hours a day. In that kind of place any sort of work was a waste of time. And why should I work there, why all that worrying about the future, when I felt that the ground was giving way beneath me, that my role here in Dubechnya was played out – in short, when I felt that I was doomed to the same fate as those farming books? It was awful in the lonely hours of the night, when every minute I feared that someone might shout that it was time I left. It wasn't Dubechnya that I regretted, but my own love, whose autumn had clearly arrived. What happiness, to love and be loved! And how dreadful to feel that you're beginning to fall off that lofty tower!

Masha returned from town the following day, towards evening. Something was annoying her, but she tried to hide it and she only inquired why all the winter window-frames had been put in – it was simply stifling, she said. So I took two frames out. We weren't very hungry, but we sat down to supper all the same.

'Go and wash your hands,' my wife said. 'You smell of putty.'

She had brought some new illustrated journals from town and after supper we looked at them together. There were supplements with fashion-plates and patterns. Masha just glanced at them and laid them to one side to have a proper look at later on. But one dress with a wide, smooth, bell-shaped skirt and full sleeves caught her eye and she seriously examined it for about a minute.

'That's not bad,' she said.

'Yes, it would suit you very well!' I said. 'Very well.'

I felt touched as I looked at the dress, admiring that grey blotch only because she liked it.

'A wonderful, charming dress!' I continued, tenderly. 'My beautiful, marvellous Masha! My dear Masha!'

And my tears fell on to the fashion-plate.

'Wonderful Masha!' I muttered. 'My dear, lovely, darling Masha.'

She went to bed, while I stayed up for another hour looking at the illustrations.

'You shouldn't have taken those window-frames out,' she called from the bedroom. 'I hope it won't be cold now. Really, you can feel the draught!'

I read something in the miscellany – about how to make cheap ink and about the largest diamond in the world. And again my attention was caught by that illustration of the dress she had liked and I imagined her at a ball, with fan, bare shoulders, brilliant, splendid, knowing all about music, painting, literature. How small and brief my role in her life seemed!

Our meeting one another, our married life, were only an episode – only one of many to come in the life of this lively, richly talented woman. All the best things in this world, as I've already pointed out, were at her feet, they were hers for nothing. Even ideas and the latest intellectual trends were a source of pleasure for her, bringing variety to her life. I was only the cab-driver, taking her from one infatuation to the other. Now that I was no longer needed, she would fly away, leaving me alone.

As if in answer to my thoughts, a desperate shout suddenly rang out in the yard.

'He-elp!'

It was a thin, female-like voice. As though trying to mimic it, the wind suddenly shrilled in the chimney. Half a minute passed and again I heard that voice through the sound of the wind, but this time it appeared to come from the other end of the yard.

'He-elp!'

'Misail, did you hear that?' my wife asked softly. 'Did you hear?'

She came out from her bedroom in her nightdress, her hair hanging loose; peering at the dark window, she listened hard.

'Someone's being murdered!' she said. 'That's the last straw!'

I took my gun and went out. It was very dark outside and the strong wind made it difficult to stand. I walked up to the gates and listened. The trees moaned, the wind whistled and a dog – most likely the village idiot's – lazily howled in the garden. Outside the gates it was pitch-dark, without one light along the railway track. From somewhere just by the outbuilding where the office had been last year, there suddenly came a strangled cry.

'He-elp!'

'Who's there?' I called.

Two men were struggling. One was pushing, the other trying to hold his ground, and both were breathing heavily.

'Let go!' one of them said and I recognized Ivan Cheprakov. So he was the one who had shouted in that shrill, woman's voice. 'Let go, damn you, or I'll bite your hands!' he said.

I recognized the other as Moisey. As I parted them I couldn't resist hitting Moisey twice in the face. He fell, stood up, and then I hit him again.

'That gent wanted to kill me,' he muttered. 'He was trying to get into his mum's chest-of-drawers. I'd like to have him locked up in the outbuilding, for safety's sake, sir.'

Cheprakov was drunk and didn't recognize me. He breathed heavily, as if filling his lungs before shouting 'He-elp!' again.

I left them and went back into the house. My wife was lying on the bed, fully dressed. I told her what had happened outside and did not even hide the fact that I had hit Moisey.

'It's terrible living in the country,' she said. 'And what a long night, damn it.'

'He-elp!' came the cry again.

'I'll go and separate them,' I said.

'No, let them tear each other's throats out,' she said with a disgusted look.

She glanced up at the ceiling, listening hard, while I sat close by, not daring to speak and feeling that I was to blame for those cries for help outside and for the interminable night.

We said nothing to each other and I waited impatiently for dawn to glimmer at the windows. Masha looked as if she had just come out of a deep sleep and now she was asking herself how such a clever, well-educated respectable woman like herself could land herself in this wretched, provincial wilderness, among a crowd of insignificant nobodies. How could she lower herself so, fall for one of these people and be his wife for more than six months? I felt that it was all the same if it were me, Moisey or Cheprakov: for her, everything had become identified with that drunken, wild cry for help – myself, our marriage, our farming and the dreadful autumn roads. When she sighed or made herself more comfortable, I could read in her face 'Oh, please come quickly, morning!'

In the morning she left. I stayed on at Dubechnya for another three days waiting for her. Then I packed all our things into one room, locked it and walked to town. When I rang the engineer's bell it was already evening and the lamps were lit on Great Dvoryansky Street. Pavel told me there was no one at home. Mr Dolzhikov had gone to St Petersburg, while Miss Dolzhikov must be at a rehearsal at the Azhogins'. I remember how anxious I felt as I went to the Azhogins', how my heart throbbed and sank as I climbed the stairs and stood for a long time on the landing, not daring to enter that temple of the muses. In the ballroom, candles in groups of three were burning everywhere – on the little table, on the piano and on the stage. The first performance was to be on the thirteenth and the first rehearsal on a Monday, an unlucky day. This was the battle against superstition! All the lovers of drama were already there. The eldest, middle and youngest sisters were walking over the stage, reading their parts from notebooks. Away from everybody stood Radish, his head pressed sideways to the wall as he watched the stage with adoring eyes, waiting for the rehearsal to begin. Everything was still the same!

I went over to greet the mistress of the house when

suddenly everyone started crying 'Ssh!' and waving at me to tread softly. There was silence. They raised the piano lid and a lady sat down and screwed up her shortsighted eyes at the music. Then my Masha walked over to the piano. She was beautifully dressed — but she looked beautiful in a strange new way, not at all like the Masha who had come to see me at the mill that spring.

'Why do I love thee, oh radiant night?'*

It was the first time since I had known her that I had heard her sing. She had a fine, rich powerful voice, and hearing her was like eating a ripe, sweet, fragrant melon. When she finished everyone applauded and she smiled and looked very pleased as she flashed her eyes, turned over the music and smoothed her dress. She was like a bird that has finally broken out of its cage and preens its wings in freedom. Her hair was combed behind her ears and she looked aggressive, defiant, as if she wanted to challenge us all or shout at us, as though we were horses, 'Whoa, my beauties!'

And at that moment she must have looked very like her grandfather, the coachman.

'So you're here as well?' she said, giving me her hand. 'Did you hear me sing? What do you think of it?' And without waiting for a reply she went on, 'You've timed it very well. Tonight I'm leaving for St Petersburg, just for a short stay. Is that all right with you?'

At midnight I took her to the station. She embraced me tenderly — most probably out of gratitude for not bothering her with useless questions, and she promised to write. For a long time I held and kissed her hands, barely able to keep back my tears and without saying a single word to her.

After she had gone I stood looking at the receding lights and fondled her in my imagination.

'My dear Masha, my wonderful Masha,' I said softly.

I stayed the night at Karpovna's in Makarikha. In the morning, Radish and I upholstered some furniture for a rich merchant who was marrying his daughter to a doctor.

* From *Night* (1850), a poem by Ya. P. Polonsky.

XVII

On Sunday my sister came for tea.

'I'm reading a lot now,' she said, showing me some books that she had borrowed from the public library on her way. 'I must thank your wife and Vladimir, they've made me aware again. They've saved me and made me feel like a human being. Up to now I couldn't sleep at night for worrying – "Oh, we've used too much sugar this week! Oh, I mustn't put too much salt on the cucumbers!" I don't sleep now, but I've other thoughts on my mind. It's sheer torture to think how stupidly, spinelessly I've spent half my life. I despise my past, I'm ashamed of it, and now I consider Father my enemy. Oh, how grateful I am to your wife! And Vladimir? He's such a wonderful man! They've opened my eyes.'

'That's no good, not sleeping,' I said.

'So you think I'm ill? Not one bit. Vladimir listened to my chest and told me I'm perfectly healthy. But it's not my health that's the problem, that's not so important ... Tell me, am I right in what I'm doing?'

She needed moral support, that was clear. Masha had gone, Dr Blagovo was in St Petersburg, and except myself there was no one in town to tell her that she was right. She stared at me, trying to read my innermost thoughts, and if I was thoughtful or silent in her company, she would take it personally and become miserable. I had to be on my guard the whole time and whenever she asked me if she was right, I would hurriedly reply that she was and that I had great respect for her.

'Did you know? I've been given a part at the Azhogins',' she continued. 'I want to act. I want to live, to drain the cup of life. I've no talent at all, and the part's only ten lines. But that's still infinitely better and nobler than pouring out tea five times a day and spying on the cook to see if she's been eating too much. But most important, Father must come and see that I'm capable of protesting.'

After tea she lay down on my bed and stayed there for some time with her eyes closed, looking very pale.

'How feeble,' she exclaimed, getting up. 'Vladimir said that all the women and girls in this town have become anaemic from laziness. How clever Vladimir is! He's right, so absolutely right. One must work!'

Two days later she went to a rehearsal at the Azhogins', notebook in hand. She wore a black dress with a coral necklace, a brooch that resembled puff-pastry from the distance, and large earrings, each with a jewel sparkling in it. I felt embarrassed looking at her and was shocked at her lack of taste. Others noticed too how unsuitably dressed she was, how out of place those earrings with the jewels were. I could see their smiles, and I heard someone laugh and say, 'Queen Cleopatra of Egypt!'

She had tried to be worldly, relaxed and assured, but she had only succeeded in looking pretentious and bizarre. Her simplicity and charm had deserted her.

'I just told Father that I was going to a rehearsal,' she began, coming over to me, 'and he shouted that he wouldn't give me his blessing and he even nearly hit me. Just imagine, I don't know my part,' she said, glancing at the notebook. 'I'm bound to mess it up. And so,' she went on, highly agitated, 'the die is cast. The die is cast . . .'

She felt that everyone was looking at her, that everyone was amazed at the decisive step she had taken, and that something special was expected of her. It was impossible to convince her that no one ever took any notice of such dull, mediocre people as she and I.

She didn't come in until the third act, and her part – a guest, a provincial scandal-monger – was merely to stand at the door as though eavesdropping and then make a short speech. For at least half an hour before her cue, while others strolled across the stage, read, drank tea, argued, she never left my side. She kept mumbling her lines and nervously crumpling her notebook. Imagining that everyone was looking at her and waiting for her to come on, she kept smoothing her hair with trembling hand.

'I'm bound to do it wrong,' she told me. 'If you knew

how dreadful I feel! It's as if I'm being led out to execution, I'm so scared!'

In the end it was her cue.

'Cleopatra Poloznev, you're on!' the producer said.

She went out into the middle of the stage and she looked ugly and clumsy. Horror was written all over her face. She stood there for about thirty seconds as if in a stupor – quite still apart from the enormous earrings swinging on her ears.

'As it's the first time, you can use the book,' someone said.

I saw quite clearly that she was shaking so much that she could neither speak nor open the book, and that she wasn't up to it at all. I was just about to go over and speak to her when she suddenly sank on to her knees in the middle of the stage and burst into loud sobs.

There was general uproar and commotion. Only I stood still as I leant on the scenery in the wings, shattered by what had happened and at a complete loss what to do. I saw them lift her up and take her away. I saw Anyuta Blagovo come up to me. Until then I hadn't noticed her in the ballroom and now she seemed to have sprung out of the floor. She wore her hat and veil and, as always, looked as if she had only dropped in for a minute.

'I told her not to try and act,' she said angrily, snapping out each word and blushing. 'It's sheer madness! You should have stopped her!'

Thin and flat-chested, Mrs Azhogin hurried over in a short blouse with short sleeves – there was cigarette ash on the front.

'It's terrible, my dear,' she said, wringing her hands and staring me in the face as usual. 'It's terrible. Your sister's in a *certain condition* . . . she's . . . mm . . . pregnant! Take her away from here, I request you to.'

She was breathing heavily from excitement. Her three daughters, as thin and flat-chested as the mother, stood nearby, huddling together in terror. They were petrified, as if a convict had been caught in their house. How disgraceful, how terrible, they would have said! And yet this honourable family had been fighting prejudice and superstition throughout its existence. In their considered opinion, three candles, the thirteenth, unlucky Monday, constituted the entire stock of the superstitions and errors of mankind.

'I must re*quest* you . . .' Mrs Azhogin repeated, pursing her lips on the 'quest'. 'I must re*quest* you to take her home.'

XVIII

A little later my sister and I were walking down the street, and I protected her with the skirt of my coat. We hurried along side-streets where there were no lamps, avoiding passers-by as if we were fugitives.

She no longer cried, but looked at me with dry eyes. It was only about twenty minutes' walk to Makarikha, where I was taking her, and, strange to relate, in that short time we managed to recall the whole of our lives. We discussed everything, weighed up our position, thought of the best course of action.

We decided that we could stay no longer in that town and that as soon as I had a little money we would move somewhere else. In some houses the people were already in bed, in others they were playing cards. We detested and feared those houses and talked about the fanaticism, callousness and worthlessness of those worthy families, those lovers of dramatic art whom we had frightened so much. 'How are those stupid, cruel, lazy, dishonest people any better than the drunken, superstitious peasants of Kurilovka?' I asked. 'Are they any better than animals, which are similarly thrown into disarray when some random incident upsets the monotony of their lives that are bounded by instincts?' What would happen to my sister now if she continued to live at home? What moral torments would she have to endure, talking to Father, or meeting her friends every single day? I saw all this quite clearly and then I recalled all those people I knew who were slowly being hounded to death by their nearest and dearest. I remembered those tormented dogs that had gone mad, those live sparrows plucked bare by street urchins and thrown into water. And I remembered the long, long unbroken sequence of muted, protracted suffering that I had observed in that town since childhood. And I could not understand how those sixty thousand people coped, why they read the Gospels, prayed, read books and magazines. What good to them was all that had been so far written and spoken by mankind if they were still spiritually unenlightened, if they still had the same horror of freedom as a hundred, three hundred years ago? A carpenter would spend all his life building houses in that town, but for all that he would go to his grave mispronouncing 'gallery'. Similarly, those sixty thousand inhabitants had been reading and hearing about truth, mercy and freedom for generations, yet to their dying day they would carry on lying from morning to night, making life hell for each other, and they feared and loathed freedom as if it were their deadly enemy.

'So, my fate is decided,' my sister said when we arrived home. 'After what has happened I can never go back *there* again. Heavens, that's good! I feel better now.'

She immediately went to bed. Tears glistened on her eyelashes, but her face was happy. She slept soundly and sweetly and I could see that she really was relaxed and able to rest now. It was simply ages since she had slept like that.

And so our life together began. She was always singing and telling me that she felt very well. Books borrowed from the library were returned by me unread, since she wasn't in the mood for reading now. Her only wish was to dream and talk of the future. While she mended my underwear or helped Karpovna at the stove, she would hum or talk about her Vladimir, praising his intellect, good manners, kindness, exceptional learning. I would agree with her, although I didn't like her doctor any more. She wanted to work and earn her own living, without any assistance. She said that she was going to be a teacher as soon as she was well enough and that she would scrub floors and do the washing herself. She loved her unborn child passionately – even though he had not entered this world yet. She knew already the colour of his eyes, what his hands were like, how he laughed. She loved talking about education, and since Vladimir was the best person in the world, all her thoughts on the subject centred around one thing – the son must be as fascinating as the father. We talked endlessly and everything she said filled her with keen joy. I felt glad too, without knowing why.

Her dreaminess must have infected me too. All I did was lounge about, and I too read nothing. For all my tiredness, I paced up and down the room in the evenings, hands in pockets, talking about Masha.

'When do you think she'll be back?' I would ask my sister. 'Towards Christmas, I think, no later. What *can* she be doing there?'

'She hasn't written, that means she'll be back soon.'

'That's true,' I would agree, although I knew very well that there was nothing in our town for Masha to come back to.

I missed her terribly and since I could no longer deceive myself, I tried to make others deceive me. My sister was waiting for her doctor, I was waiting for Masha, and we both talked and laughed incessantly without ever noticing that we were keeping Karpovna awake. She would lie over the stove in her room forever muttering, 'This morning the samovar was a-humming, oh, how it was humming! That means bad luck, my dears. Bad luck!'

The only caller was the postman, who brought my sister letters from the doctor, and Prokofy, who sometimes dropped in during the evening. He would look at my sister without saying a word and then go back into the kitchen.

'Everyone should stick to his calling,' he would say, 'and those what are too proud to understand will walk through a vale of tears in this life.'

He loved his 'vale of tears'. Once, around Christmas, when I was walking through the market, he called me to his butcher's stall and without shaking my hand declared that he had something very important to discuss. He was red in the face from frost and vodka. Next to him, at the counter, stood Nikolka of the murderous face, holding a bloody knife.

'I want to tell you what I think,' Prokofy began. 'This business here can't go on because you yourself know this vale of tears can blacken our name. Of course, Ma's too sorry for you to tell you anything unpleasant – I mean, that your sister should move somewhere else because she's expecting, like. But I want no more of it, seeing as I can't approve of the way she's been carrying on.'

I understood and walked away from the stall. That same day my sister and I moved to Radish's. We had no money for a cab, so we walked. I carried our things in a bundle on my back, but my sister carried nothing. She kept gasping and coughing and asking if we would be there soon.

XIX

At last a letter from Masha arrived.

My dear, kind M. [she wrote], my kind, gentle 'guardian angel', as our old painter calls you. Goodbye. I'm going with Father to the Exhibition in America. In a few days I shall see the ocean – it's so far from Dubechnya it frightens me to think of it! It's as distant and boundless as the sky and it's there I long to go, to be free. I'm exultant, as happy as a lark, I'm insane – you can see what a mess this letter is. My dear Misail, give me my freedom, please hurry and snap the thread which is still binding you and me. To have met and known you was like a ray of heavenly light that brightened my existence. But becoming your wife was a mistake, you understand that, and the realization of this mistake weighs heavy on me. I go down on my knees and beg you, my dear generous friend, to send me a telegram as quick as you can, before I travel over the ocean. Tell me that you agree to correct the mistake both of us made, to take away the only stone that drags my wings down. Father will make all the arrangements and he's promised not to trouble you too much with formalities. And so, am I as free as a bird? Yes? Be happy, God bless you. Forgive me for having sinned.

I'm alive and well. I'm throwing money away, I do many stupid things and every minute I thank God that a silly woman like me has no children. I'm having success with my singing, but it's no idle pastime, it's my refuge, my cell where I retire to find peace. King David had a ring with the inscription 'All things pass'. Whenever I feel sad those words cheer me up, but when I'm cheerful they make me sad.

I have a ring now with Hebrew letters and it's a talisman that will keep me from temptation. All things pass, and life itself will pass, which means one needs nothing. Or perhaps all one needs to know is that one is free, because free people need nothing, absolutely nothing. Break the thread. My fondest love to you and your sister.

Forgive and forget your M.

My sister was lying in one room; in another lay Radish, who had been ill again and was just convalescing. When the letter arrived my sister had quickly gone into the painter's room, had sat down and started reading to him. Every day she read Ostrovsky or Gogol, and he would listen very seriously, staring into space. Now and then he would shake his head and mutter to himself 'All things are possible, all things!'

If something ugly, nasty was depicted in a play he would poke the book with his finger and start gloating, 'There's a pack of lies. That's what lying does for you!'

He liked plays for their plot, moral message and intricate artistic structure, and he always called the author *him*, *he*, never actually mentioning names. 'How skilfully *he's* made everything fit together!' he would say.

This time my sister read only one page to him; she could not go on as her voice was too weak. Radish took her by the arm, twitched his dry lips and said in a barely audible, hoarse voice, 'The righteous man's soul is white and smooth as chalk, but a sinner's is like pumice stone. A righteous man's soul is like bright oil, but a sinner's is like tar. We must toil, endure sorrow, suffer illness,' he went on. 'But he who does not toil or grieve will never enter the kingdom of heaven. Woe to the well-fed, woe to the strong, woe to the rich, woe to the usurers. They will never enter the kingdom of heaven. Grass withers, iron rusts . . .'

I read the letter once more. Then the soldier came into the kitchen – the same soldier who twice weekly brought us tea, French rolls and grouse that smelled of perfume. Who the sender was remained a mystery. I had no work, so I had to stay at home for days on end, and whoever sent the rolls must have known that we were hard up.

I could hear my sister talking to the soldier and cheerfully laughing. Then she ate a small roll, lay on the bed and told me, 'From the very start, when you said you didn't want to work in an office and became a house-painter, Anyuta Blagovo and I knew that you were in the right, but we were too scared to say it out loud. Tell me, what is this strange power that prevents us from saying what we think? Take Anyuta Blagovo, for example. She loves you, she adores you, and she knows that you're right. She loves me like a sister and knows that I'm right as well. Perhaps in her heart of hearts she envies me. But something is stopping her from coming to see us. She avoids us, she's scared.'

My sister folded her hands on her breast and said excitedly, 'If only you knew how she loves you! She confessed it to me alone, and in secret, in the dark. She used to take me to a dark avenue in the garden and whisper how dear you are to her. You'll see, she'll never marry, because she loves you. Don't you feel sorry for her?'

'Yes.'

'*She* was the one who sent those rolls. She really makes me laugh. Why should she hide it? I was once funny and silly too, but now I've left that place I'm no longer scared of anyone. I think and I say what I like out loud and that's made me happy. When I was living at home I had no idea what happiness was; now I wouldn't change places with a queen.'

Dr Blagovo arrived. He had received his doctor's degree and was staying in town at his father's place for a little rest. He said that he would soon be off to St Petersburg again, as he wanted to do research in typhus and cholera inoculations, it seemed. He wanted to go abroad to complete his studies and then become a professor. He had resigned from the army and wore loose-fitting cheviot jackets, very wide trousers and superb ties. My sister was in raptures over the tie-pins, the cuff-links, and the red silk scarf he sported in the top pocket of his jacket. Once, when we had nothing to do, we tried to remember how many suits he had and concluded that there were at least ten. He clearly loved my sister as much as before, but not once, even as a joke, did he suggest taking her with him to St Petersburg or abroad. I just couldn't imagine what would happen to her if she survived, what would become of the child. All she did was daydream, however, without giving any serious thought to the future: she said that he could go where he liked, even abandon her, as long as he was happy, and that she was quite content with things as they had turned out.

When he visited us he usually listened very carefully to her and insisted she had drops in her milk. And this time it was the same. He listened to her chest, then made her drink a glass of milk, after which our rooms smelled of creosote.

'That's my clever girl!' he said, taking her glass. 'You mustn't talk too much, you've been chattering ten to the dozen lately. Now, please don't talk so much!'

She burst out laughing. Then he went into Radish's room, where I was sitting, and gave me an affectionate pat on the shoulder.

'Well, how are you, old man?' he asked, bending over the invalid.

'Sir,' Radish said, quietly moving his lips. 'If I may be so bold as to inform you, sir . . . all of us are in God's hands, we all have to die some time . . . Allow me to tell you the truth, sir . . . *you* won't enter the kingdom of heaven!'

'What can I do about it?' the doctor joked. 'Someone has to go to hell.'

And then, suddenly, I seemed to lose consciousness and felt that I was dreaming: it was a winter's night and I was standing in the slaughter-house next to Prokofy, who smelt of pepper-brandy. I tried to pull myself together, rubbed my eyes and seemed to be on my way to the Governor's, for the interview. Nothing like this has ever happened to me before or since and I can only put these strange, dream-like memories down to nervous strain. I lived through the scene at the slaughter-house and my interview at the Governor's, vaguely conscious all the time that it wasn't real. When I came to, I realized that I wasn't in the house, but standing near a street-lamp with the doctor.

'It's sad, so sad,' he was saying, the tears running down his cheeks. 'She's cheerful, always laughing and full of hope. But her condition is hopeless, my dear friend. Your Radish hates me and keeps trying to drum into me how badly I've behaved towards her. In his way he's right, but I have my views as well and I don't regret what happened at all. One must love, we should all love, shouldn't we? Without love there wouldn't be any life and the man who fears love and runs away from it is not free.'

Gradually he turned to other topics – science, his thesis, which had a good reception in St Petersburg. He spoke very enthusiastically and quite forgot my sister, his own sorrows, and me. He was thrilled with life. 'She has America and a ring with an inscription,' I thought, 'and he has a higher degree and an academic career in front of him. Only my sister and I are in the same old rut.'

I said goodbye and went over to a street-lamp to read the letter again. And I remembered vividly how she had come down to the mill one spring morning to see me, how she lay down and covered herself with a sheepskin coat, trying to look like a simple old peasant woman. Another time, when we were pulling the fish-trap out of the water, large rain-drops scattered over us from the willows along the bank and made us laugh.

Everything was dark in our house in Great Dvoryansky Street. I climbed the fence and went into the kitchen by the back door, as in former days, to fetch a lamp. No one was there. A samovar was hissing by the stove, all ready for Father. 'Who's going to pour Father's tea for him now?' I wondered. Taking the lamp, I went into my hut, made up a bed from old newspapers and lay down. The spikes on the wall looked as ominous as before and their shadows flickered. It was cold. I expected my sister to come in with my supper at any moment, but immediately I remembered that she was ill at Radish's. Climbing that fence and lying in my unheated hut struck me as bizarre. Everything seemed confused and my imagination conjured up the oddest things.

The bell rang. I remember those sounds from childhood: at first the wire rustling along the wall, then a short, plaintive tinkle. This was Father returning from his club. I got up and went into the kitchen. When Aksinya the cook saw me she clasped her hands and, for some reason, burst out crying.

'My dear boy!' she said softly. 'My dear! Oh, good heavens!'

She was so excited she began crumpling her apron. Half-gallon jars of berries in vodka stood in the window. I poured out a teacupful and gulped it down, I was so thirsty. Aksinya had just scrubbed the table and benches and there was that smell which bright, comfortable kitchens always have where the cook keeps everything clean and shining. This smell, with the chirping of crickets, always used to tempt us into the kitchen when we were children and put us in the mood for fairy tales and card games.

'Where's Cleopatra?' Aksinya asked, quietly and hurriedly, holding her breath. 'And where's your cap, dear? I hear your wife's gone to St Petersburg.'

She had worked for us when Mother was alive and used to bath me and Cleopatra in a tub. And for her we were still children who had to be told what to do. Within a quarter of an hour she had revealed to me, in that quiet kitchen, with all the wisdom of an old servant, the ideas she had been accumulating since we last met. She told me that the doctor ought to be forced to marry Cleopatra – he only needed a good fright, and that, if the application were made in the right way, the bishop would dissolve his first marriage. She said that it would be a good idea to sell Dubechnya without my wife knowing anything about it and to bank the money in my own name; that if my sister and I went down on bended knees before our father and begged hard enough, he would perhaps forgive us; and that we should say a special prayer to the Holy Mother.

'Well, off with you, dear, go and talk to him,' she said when we heard Father coughing. 'Go and talk to him, bow down before him, your head won't fall off.'

So I went. Father was at his desk sketching a plan for a villa with Gothic windows and a stumpy turret that resembled the watch-tower of a fire-station — all very heavy-handed and amateurish. I entered his study and stopped where I could see the plan. I didn't know why I'd come to see Father, but when I saw his gaunt face, his red neck, his shadow on the wall, I remember that I wanted to throw my arms around his neck and go down on my bended knees as Aksinya had instructed. But the sight of that villa with its Gothic windows and stumpy turret held me back.

'Good evening,' I said.

He looked at me and immediately looked down at his plan.

'What do you want?' he asked after a while.

'I've come to tell you that my sister is very ill. She doesn't have long to live,' I added in an empty voice.

'Well, now,' Father sighed, taking off his spectacles and laying them on the table. 'As ye sow, so shall ye reap. As ye sow, so shall ye reap,' he repeated, getting up from the table. 'I want you to remember when you came here two years ago. In this very place I asked you, I begged you, to abandon the error of your ways. I reminded you of your duty, your honour, your debt to your ancestors, whose traditions must be held sacred. You ignored my advice and stubbornly clung to your erroneous ideas. What's more, you led your sister astray and made her lose her moral sense and all sense of decency. Now you're both paying for it. Well, then, as ye sow, so shall ye reap!'

He said all this pacing the study. Probably he thought that I'd come to apologize and probably plead for myself and my sister. I was cold, I shivered feverishly and spoke in a hoarse voice and with great difficulty.

'And I would also ask you to remember something,' I

said. 'In this very room I begged you to try and understand my viewpoint, to think hard about what we're living for and how we should live. But your only answer was to talk about ancestors, about the grandfather who wrote poetry. Now, when you're told that your only daughter is hopelessly ill, all you can do is go on about ancestors and tradition. How can you be so thoughtless in your old age, when death is just round the corner and you have only five or ten years left?'

'Why have you come here?' Father asked sternly, clearly annoyed with me for calling him thoughtless.

'I don't know. I love you and can't say how sorry I am that we're so far apart. That's why I came. I still love you, but my sister's finished with you for good. She won't forgive you, she never will. The mere mention of your name fills her with revulsion for the past, for life.'

'And who's to blame?' Father shouted. '*You're* to blame, you scoundrel!'

'All right, I'm to blame,' I said. 'I admit that I'm to blame for many things. But why is the type of life you're leading — which you insist *we* have to follow — so boring, so undistinguished? In all the houses you've been building for thirty years now, why isn't there a single person who could teach me how to live the way you want? There's not one honest man in the whole town! These houses of yours are thieves' kitchens, where life is made hell for mothers and daughters and where children are tortured. My poor mother!' I went on despairingly. 'My poor sister! One has to drug oneself with vodka, cards, scandal, one has to cringe, play the hypocrite, draw up plan after plan for years and years to blind oneself to the horrors lurking in those houses. Our town has existed for hundreds of years and not once in all that time has it given one useful person to the country — not one! Anything at all bright and lively has been stifled at birth by you. This is a town of shopkeepers, publicans, clerks, priests. It's a useless town, no good to anyone. Not one person would be sorry if the earth suddenly swallowed it up.'

'I don't want to hear any more, you scoundrel!' my father said, picking up a ruler from the table. 'You're drunk! How dare you visit your father in that state! I'm telling you for the last time – and you can tell this to your slut of a sister – that you will get nothing from me. There's no place in my heart for disobedient children, and if they suffer for their disobedience and obstinacy they'll get no pity from me. You can go back to where you came from. It was God's will to punish me through you, but I endure this trial with all humility. I'll find consolation in suffering and never-ending toil, as Job did. You will never cross my doorstep again unless you reform. I'm a just person, everything I'm telling you is good sense. If you want to do yourself some good, remember what I said to you before and what I'm telling you now – remember it for the rest of your life!'

I gave up and left. I don't remember what happened that night or on the next day. People said that I staggered bareheaded through the streets, singing out loud, with crowds of boys following me and shouting 'Better-than-Nothing! Better-than-Nothing!'

XX

If I had wanted a ring I would have chosen the following inscription for it: 'Nothing passes'. I believe that nothing actually disappears without trace and that the slightest step we take has some meaning for the present and future.

What I have lived through has not been in vain. The people in the town have been touched by my misfortunes and my powers of endurance. No longer do they call me 'Better-than-Nothing', no longer do they laugh at me or pour water over me when I walk through the market. Now they are used to my being a workman and they see nothing strange in a gentleman like myself carrying buckets of paint and fitting window-panes. On the contrary, they willingly give me jobs to do and I'm considered an excellent workman and the best contractor after Radish. Although his health is better – he still paints church belfry cupolas without using scaffolding – he can no longer keep the men under control. I run around town now instead of him, looking for orders. I take men on, sack them, I borrow money at high interest. And now that I've become a contractor I can understand how a man can run round town for three days looking for roofers, for the sake of some lousy little job. People are polite to me, call me 'Mr', and in the houses where I'm working I'm given tea and asked if I want a hot meal. Children and girls often come and watch me, with sad, inquisitive looks.

One day I was working in the Governor's garden, painting a summer house to look like marble. The Governor was out strolling and came into the summer house. Having nothing else to do he started talking to me. I reminded him how once he had ordered me to his office for an interview. He stared into my face for a while, then he made an 'O' with his mouth, spread his arms out helplessly and said, 'I don't remember!'

I have aged and become taciturn, stiff and stern, and I rarely laugh. People say that I've come to resemble Radish, and I bore my workmen with useless moral exhortations.

My ex-wife Masha Dolzhikov now lives abroad, and her father, the engineer, is building a railroad in some eastern Russian province and buying up estates there. Dr Blagovo is also abroad. Dubechnya has once again passed to Mrs Cheprakov, who bought it back after getting the engineer to cut twenty per cent off the price. Moisey now goes around in a bowler hat. He often comes into town on a racing-drozhky and stops near the bank. They say he's bought himself an estate on a mortgage and he's always inquiring at the bank about Dubechnya, which he intends buying as well. For a long time poor Ivan Cheprakov roamed around the town, doing nothing and drinking heavily. I had tried to fix him up with a job with us and for a while he worked with us, painting roofs and doing some glazing. He even grew to like the work. Like any regular house-painter, he stole linseed oil, asked for tips and got drunk. But he soon grew sick and tired of it and went back to Dubechnya. Later on the lads confessed to me that he had been inciting them to help him kill Moisey at night and rob Mrs Cheprakov.

Father has aged terribly and become round-shouldered. In the evenings he takes a little stroll near his house. I never go and see him.

During the cholera epidemic Prokofy treated the shop-keepers with pepper-brandy and tar, and took money for it. As I later learned from our newspaper, he was flogged for saying nasty things about doctors in his butcher's stall. Nikolka, the boy who helped him, died of cholera. Kar-povna is still alive and, as ever, loves and fears her Prokofy. Whenever she sees me she shakes her head sadly.

'You're finished, you poor devil!' she says, sighing.

On weekdays I'm usually busy from morning to night. On holidays, when the weather is fine, I pick up my little niece (my sister was expecting a boy, but she had a girl) and walk, taking my time, to the cemetery. There I stand or sit down and gaze for a long time at the grave that is so dear to me, and I tell the little girl that her mother lies there.

Sometimes I meet Anyuta Blagovo at the graveside. We greet one another and stand in silence, or we talk about Cleopatra, about the little girl, and about the sadness of life. Then we leave the cemetery and walk silently – she walks slowly, so that she can stay next to me as long as possible. The little girl, happy and joyful, screws up her eyes in the bright sunlight and laughs as she stretches her small hands out towards me. We stop and together we fondle that dear little girl.

As we enter the town, Anyuta Blagovo becomes agitated and she blushes as she says goodbye and walks on alone, solemn and demure. And no one in that street looking at her now would have thought that only a moment ago she had been walking at my side and had even fondled that little child.

An Unpleasant Business

Grigory Ovchinnikov, a country doctor of about thirty-five, gaunt and nervous-looking, was known to his colleagues for his minor contributions to medical statistics and keen interest in so-called 'social problems'. One morning he was doing the rounds in the hospital wards, followed as usual by his assistant Mikhail Smirnovsky, an elderly man with a fat face, flattened hair and an earring in one ear.

Hardly had the doctor started his rounds than one trivial little detail struck him as most suspicious: his assistant's jacket was badly creased and kept obstinately riding up, despite his repeated efforts to straighten it. His shirt was slightly crumpled and creased too; there were bits of fluff on his long black frock-coat, his trousers and even on his tie. He had obviously slept in his clothes, and from the look on his face as he tugged at his jacket and adjusted his tie it was obvious that the clothes were too tight for him.

The doctor stared at him and guessed what was wrong. His assistant was standing quite steadily and answered questions coherently, but his sullen, dull face, his bleary eyes, the way his neck and hands were trembling, his untidy clothes – above all, his intense efforts to control himself and his desire to hide the state he was in – all this testified that he had just got up, that he had slept poorly, and that he was still extremely drunk from what he had knocked back the night before. He was having a murderous hangover, was going through absolute agony and clearly was very upset with himself.

The doctor, who had his own reasons for disliking this medical orderly, felt a strong urge to tell him 'You're drunk, I see!' Suddenly that waistcoat, the long frock-coat, the earring in that fleshy ear disgusted him. But he held his anger back and said in his usual soft polite voice, 'Has Gerasim had his milk?'

'Yes, doctor,' Smirnovsky answered – also in a soft voice.

While he talked to the patient called Gerasim, the doctor glanced at the temperature chart and felt a fresh surge of loathing. He held his breath to stop himself saying something, but just could not help asking, in a rude, gasping voice, 'Why hasn't his temperature been entered?'

'Oh, but it has, doctor!' Smirnovsky replied. But after he had taken a look at the chart and convinced himself that it hadn't, he shrugged his shoulders in bewilderment and muttered, 'I just don't understand. It's Sister Nadezhda's fault!'

'And it wasn't entered last night either!' the doctor went on. 'All you can do is get drunk, blast you! Even now you're plastered! Tell me, where's Sister?'

Sister Nadezhda the midwife wasn't in any of the wards, although it was her job to supervise the change of dressings every morning. The doctor looked and began to notice that the ward hadn't been tidied up, that everything was in a terrible mess, that none of the normal jobs had been done and that everything was as billowing, crumpled and fluff-covered as the orderly's obnoxious waistcoat. He felt like tearing off his white apron, shouting, throwing everything on to the floor, saying to hell with everything and leaving. But he made a strong effort of will and continued his rounds.

After Gerasim there was a surgical case – tissue inflammation of the entire right arm. This patient needed a change of dressing. The doctor sat down on a stool at his side and got to work on the arm.

'They had a wild party yesterday, someone's name-day,' he thought, slowly removing the bandage. 'You just wait, I'll give you parties! But what can I do? I can't do a thing.'

He felt an abscess on the swollen, purple arm and said, 'Scalpel!'

Trying to prove that he was steady on his feet and capable of work, Smirnovsky rushed off and quickly returned with a scalpel.

'Not that one! A new one!' said the doctor.

The orderly took mincing steps over to the chair where the box of dressing material was and hurriedly started rummaging around in it. He spent a long time whispering to the nurses, moving the box on the chair, made a rustling noise and twice dropped something while the doctor sat there waiting and feeling a severe irritation in his back from all the whispering and rustling.

'Are you going to be much longer?' he asked. 'You must have left them downstairs.'

The orderly ran up to him and handed him two scalpels, making the mistake of breathing in the doctor's direction.

'Not those!' the doctor said, flaring up. 'I'm telling you in plain language, give me the new ones. Oh, forget it! Go and sleep it off. You smell just like a pub! I can't rely on you for *anything*!'

'But what other knives do you need?' the orderly asked irritably and slowly shrugged his shoulders. He was annoyed with himself and ashamed that all the patients and the nurses were staring at him. To try and conceal his embarrassment he forced a smile and repeated, 'But what other knives do you need?'

The doctor felt tears in his eyes; his fingers were trembling. He made a strong effort to control himself. 'Go and sleep it off,' he said in a shaking voice. 'I don't want to talk to drunks.'

'You can't tell me off for what I do in my free time,' the orderly went on. 'What if I did have a few, no one's got the right to pull me up for that. Don't I do my job properly?'

The doctor leapt to his feet and, not aware of what he was doing, took a swing and hit the orderly on the face with his full force. He couldn't say why he did it, but he derived great pleasure from the fact that his fist had landed right in his face, from the fact that this respectable, church-going family man, a responsible member of society with an inflated opinion of himself, bounced like a ball and then slumped on to a stool.

He had a strong urge to hit him again, but when he saw

those pale, anxious faces in the proximity of that loathsome face, his feeling of pleasure subsided. He threw up his hands in despair and tore out of the ward.

Outside in the hospital grounds he met Sister Nadezhda on her way in. She was a twenty-seven-year-old spinster, with a pale, yellowish face and loose hair. Her pink cotton-print dress was very tight in the skirt, which made her take very short, quick steps. She rustled her dress, twitched her shoulders in time with each step and tossed her head as if she was humming a cheerful little tune to herself.

'Aha, the Mermaid!' the doctor thought, remembering that the hospital staff teased her by calling her this name, and he was pleased at the thought of making that mincing, self-enamoured lady of fashion look small.

'Why are you always somewhere else?' he shouted as he drew level. 'Why can I never find you in the hospital? The temperatures haven't been entered, there's chaos everywhere, my orderly's drunk – and you stay in bed until twelve o'clock. You'd better look for another job, you're no longer employed here!'

When he reached his flat the doctor tore off his white apron and the towel he wore to keep it belted, furiously flung both towel and apron into a corner and paced his study.

'My God, what a crowd, what people!' he said. 'They're no assistants of mine – they're my enemies! I can't stay in this place any longer! I just can't. I shall leave!'

His heart was pounding. He trembled all over and he felt like crying. To rid himself of these sensations he tried calming himself with the thought that he was absolutely in the right and that hitting his assistant had been an excellent idea. The nasty thing about it was, so the doctor thought, this man had not obtained his job at the hospital in the usual way, but through the influence of an aunt, a nanny who worked for the chairman of the local council. It really revolted him when this formidable aunt came for treatment, behaving as if the place belonged to her and jumping the queue. That assistant of his knew nothing about discipline, and what he did know he failed to understand. He was always drunk, insolent, didn't keep himself clean, took bribes from the patients and sold government medicine on the quiet. Moreover, it was common knowledge that he had his own little practice, treating young people in the town for unspeakable diseases with methods he himself had devised. It would have been quite bad enough had he been just another ordinary quack. But he was a quack of the 'up-in-arms' variety, harbouring rebellious ideas! Without the doctor knowing a thing about it, he would cup and bleed out-patients, assisted at operations with unwashed hands, picked at wounds with a perpetually filthy probe: all this was enough to show how deeply and audaciously he despised the doctor's medicine with all its erudition and pedantry.

Waiting until his fingers stopped shaking, the doctor sat at his desk and wrote a letter to the chairman of the local council.

Dear Leo Trofimovich

If, on receipt of this letter, the council fails to dismiss male orderly Smirnovsky and refuses me the right to select my own assistants, then I shall be obliged (not without regret, may I add) to ask you to consider me no longer a doctor at N— Hospital and to set about finding a replacement.

My respects to Lyubov Fyodorovna and Yus.

Yours faithfully
G. Ovchinnikov

Re-reading the letter, the doctor found it too brief and not formal enough. Moreover, paying his respects to Lyubov Fyodorovna and Yus (this was the nickname of the chairman's younger son) was quite improper in an official letter of resignation.

'What the hell has Yus got to do with it?' the doctor reflected. He tore the letter up and tried to concoct something different. 'Dear Sir,' he thought, sitting at the open window and watching the ducks and ducklings hurrying down the path, stumbling and waddling, doubtless on their way to the pond. One duckling had picked up a piece of offal, choked on it and squealed in alarm. Another ran up to it, tugged the piece of offal out of its mouth and started choking too. Far off, by the fence, in the lace pattern of the shadows cast by the young limes, Darya the cook was wandering about gathering sorrel for the cabbage soup.

The doctor could hear voices. Zot the coachman, bridle in hand, and Manuylo the hospital handyman, in a filthy apron, were standing near the shed talking about something and laughing.

'They're going on about my hitting that orderly of mine,' the doctor thought. 'By this evening the whole district will know about this scandal. All right. "Dear Sir, Unless your council dismisses . . ." '

The doctor knew perfectly well that on no account would the council employ an orderly in place of him and it would sooner discharge every male nurse in the district than deprive itself of such a first-rate man as Dr Ovchinnikov. The moment Leo Trofimovich received the letter he would be certain to turn up in his troika saying, 'What's got into your head, old man? What's it all about, God forgive you! Why? For what reason? Where is he? Send him here, the swine! Kick him out! He must be sacked! I want that scoundrel out of here by tomorrow!' Then he would dine with the doctor and lie afterwards on that crimson sofa, belly upwards, cover his face with a newspaper and start snoring. After a nice little snooze he would have tea and drive the doctor off to spend the night at his place. And the whole drama would finish with the male nurse staying on at the hospital and the doctor not resigning after all.

But, deep down, the doctor did not want things to turn out this way. He wanted the orderly's aunt to triumph, he wanted the council to accept his resignation without further discussion – and with pleasure, even, despite his eight years' conscientious service. He dreamed of driving away from that hospital he had grown so used to, of writing a letter to *The Physician*, of the address of sympathy that his colleagues would present him with.

The Mermaid came into sight along the road. Taking tiny steps and rustling her dress, she came up to the window.

'Dr Ovchinnikov, are you going to see the patients yourself?' she asked. 'Or do you want us to do it?'

But her eyes said, 'You lost your temper. You've calmed down and feel ashamed now. But I'm the forgiving type and I'm turning a blind eye to it!'

'All right, I'll be right over,' the doctor said. He put his apron on again, used the piece of towel as a belt and went off to the hospital.

'I did the wrong thing, running off like that after I hit him,' he thought on the way. 'It gave the impression that I was embarrassed or frightened. I acted like a schoolboy. It's not very nice!'

He imagined the awkward glances of the patients when he entered the ward, and feeling ashamed of himself. But when he went in they were quietly lying in their beds hardly taking any notice of him. The tubercular Gerasim's face expressed total indifference, and seemed to be telling him, 'He did something that upset you, so you gave him a little lesson. There's no other way.'

The doctor lanced two abscesses on the purple arm, bandaged it, then went to the women's wards, where he operated on one peasant woman's eye. The Mermaid kept following him, helping him as if nothing had happened, and all was well. After the rounds there was the out-patients' clinic. The window was wide open in the doctor's small consulting-room. If you sat on the window-sill and bent down a little, you could see the young grass a couple of feet away. The evening before, there had been thunder and heavy rain, and the grass was rather trampled and shiny. The path that led from just beyond the window down to a gully seemed to have been washed by the rain, and the bits of broken dispensary jars scattered along both sides seemed to have been washed too, and they glinted in the sun, shooting out dazzling rays of light. Further off, beyond the path, young firs clothed in sumptuous green robes huddled together. Beyond them were birches with trunks like white paper, and the fathomless blue sky could be glimpsed through their leaves that barely stirred in the breeze. If you looked out, you could see the starlings hopping along the path, turning their silly beaks towards the window and trying to make up their minds whether to take fright or not. Deciding on the former, they winged their way to the tops of the birches, one after the other, chirping merrily, as if making fun of the doctor for not being able to fly.

Through the oppressive smell of iodoform you could sense the fragrance and freshness of the spring day. It was good to breathe.

'Anna Spiridovna!' the doctor called.

A young peasant woman in a red dress came in and prayed before the icon.

'What's wrong?' the doctor asked.

The woman darted a suspicious glance at the door through which she had just come, went close to the doctor and whispered, 'I ain't got no children!'

'Who else hasn't registered?' the Mermaid shouted in the dispensary. 'Come and sign here!'

'He's a swine,' thought the doctor while he examined the woman, 'because he made me use my fists for the first time in my life. I never came to blows before.'

Anna Spiridovna left. Then an old man with venereal disease came in, then a peasant woman with three children suffering from scabies – work was in full swing. The orderly didn't show his face. Behind the dispensary door the Mermaid twittered away cheerfully, rustling her dress and clinking bottles. Now and again she came into the consulting-room to help with a minor operation or to fetch a prescription – all this being performed with a look that apparently said all was well.

'She's glad I hit that orderly,' the doctor thought, listening to the midwife's voice. 'They've always been at each other's throat; she'll be celebrating if he's given the sack. I do believe the nurses are glad too . . . Oh, how revolting!'

When the clinic was at its busiest he began to feel that Sister, the nurses and even the patients were trying to look unconcerned, cheerful, as if they understood how painfully embarrassing it was for him, but out of delicacy they pretended not to understand. He started shouting at them angrily, to demonstrate that he wasn't in the least embarrassed.

'Hey, you there! Close the door, there's a terrible draught!'

But he really was embarrassed and depressed. After seeing forty-five patients he slowly left the hospital. The Sister had already been back to her flat, where she put a bright crimson shawl around her shoulders. With a cigarette between her teeth and a flower in her loose-hanging hair she was hurrying somewhere, probably to see a patient or to visit someone. Patients sat in the hospital doorway silently sunning themselves. The ever-noisy starlings were hunting beetles. Looking around him, the doctor thought that, among all those settled, unruffled lives, only two stuck out like sore thumbs and were clearly useless: the orderly's and his own. The orderly must be in bed by now, trying to sleep it off, but most likely he was being kept awake by the thought that he was to blame, had been insulted and had lost his job. He was in a dreadful position. On the other hand the doctor, who had never hit anyone in his life, felt as if he had surrendered his virginity. He no longer blamed the orderly or tried to excuse himself, but he was purely and simply puzzled by the fact that a respectable person like himself, who had never even hit a dog, could have dealt that man a blow. Returning to his flat, he lay on the study couch, facing the back. 'He's a bad type,' he thought, 'and a menace. During the three years he's been working here things have been coming to a head. But for all that, there's no excuse for the way I behaved. I abused my authority. He's my subordinate, he was in the wrong, and drunk into the bargain. I'm his superior, I was in the right, and sober. That means my position is the stronger. Secondly, I hit him in front of people who look up to me, therefore I set them a rotten example.'

The doctor was called to dinner. He ate just a few spoon-fuls of cabbage soup, then left the table to lie down again on his couch.

'What should I do now?' he wondered. 'I must offer him the chance of satisfaction as soon as possible. But how? As a practical man, he probably thinks duelling is stupid or just doesn't understand it. If I apologized in that same ward, in front of the nurses and patients, then the apology would satisfy only me, not him. As he's a rotter, he would think that I was being a coward, that I was scared he might complain to the authorities. What's more, any apology would wreck all discipline in the hospital. Should I offer him money? No, that's immoral and amounts to bribery. Supposing I asked the direct authorities, the council, that is, to try and solve the problem. They might give me a repri-mand or dismiss me . . . but they wouldn't go as far as that. And after all, it wouldn't be very nice dragging the council into the hospital's private affairs, because it has no authority there anyway.'

Three hours after dinner he was on his way to the pool for a bathe. 'Shouldn't I act like anyone else in the circum-stances? I mean, let him take me to court. As there's not the slightest doubt that I'm in the wrong, I won't offer any defence and the judge will send me to prison. In this way the injured party will have satisfaction and those who consider me a person of authority will see that I was wrong.'

This idea pleased him. He was delighted and thought that this was the best solution, that it was impossible to be any fairer.

'Well, that's excellent!' he thought as he waded into the water and watched shoals of tiny golden crucians dart away from him. 'Let him sue me. That will suit him all the more, since our working relationship is finished now, and after this scandal one of us will have to leave the hos-pital.'

In the evening the doctor ordered the cabriolet to be brought round, to take him to the commander of the local

barracks for a game of bridge. While he was standing in his
study putting on his gloves, with his hat and coat on and
ready to leave, the outer door creaked open and someone
came quietly into the hall.

'Who's there?' the doctor asked.

A voice answered dully, 'It's me, doctor.'

The doctor's heart suddenly started pounding and a feeling of embarrassment, together with a strange kind of panic,
made him go cold all over. Smirnovsky the orderly (it was
he) quietly coughed and timidly entered the study. After a
short silence he said in a hollow guilty voice, 'Please forgive
me, Dr Ovchinnikov!'

The doctor was taken aback and at a loss for words. He
saw that the orderly had come to grovel and ask forgiveness,
not to mortify the offending party by any display of Christian humility but simply to further his own cause: 'I'll force
myself to apologize and perhaps I won't be sacked and have
to starve.' What could be more insulting to the dignity of
man?

'Forgive me,' said the orderly.

'Now, listen,' the doctor began, trying not to look at him
and still not knowing what to say. 'Look here . . . I assaulted
you and I must be punished. That is, I must give you satisfaction. You've no time for duels. Nor have I, come to that.
I have assaulted you and you . . . hm . . . you can file a
complaint against me with the Justice of the Peace and I'll
have to take the consequences. But the two of us can't stay
on. One of us will have to go.' ('Good God, I'm telling him
all the wrong things,' the doctor thought, horrified. 'How
absolutely stupid!') 'To cut it short, go ahead and sue. We
can't go on working together! It's you or me! File the action
tomorrow!'

The orderly gave the doctor a sullen look and the most
brazen contempt gleamed in his dark, dim eyes. He had
always thought the doctor an impractical, unpredictable
little boy, and now he despised him for that trembling, for
that hectic verbal rigmarole.

'And I *will* sue you,' he said morosely and spitefully.

'Then go ahead and sue!'

'You think that I won't, don't you? I *will* go ahead, so there. You have no right to strike me. You should be ashamed! Only drunken peasants do that, and you're an educated man.'

Suddenly the hatred inside the doctor welled up and he shouted in a voice that wasn't his at all, 'Clear off!'

The orderly reluctantly retreated (it seemed he had something else to say), went into the hall and stayed there, deep in thought. Then, having thought of something, he made a determined exit.

'How stupid!' the doctor muttered as he left. 'How stupid and vulgar all this is!'

He felt that he had behaved childishly towards the orderly, and now he could see that all his ideas about lawsuits were not clever at all, that they did not solve the problem, but only complicated it.

'How stupid!' he thought as he sat in his cabriolet, and later when playing bridge at the commander's. 'Can I really be so ignorant, do I really know so little of life that it's too much for me to solve a simple problem? Well, what can I do?'

Next morning the doctor saw the orderly's wife getting into a carriage and driving off somewhere. 'She's going to that aunt's. Let her, then!'

The hospital had to cope without an orderly. A statement should have been sent to the council, but the doctor still could not compose the correct sort of letter. The main drift of it should now be: 'I request you to dismiss my orderly, although I'm to blame, not he.' But expressing this thought so that it did not sound stupid or degrading was well-nigh impossible for any decent man.

Two days later the doctor was informed that his orderly had complained to Leo Trofimovich. The chairman of the council had not let him get a word in, had stamped his feet and sent him on his way: 'I know your type!' he shouted. 'Clear off! I don't want to hear any more!'

From Leo Trofimovich's place the orderly went to the

council offices, where he filed a complaint in which, without mentioning the blow or asking for anything for himself, he informed the members that the doctor had made derogatory remarks about the council and the chairman in his presence; that he was giving his patients incorrect treatment; that he was neglecting his rounds in the vicinity and so on. The doctor burst out laughing when he heard this, and he thought 'What an idiot!' He felt ashamed and sorry that the orderly was being so silly. The more stupid things a man does to defend himself, the more defenceless and weak he is.

Exactly one week after the morning described above, the doctor received a summons from the Justice of the Peace.

'It's just too silly for words,' he thought as he signed the papers. 'I can't think of *anything* more stupid than this!'

As he drove over to the court-house on that calm, overcast morning he felt far from embarrassed: he was annoyed and disgusted. He was angry with himself, with the orderly and with the whole affair.

'I shall tell everyone in court to go to hell,' he fumed. 'You're all asses and understand nothing!'

When he drove up to the court-house he saw three of his nurses on the doorstep, together with the Mermaid. They had been summoned as witnesses. Seeing these nurses and the vivacious Sister – she was shifting from one foot to the other in impatience and even blushed with pleasure when she saw the leading figure in the impending trial – the furious doctor felt like swooping down on them like a hawk and stunning them by saying 'Who gave you permission to leave the hospital? Will you please return immediately.' But he held himself back, tried to appear calm and made his way through the crowd of peasants into the court-house. The chamber was empty and the judge's chain of office was hanging over the back of his armchair. The doctor went into the clerk's room, where he saw a gaunt-faced young man in a linen jacket with bulging pockets (this was the clerk), and the doctor's orderly, sitting at the table looking through a book of case records, for want of something better to do. The clerk stood up when the doctor entered; so did the orderly, and he looked rather embarrassed.

'So Alexander Arkhipovich hasn't arrived yet?' the doctor asked nervously.

'Not yet . . . he's still at home,' the clerk replied.

The court-house was in one of the outbuildings of the judge's country estate, and the judge himself lived in the main house. The doctor left the court-house and slowly made his way towards the main house. He found Alexander Arkhipovich near a samovar in the dining-room. He wasn't wearing a coat or waistcoat, his shirt was unbuttoned and he stood near the table, teapot in both hands, pouring tea as dark as coffee into a glass. When he saw his visitor he quickly reached for another glass and filled it.

'With or without sugar?' he asked, without saying good morning. At one time, very long ago, the judge had served in the cavalry. Now, after many years' service as electoral officer, he had reached senior rank in the civil service, but had never relinquished his uniform or military habits. He had the long whiskers of a chief of police, piped trousers, and his every action and word was imbued with martial elegance. When he spoke he threw his head back slightly, embellishing his speech with a general's fruity 'My deah sir,' exercising his shoulder muscles and flashing his eyes. When he greeted someone or offered them a light, he scraped his heels; and when he walked, he clinked his spurs so carefully and exquisitely, it seemed that with every jingle he had an intolerable surge of pain. After making the doctor sit down to tea, he stroked his broad chest and stomach, sighed deeply and said, 'Hm . . . yes . . . my deah sir, perhaps you would care for a drop of vodka and a little something to eat? Yes, my deah sir?'

'No, thanks, I've eaten.'

Both gentlemen felt that a discussion about the hospital scandal was inevitable, and both felt awkward. The doctor did not say a word. With a graceful motion of the hand, the judge caught a gnat that had bitten him on the chest, carefully scrutinized it from all angles and released it. After that he sighed deeply, looked up at the doctor and asked in a slow, measured voice, 'Now, why don't you get rid of him?'

The doctor detected a note of sympathy in his voice; suddenly he felt sorry for himself, and weary and jaded after the week's upsets. Looking as if his patience had finally snapped, he got up from the table, frowned irritably and said, shrugging his shoulders, 'Get rid of him! Good God, the things you people say! It really is amazing. How am I to get rid of him? You sit there and think that I'm in charge of the whole hospital and that I can do anything I like! It's quite amazing the ideas you people get! Do you think I can sack an orderly when his aunt is nanny to Leo Trofimovich's children, and when that gentleman relies on little sneaks and crawlers like that Smirnovsky? What can I do about it if the council doesn't think we doctors are worth a brass farthing, if it tries to trip us up with every step we take? To hell with all of them, they can keep their job! I don't want it.'

'Now, now, my deah chap, you're exaggerating the whole thing, so to speak . . .'

'The Marshal of the Nobility bends over backwards to prove that we're all nihilists. He spies on us and treats us like common clerks. What right has he to visit the hospital when I'm away and to cross-examine the nurses and patients? Wouldn't you call that an insult? And that holy idiot of yours, Semyon Alexeyevich, who does his own ploughing and doesn't believe in medicine because he's healthy and as well-fed as an ox. He calls us parasites to our faces – shouting the odds so everyone can hear – and he begrudges us our living. To hell with him! I work from dawn to dusk, I don't know what it is to relax, and they need me here more than all these holy fools, bigots, reformers and clowns put together! The work has cost me my health, and instead of being grateful they begrudge me my living! Thanks very much! Everyone thinks he's entitled to poke his nose into someone else's business, to issue instructions and order them around. That old councillor friend of yours, Kamchatsky, gave us doctors a wigging at the committee meeting for wasting potassium iodide and told us to be careful with the cocaine! What does he know about it? What business is it of his? Why doesn't he try and teach you to be a judge?'

'But he's such a boor, old chap, a real creep ... You should ignore him.'

'He is a boor and a creep, yet *you* elected this loud-mouth to the committee, and *you* allow him to poke his nose in everywhere. Yes, you can smile! You think it's all trifles, mere nothings. Just get it into your head, if you can, that these trifles are so numerous that our whole lives are made up of them, just as mountains consist of grains of sand! I can't take any more! I've no strength, Alexander Arkhipovich. Any more of this and I'll not only be punching fat faces, I'll be firing bullets at people, you can be sure of that! Please understand that I don't have nerves of steel. I'm a human being, like yourself.'

The doctor's eyes filled with tears and his voice shook. He turned round and started looking through the window. Silence fell.

'Hm ... my deah chap,' the judge muttered pensively. 'On the other hand, if one looks at things coolly' (the judge caught the gnat, screwed his eyes up tight as he examined it from all angles, then squashed it and threw it into the slop-basin) 'then ... don't you see? There's no reason to give him the sack. If we dismiss him, then another, just the same – perhaps even worse – will take his place. You can go through a hundred men without finding a good one. They're all scoundrels.' (Here the judge stroked his armpits and slowly lit a cigarette.) 'You have to come to terms with this evil. Let me tell you that these days you'll only find honest, sober, trustworthy workmen among the professional classes and the peasantry. That's to say, at the two extremes of society, nowhere else. You might find a terribly honest doctor, an excellent teacher, a really decent ploughman or blacksmith. But as for the people in between – I mean those who have drifted away from the peasantry and haven't become professionals – they are the unreliable element. It's dreadfully difficult finding an honest, sober, orderly, clerk, bailiff and so on. Extraordinarily difficult! I've been working in the justice department since the year dot and all that time I've never had one honest, sober clerk, although I've given whole batches of them the push in my time. People without moral discipline, not to mention hm . . . principles, so to speak . . .'

'What's he on about?' the doctor thought. 'It's got nothing to do with it.'

'Only last Friday,' the judge continued, 'my clerk Dyuzhinsky was up to his tricks. He got some drunks together – the devil knows who – and spent the whole night drinking with them in my court-house. How do you like that? I've nothing against drink. Hell, they can knock back as much as they like, but why let strangers into the court-house? You can see for yourself, it only takes a few seconds to steal some documents, a promissory note or something of the sort, from the files. So, what do you think happened? After that orgy I was forced to spend two days checking the files to see if anything *was* missing. Well, what would *you* do with a swine like that? Get rid of him? Right. But what guarantee do you have that the next won't be worse?'

'But how would you get rid of him?' the doctor asked. 'It's easy enough to speak, but how can I dismiss him and deprive him of a crust of bread if I know that he's a family man, that he's hard up? What would he and his family do?'

'To hell with it, that's not what I mean,' he thought, and it struck him as strange that he couldn't concentrate on a definite thought or feeling. 'That's because I'm shallow, incapable of lucid thought,' he reflected.

'This man in between, as you call him, can't be relied upon,' he continued. 'We hound him, abuse him, hit him in the face, but surely we should see things his way, shouldn't we? He's neither peasant nor gentleman, neither fish nor fowl. His past has been awful, his present is earning a mere twenty-five roubles a month, his family's starving and he's under someone's foot the whole time. His future consists of the same twenty-five roubles, that same menial position, even if he lives a hundred years. He has no education, no property. He has no time to read or go to church, he can't hear us, as we won't let him get near. And so he muddles along from day to day until he dies, half-starved and fearing that he can be thrown out of his tenement flat at any time without knowing where to find a roof for his children. So, what's there to stop a man getting drunk, stealing, with that sort of life? What principles do you expect him to acquire?'

'Seems we're solving social problems now,' he thought. 'Good God, and how clumsily! What's the point of all this?'

Bells tinkled – someone had driven into the yard, right up to the court-house first, then to the porch of the main house.

'It's him,' the judge said, looking through the window. 'Well, you're for it now!'

'Please deal with it as quickly as you can,' the doctor asked. 'Please put my case at the top of the queue, if that's possible. I really haven't much time, honestly.'

'All right. Only I still don't know whether the case falls within my jurisdiction, old chap. Your relations with your orderly are, in a manner of speaking, confined to the hospital, are they not? What's more, you clumped him while he was fulfilling his official duties. I really can't say for certain, though. But here's Leo Trofimovich, we can ask him.'

There were hurried footsteps and heavy breathing: Leo Trofimovich, the chairman of the council, appeared in the doorway. He was a balding, grey-haired old man with a long beard and red eyelids.

'Good day to you, gentlemen!' he said, panting. 'Ugh! Please get me some kvass, my dear judge. This will be the finish of me . . .'

He sank into an armchair but immediately leapt up, ran over to the doctor, and glared at him. In a shrill voice he said, 'I'm extremely grateful, Grigory Ovchinnikov. Many thanks for the great favour you've done me. I shall never forget you, until the end of time! But friends don't carry on like this, do they? Think what you like, you haven't really played the game. Why didn't you let me know? What do you take me for? Your enemy or a stranger? Have I ever refused you anything, eh?'

Staring angrily and twiddling his fingers, the chairman drank some kvass, quickly wiped his lips and continued, 'So deeply, deeply obliged to you! Now, why didn't you let me know? If you'd had any feeling for me you would have driven over and told me all about it, as a friend. "My dear Leo Trofimovich," you would have said, "it's like this, these are the facts. Such and such a thing happened . . ." I would have had it sorted out in a jiffy and there would have been no need for this scandal. But now that moron seems to have gone crackers, wandering around the district spreading muck, gossiping with village crones, while you, I'm ashamed to say, have stirred up a real hornet's nest, if you'll pardon the expression, and you've forced that imbecile to sue you! It's a downright disgrace! Everyone keeps asking me what it's all about, who's right or wrong. And just fancy, I, the chairman, don't know what you're cooking up! You don't need me, that's for sure! Thank you very, very much, Grigory Ovchinnikov!'

The chairman bowed so low he even turned purple. Then he went over to the window and shouted, 'Zhigalov, send in Smirnovsky! Tell him I want him here this instant!'

He turned away from the window and continued, 'It's not very nice, doctor! Even my wife felt hurt, and she's always had a soft spot for you. You gentlemen pride yourselves on your grey matter a bit too much! You're all dead set on trying to reason things out, you're always on about principles and all that fancy claptrap. But it's no use. All it does is cloud the issue.'

'But you never exercise your grey matter, and where does it get you?' asked the doctor.

'Where does it get me? Simply, if I hadn't come here right away you would have brought disgrace on yourself and on us. Consider yourself lucky that I came!'

The orderly came in and stopped by the door. The chairman stood sideways to him, stuffed his hands in his pockets, cleared his throat and said, 'Apologize to the doctor immediately!'

The doctor turned red and ran into another room.

'So, you see, the doctor doesn't wish to accept your apology,' the chairman went on. 'He wants you to show in deeds, not words, that you're sorry. Will you give me your word that from this day on you'll do what you're told and stay sober?'

'You have my word,' the orderly said in a gloomy, deep voice.

'Watch your step now, or God help you. You'll be fired before you can say knife, you will. If anything else happens don't come asking for favours. All right, then, off with you.'

This turn of events came as a complete surprise for the orderly, who was already reconciled to his fate. He even went pale with joy. He wanted to speak and stretched his arm out, but the words would not come. Then he smiled dumbly and left.

'So that's it!' the chairman said. 'And there's no need for a trial.' He sighed with relief, inspected the samovar and glasses with the look of one who has accomplished something very difficult and important, and wiped his hands.

'Blessed are the peacemakers,' he said. 'Pour me another glass, please, Alexander. But first tell them to bring me something to eat. Oh, yes, and some vodka.'

'Gentlemen, this situation is impossible!' the doctor said, entering the dining-room, still red-faced and wringing his hands. 'This is an absolute farce ... It's disgusting! Better twenty lawsuits than solving problems in this music-hall manner! I can't stand it!'

'So what do you want?' the chairman snapped. 'To sack him? All right, I'll sack him.'

'No, don't do that ... I don't know what I want, but this attitude to things, gentlemen ... God, it's sheer torture!'

The doctor fidgeted nervously as he looked for his hat. Unable to find it he slumped into an armchair, utterly exhausted. 'It's disgusting,' he repeated.

'My dear fellow,' the judge whispered. 'I don't altogether understand you, so to speak. After all, *you* were to blame in this incident. Swiping people in the mug at the end of the nineteenth century is somehow, so to speak, not the done thing. The fellow's a swine, but you must agree that you acted imprudently yourself.'

'Of course,' the chairman agreed.

Vodka and snacks were served. The doctor mechanically drank a glass of vodka and ate a radish before departing.

On his way back to the hospital his thoughts became veiled in mist, like grass on an autumn morning.

'What was the point of all the sufferings, all those changes of heart, all that talk of the past week for everything to peter out in this stupid, trite way? How stupid, how stupid!'

He felt ashamed of having involved strangers in his personal problems, ashamed of what he had said to these people, ashamed of the vodka he had drunk just out of habit and because he was used to an idle existence. Back at the hospital he immediately started on his rounds. The orderly followed him around, treading softly as a cat and quietly answering questions. The orderly, the Mermaid, the nurses – all pretended that nothing had happened and that all was well. And the doctor himself did his utmost to appear unconcerned. He gave orders, got angry, joked with the patients, while all the time the word 'stupid' kept stirring in his brain.

A Nervous Breakdown

I

One evening a medical student called Mayer, and
Rybnikov, a pupil at the Moscow Institute of Painting,
Sculpture and Architecture, called on their law-student
friend Vasilyev and invited him to pay a visit to S— Street *
with them. Vasilyev took a long time to make up his mind
but finally put his coat on and went off with them.

He knew of fallen women only by hearsay and from
books, and he had never been in their houses. He knew that
there were immoral women forced to sell their honour for
money under pressure of circumstances – environment, poor
upbringing, poverty and so on. These women knew nothing
of pure love, had no children, no legal rights. Their mothers
and sisters mourned them as if they were dead, science
treated them as an evil and men spoke to them with contempt. But for all this they had not lost the image and
likeness of God. All of them acknowledged their sin and
hoped to be saved – and the paths to salvation open to them
were innumerable. It is true that society does not forgive
people their past, but Mary Magdalene is no lower than
other saints in the sight of God. Whenever Vasilyev
happened to recognize a prostitute in the street from her
dress or manner, or whenever he saw a picture of one in a
humorous paper, he always remembered a story that he had
once read somewhere: a certain pure and selfless young man
falls in love with a prostitute and asks her to become his
wife, but she considers herself unworthy of such happiness
and poisons herself.

Vasilyev lived in one of the side-streets leading off the

* The notorious Sobolev Alley in Moscow, mentioned damningly by
Chekhov in a letter to Suvorin.

Tver Boulevard. It was about eleven o'clock when he left the house with his friends. The first winter snow had only just begun to fall and the whole of nature was held captive by this fresh snow. The air smelt of snow; snow softly crunched underfoot; the ground, roofs, trees, boulevard benches – all was soft, white and new, and the houses looked quite different from the day before. The lamps shone more brightly, the air was clearer and the clatter of carriages was muffled. And one's sensations became just like the touch of white, new, fluffy snow in that fresh, light frosty air.

> 'Unwilling to these sad shores
> A mysterious force is drawing me'★

sang the medical student in a pleasant tenor.

> 'See the windmill now in ruins'

the art student joined in.

> 'See the windmill now in ruins'

repeated the medical student, raising his eyebrows and sadly shaking his head.

He stopped singing for a moment, rubbed his forehead as he tried to recall the words, then he sang so loudly, so well that passers-by looked round at him.

'Here once I did meet light-hearted love, as free as myself.'

The three entered a restaurant and each drank two glasses of vodka at the bar without taking their coats off. Before they swallowed the second, Vasilyev noticed a piece of cork in his, raised the glass to his eyes and gazed at it for a long time, blinking shortsightedly. His expression appeared strange to the medical student.

'Why are you staring like that?' he asked. 'Please, don't start philosophizing! Vodka's for drinking, sturgeon's for eating, women for visiting and snow for walking over.

★ From Pushkin's *Rusalka*, set to music by A. S. Dargomyzhsky in his opera of that name (1855).

Please try and behave like a normal human being, at least for one evening!'

'Don't worry, I'm not chickening out!' Vasilyev laughed.

The vodka warmed his chest. He looked at his friends affectionately, and admired and envied them. How well-balanced these healthy, strong, cheerful men were, how well-rounded and smooth their minds and hearts! They sang, loved the theatre passionately, sketched, talked a great deal, drank without having hangovers the next day. They were romantic, dissolute, gentle and audacious. They could work, be deeply indignant, laugh at nothing and talk rubbish. They were warm, decent, selfless and as human beings were in no way inferior to Vasilyev himself, who was so careful with his every word and step, so mistrustful, so cautious, so prone to make an issue out of the least trifle. And so he had felt the urge to spend just one evening in the same way as his friends, to unwind, let himself go a little. Would he have to drink vodka? Then drink it he would, even if he had a splitting headache the next morning. Would they take him to visit some girls? Then he would go. He would laugh, play the fool, cheerfully respond to passers-by.

He was laughing as he left the restaurant. He liked his friends – the one with pretensions to artistic eccentricity in that crumpled, broad-brimmed hat, the other in his sealskin cap – he had money, but he liked to play the academic Bohemian.

He liked the snow, the pale street-lamps, the sharp black prints left on the snow by the feet of passers-by. He liked the air and particularly that crystal-clear, gentle, innocent, almost virginal mood that one sees in nature only twice a year – when all is covered with snow, and on bright days or those moonlit nights in spring, when the ice breaks up on the river.

> 'Unwilling to these sad shores
> A mysterious force is drawing me . . .'

he sang under his breath.

For some reason he and his friends could not get that tune

out of their minds and the three of them sang it mechanically, out of time with each other.

Vasilyev pictured himself and his friends knocking at some door in ten minutes' time, creeping down dark passages, through dark rooms, to the women. Taking advantage of the darkness he would strike a match and suddenly illumine a suffering face and guilty smile. The woman – a mysterious blonde or brunette – would doubtless have her hair hanging down and be wearing a white nightdress. She would be frightened by the light and be terribly embarrassed. 'For goodness' sake, what are you doing?' she would ask. 'Put that light out.' It was all very terrifying, yet intriguing and novel.

II

The friends turned off Trubny Square into Grachovka Street and quickly went down the side-street which Vasilyev knew only by hearsay. Seeing two rows of houses with brightly lit windows and wide-open doors, hearing the gay sounds of pianos and fiddles floating out of all the doorways and mingling to create some weird musical jumble as if an invisible orchestra was tuning up in the darkness above the roofs, he was amazed and said, 'So many houses!'

'That's nothing!' the medical student said. 'There's ten times as many in London – there's about a hundred thousand women like these living there.'

The cab-drivers sat on their boxes as calmly and apathetically as in any other street. And, as in any other street, pedestrians walked the pavements. No one hurried, no one hid his face in his coat-collar, no one shook his head reproachfully . . . In this indifference, this cacophony of pianos and fiddles, in those bright windows and wide-open doors, there was something quite blatant, brazen, bold and happy-go-lucky. In slave markets long ago it must have been just as busy and bustling, people's faces and walk must have shown the same indifference.

'Let's begin at the beginning,' the art student said.

The friends entered a narrow passage lit by a lamp with a reflector. When they opened the door a man in a black frock-coat, with the unshaven face and sleepy eyes of a flunkey, lazily got up from a yellow sofa. The place smelt like a laundry with a splash of vinegar. A door led from the hall into a brightly lit room. The medical student and the artist stopped in this doorway, craned their necks and looked into the room together.

'*Buona sera, signori!*' the artist began, making a theatrical bow. 'Rigoletto, Huguenotti, Traviata!'

'Havana, Cucaracha, Pistoletto!' the medical student said, pressing his cap to his chest and bowing low.

Vasilyev stood behind them. He too wanted to perform a theatrical bow, to say something ridiculous, but he could only smile, and the embarrassment he felt was almost a feeling of shame. Impatiently, he waited to see what would happen next. A small, fair girl of about seventeen or eighteen appeared in the doorway. Her hair was closely cropped and she wore a short blue frock with a white metallic pendant on her breast.

'Why are you standing in the doorway?' she asked. 'Take your coats off and come into the lounge.'

The medical and art students still talked mock-Italian as they entered the lounge. Hesitantly, Vasilyev followed them.

'Gentlemen, please take your coats off,' a servant said sternly. 'We can't have this.'

Besides the blonde, there was another girl in the lounge – very tall and plump, with a foreign-looking face and bare arms. She was sitting by the piano with patience cards spread out on her lap. She completely ignored the visitors.

'Where's the other young ladies?' the medical student asked.

'Having tea,' the blonde said. 'Stepan,' she called, 'go and tell the girls some students have come.'

A little later a third girl came into the lounge. She wore a bright red dress with blue stripes. Her face was heavily and clumsily made up, her forehead was hidden beneath her hair and her unblinking eyes had a frightened look. After she came in she immediately started singing some song in a strong, coarse contralto. A fourth girl appeared, then a fifth . . .

Vasilyev found nothing novel or interesting in any of this. He felt as if it was not the first time he had seen a lounge, piano, mirror with cheap gilt frame, pendant, blue striped dress and empty indifferent faces like these. There was no trace of the darkness, the quiet, the secrecy, the guilty smile and all that he had been expecting and fearing.

It was all so ordinary, prosaic and uninteresting. Only one thing aroused his curiosity a little – this was the strange, seemingly deliberate bad taste evident in the cornices, the ludicrous paintings, dresses, pendant. There was something special, unusual, about this lack of taste.

'How cheap and stupid it all is!' thought Vasilyev. 'What is there in all this rubbish I can see now that might tempt any normal man, that would make him commit the dreadful sin of buying a human being for a rouble? Sinning for the sake of magnificence, beauty, grace, passion, good taste – that I can understand. But this is something different. What's worth sinning for in this place? But I mustn't think about it.'

'You there with the beard, get me some porter!' the blonde said to him. Vasilyev was suddenly embarrassed.

'With pleasure,' he said, politely bowing. 'Only you must forgive me, madam, I . . . hm . . . won't join you. I don't drink.'

Five minutes later the friends were heading for another brothel.

'Now then, why did you get her porter?' the medical student asked angrily. 'Think you're a millionaire! That's six roubles down the drain!'

'Why not let her have the pleasure if that's what she wanted?' Vasilyev said, defending himself.

'It was *Madam's* pleasure, not hers. They tell the girls to ask customers to treat them to drinks, and they're the ones who make the profit.'

'See the windmill,' the art student sang, 'now in ruins.'

After arriving at another brothel the friends stayed out in the hall without going into the lounge. As in the first house, a frock-coated figure with a flunkey's sleepy face rose from a sofa in the hall. As he looked at this servant, his face and shabby frock-coat, Vasilyev thought, 'What sufferings an ordinary simple Russian must have gone through before landing up here as a footman! Where was he before and what did he do? What lay in store for him? Was he married? Where was his mother, and did she know he was a servant in this place?' And now Vasilyev could not help paying attention first and foremost to the male servant in each house he called at. In one house – he reckoned it was the fourth – there was a frail, shrivelled-looking little flunkey with a watch-chain on his waist-coat. He was reading *The Leaflet* and paid no attention to the new arrivals. As he looked at his face Vasilyev concluded, for some reason, that a person with a face like his was capable of robbery, murder and perjury. And it really was a fascinating face, with its large forehead, grey eyes, squashed little nose, thin, tight lips and an expression that was at once stupid and insolent – like that of a young beagle in pursuit of a hare. Vasilyev thought that it would be nice to touch that man's hair to see if it was wiry or soft. It was probably wiry, like a dog's.

III

After two glasses of porter the art student suddenly became drunk and unnaturally lively.

'Let's go to another!' he commanded, waving his arms. 'I'll take you to the best!'

After taking his friends to what was, in his opinion, the best brothel, he expressed an urgent desire to dance a quadrille. The medical student started grumbling about having to pay the musicians a rouble, but agreed to join him. They started dancing.

The best house was just as dreadful as the worst. Here there were exactly the same mirrors, pictures, exactly the same hair-styles and dresses. Examining the furniture and costumes, Vasilyev understood that this was not exactly bad taste, but something that could be called the taste (and the style even) of S— Street. This style was to be found nowhere else, and there was something honest about its very ugliness, which had not come about by chance, but was the result of a long process of development. After visiting eight brothels, he was no longer startled by the colours of the dresses, the long trains, the garish ribbons, the sailor suits and the thick, violet make-up on the girls' cheeks. He saw that all this was correct and that if only one of these women had been dressed like a normal human being, or if one decent engraving had hung on the walls, then the entire tone of the whole street would have suffered.

'How clumsily they sell themselves!' he thought. 'Can't they understand that vice is tempting only when it's attractive and concealed – when it's wrapped up as virtue? Modest black dresses, pale faces, sad smiles and even darkness would have more of an effect than all this crude tinsel. The stupid girls! If they can't see that for themselves, then their customers should have taught them, shouldn't they?'

A young lady in Polish costume, with white fur trimming, came over and sat by him. 'You're a nice dark and handsome man, why aren't you dancing?' she asked. 'Why do you look so bored?'

'Because I *am* bored.'

'Treat me to some claret, then you won't be bored.'

Vasilyev didn't reply. After a short pause he asked, 'What time do you go to bed?'

'After five.'

'And when do you get up?'

'Sometimes at two, sometimes three.'

'And what do you do when you're up?'

'We drink coffee and have dinner between six and seven.'

'And what do you eat?'

'Nothing special. Soup or cabbage stew, steak, dessert. Madam looks after her girls well. But why are you asking all this?'

'Hm, well, just to make conversation.'

Vasilyev wanted to discuss many things with the girl. He felt a strong urge to know where she was born; whether her parents were still alive; if they knew she was in this place; how had she come here; whether she was cheerful and contented, or if she was sad and oppressed by dismal thoughts; if she had hopes of escaping from her present situation one day. But try as he might, he just did not know where to start and how to frame his questions without appearing indiscreet. After a long, thoughtful silence he asked, 'How old are you?'

'Eighty,' the girl said, joking and laughing at the way the art student was comically waving his arms and legs about.

Suddenly she burst out laughing at something and produced a long, obscene sentence that everyone could hear. Vasilyev was struck dumb and, not knowing what kind of face to make, forced himself to smile. But only he was smiling, all the others – his friends, the musicians and the women – didn't even look at the girl sitting next to him. It was just as if they hadn't heard.

'Bring me some claret!' the girl repeated.

Vasilyev felt disgusted by those white trimmings and the girl's voice and he left her. He felt hot, that he was suffocating, and his heart started beating slowly, with strong hammer-like beats.

'Let's get out of here!' he said, tugging the art student's sleeve.

'Wait a minute, let me finish.'

While the art student and medical student were finishing their quadrille, Vasilyev scrutinized the musicians to avoid looking at the women. At the piano was a fine-looking old man in spectacles who resembled Marshal Bazaine. The violinist was a young man dressed in the latest fashion, and he had a fair, diminutive beard. His face was far from stupid, didn't look haggard – on the contrary, it was young, clever and fresh. He was fastidiously, tastefully dressed and he played with feeling. There was one problem: how did he and that respectable, handsome old man come to be here? Why weren't they ashamed to be playing in such a place?

What did they think when they looked at the women?

If the pianist and violinist had been scruffy, hungry, miserable, drunken, with gaunt or stupid faces, their presence would perhaps have been understandable. But as things were, Vasilyev understood nothing. He remembered the story of the fallen woman that he had once read, but he found that image of humanity with the guilty smile had nothing in common with what he was seeing now. He felt that he wasn't watching prostitutes, but some kind of different, decidedly peculiar, alien and incomprehensible world. Had he seen that world before in the theatre, or read about it in a book, he would never have believed in it . . .

The woman with the white fur trimmings produced another loud laugh and called out something quite revolting. Overcome with disgust, Vasilyev blushed and left.

'Wait a moment, we're coming too!' the art student shouted after him.

IV

'I had a little chat with my partner while we were dancing,' the medical student told them when all three were out in the street. 'It was about her first love affair. The hero was some book-keeper from Smolensk, with a wife and five children. She was seventeen and lived with her mother and father who sold soap and candles.'

'How did he win her heart?' Vasilyev asked.

'He bought her fifty roubles' worth of underwear. The devil only knows what!'

'All the same, the medical student made his partner tell him all about her affair,' Vasilyev thought. 'But I didn't manage to . . .'

'Gentlemen, I'm going home,' he said.

'Why?'

'Because I don't know how to behave in a place like this. Besides, I feel bored and disgusted. It doesn't exactly cheer you up, does it? If only they were human, but they're savages, animals. I'm off, do what you like!'

'Oh, come on, dear Grigory, Grig . . .' the art student said, trying to coax him and putting his arm around him. 'Let's visit just one more, then to hell with them. Please, Gregorius!'

They persuaded Vasilyev and led him up some staircase. The carpet, gilt banisters, the porter who opened the door, the panelling in the hall were all in S— Street style, but elegant and imposing.

'Really, I ought to go home,' Vasilyev said, taking off his coat.

'Come on, old man,' the art student said, kissing his neck. 'Don't be childish, Grig-Grig, be a sport! Together we came, together we shall leave. You really are an ass, you know.'

'I can wait in the street. Christ, it's really disgusting here!'

'Now, now, Grigory. If it disgusts you, then you can make some observations. Do you understand? Make observations!'

'One should look at things objectively,' the medical student said pompously.

Vasilyev went into the lounge and sat down. Besides him and his friends there were several other visitors: two infantry officers, a balding, grey-haired man in gold-rimmed spectacles, two beardless young men from the Institute of Surveyors and one very drunken man with the face of an actor. The girls were all busy with them and paid no attention to Vasilyev. Only one of them, dressed as Aida, gave him a sidelong glance, smiled for some reason and said with a yawn, 'Someone with dark hair has arrived.'

Vasilyev's heart pounded and his face burned. He was ashamed to face the other visitors, and it was a nasty, painful feeling. It was sheer agony to think that a respectable, loving person like himself (he had always looked upon himself as such) hated those women and felt only revulsion for them. He felt no pity for the women, nor the musicians, nor the servants.

'It's because I'm not trying to understand them,' he thought. 'They're more like animals than human beings – all of them – but they are human beings nonetheless, they have souls. One must understand them first and then judge them.'

'Grigory, don't go, wait for us!' the art student shouted and disappeared. The medical student soon disappeared too.

'Yes, I must try and understand them, this is no good,' Vasilyev kept thinking.

He began staring intensely into each woman's face, looking for a guilty smile. Either he was no good at reading expressions or not one of the women in fact felt guilty, but all he discovered on each face was a blank look of banal, workaday boredom and contentment. Stupid eyes, stupid smiles, harsh, stupid voices, provocative movements – that was all. In the past every one of them had clearly had an affair with a book-keeper and had fifty roubles' worth of underclothes, and now their only pleasures in life were the coffee, three-course dinners, wine, quadrilles and sleeping until two in the afternoon.

Not finding one guilty smile, Vasilyev looked for an intelligent face. His attention was caught by one that was pale, rather sleepy and tired: this was a brunette, no longer young, with a dress covered in sequins. She was sitting in an armchair looking thoughtfully at the floor. Vasilyev paced up and down and then sat by her, as if by accident.

'I must begin with something trite,' he thought, 'and then gradually move on to serious matters.'

'That's a pretty dress you're wearing!' he said and touched the gilt fringe of her shawl.

'Am I?' the brunette said lifelessly.

'Where are you from?'

'Me? A long way away, from Chernigov.'

'It's nice there, very pleasant.'

'The grass grows greener . . .'

'A pity I'm no good at describing nature,' Vasilyev thought. 'I could move her with descriptions of the Chernigov countryside. She must have loved it if that's where she was born.'

'Don't you find it boring here at times?' he asked.

'Of course.'

'Then why don't you leave if you're bored?'

'Where could I go? Begging for charity?'

'Begging would be easier than living here.'

'How do you know? Have you ever tried it?'

'Yes, I have, when I couldn't pay my tuition fees. Even if I hadn't, the thing should be obvious. Whatever you may say, a beggar is a free person, but you're a slave.'

The brunette stretched and sleepily watched a waiter carrying glasses and soda-water on a tray.

'Get me some porter,' she said, yawning again.

'Porter?' thought Vasilyev. 'But what if your brother or mother were to come in right now? What would you say? What would they say? They'd give you porter all right!'

Suddenly there was a sound of crying. Out of the adjoining room where the waiter had taken the soda-water rushed a fair-haired man with red face and angry eyes, followed by the tall, plump Madam.

'No one gave you permission to slap girls' faces,' she screeched. 'We have better-class clients than you and they don't start fights! You lousy fraud!'

A great racket ensued, startling Vasilyev and making him turn pale. In the next room someone was sobbing the deeply felt sobs of the cruelly abused. And he understood that here were real human beings who were being badly treated, who suffered, wept and cried out for help like people anywhere else. Intense loathing and disgust gave way to a feeling of acute pity and of anger with the offender. He rushed to the room where the sobs were coming from and between rows of bottles on a marble table top he could make out a martyred, tear-stained face. He stretched his hands towards this face, took one step towards the table, but immediately recoiled in horror. The weeping girl was drunk.

As he forced his way through the noisy crowd that had gathered around the fair-haired man, his heart sank, he felt the terror of a child, imagining that the inhabitants of this alien, incomprehensible world wanted to chase him, beat him and shower him with obscenities. He grabbed his coat from the hook and dashed headlong downstairs.

V

Pressing himself to the fence, Vasilyev stood near the house and waited for his friends to come out. The cheerful, bold, impudent and melancholy sounds of pianos and fiddles blended into a musical jumble which again resembled an invisible orchestra tuning up in the darkness over the roofs. If one looked up at this darkness the entire black background was sprinkled with moving white dots – falling snow. When the flakes came into the light they circled lazily in the air, like down, and fell even more lazily to earth. A mass of them swirled around Vasilyev and clung to his beard, eyelashes, eyebrows. Cabmen, horses and passers-by were white all over.

'How can snow fall in *this* street!' Vasilyev wondered. 'Damn these brothels!'

His legs were giving way from the effort of running downstairs, he gasped as though he were climbing a hill, he heard his heart pounding, and he had an overwhelming desire to escape from that street as quickly as he could and go home. But he felt an even stronger desire to wait for his friends and vent his spleen on them. There was a great deal that he did not understand about these houses, and the minds of those doomed women were just as much of an enigma as before. But things were far worse than he ever could have imagined – that was clear. If the guilty woman in the story could be called 'fallen' then it was difficult to find a suitable name for all those who were dancing now to that jumble of sounds, who were producing those long, obscene sentences. They were not merely doomed, they were ruined.

'There is vice here,' he thought, 'but no awareness of guilt or hope of salvation. Those women are bought and sold, they are swamped with wine and all kinds of loathsome things, but they are just like sheep – unquestioning, complacent. Oh, good God!'

He could also see that all that went under the name of human dignity, individuality, the image and semblance of God, was defiled – 'down to the last drop' as drunks put it, and that not only were the street and stupid women to be blamed for this.

A crowd of students passed by, white with snow and cheerfully talking and laughing. One of them, tall and thin, stopped, peered into Vasilyev's face and said in a drunken voice, 'He's from our year! Sloshed are you, old chap? Aha! Never mind, enjoy yourself! Let yourself go! Don't be down in the dumps, old man!'

He took Vasilyev by the shoulders, pressed his cold wet moustache to his cheek, then slipped and staggered. Throwing up both arms he shouted, 'Hold on, mind you don't fall!'

In fits of laughter he ran off to catch up with his friends.

Through all the noise the art student's voice could be heard: 'How dare you strike a woman! I won't stand for it, blast you! You rotten swine!'

The medical student appeared in the doorway. He looked to both sides and when he saw Vasilyev he said anxiously, 'So here you are. Listen to me, you can't take Yegor anywhere! I don't understand him. He's made a real scene! Yegor, can you hear?' he shouted into the doorway. 'Yegor!'

The art student's shrill voice rang out from above: 'I won't allow you to strike a woman!'

Something heavy and cumbersome rolled down the stairs. It was the art student, flying head over heels: evidently he was being thrown out.

He struggled to his feet, shook his hat and brandished his fist upwards with a spiteful, outraged look.

'Bastards!' he shouted. 'Crooks! Bloodsuckers! I won't allow beating! Striking a defenceless, drunken woman! Oh, you . . .'

'Yegor! Come on, Yegor!' the medical student pleaded. 'I give you my word of honour that I'll never go out with you again. Word of honour!'

The art student gradually calmed down and the friends went home.

224

'Unwilling to these sad shores
A mysterious force is drawing me . . .'

sang the medical student.

'See the windmill now in ruins'

the art student joined in a little later. 'God, how it's snowing! Grigory, why did you leave? You're a coward, an old woman, that's what!'

Vasilyev walked behind his friends and looked at their backs. 'It's one thing or another,' he thought. 'Either we only imagine prostitution's an evil and we exaggerate it. Or else, if it is in fact such a great evil as is commonly thought, then my dear friends are slave-owners, rapists and murderers just as much as those inhabitants of Syria and Cairo whose pictures one sees in *Niva*.★ Now they're singing away, roaring with laughter, soberly arguing, but haven't *they* just been exploiting hunger, ignorance and stupidity? What they did . . . well, I saw it. What became of their humanity, their medicine, their painting? The learning, fine arts and elevated feelings of those murderers reminds me of the story of the bacon. Two robbers cut a beggar's throat in a forest. They start sharing out his clothes and find a piece of bacon in his bag. "That's good," one of them says. "Let's eat it." "Have you gone crazy?" the other asks, horrified. "Have you forgotten today's Wednesday, a fast day?" So they left it. Two men cut someone's throat and then emerge from the forest convinced they are devout Christians! Those two are the same, they buy women and go around thinking what fine artists and scholars they are . . .'

'Now listen!' he snapped. 'Why do you come here? Can't you see what horrors lie here? Medicine tells you that every single one of these women dies prematurely from tuberculosis or some other illness. The arts tell us that, morally, she's dead long before that. Let's suppose one of these women dies from entertaining an average of five hundred men in her life. Each of them is killed by five hundred men.

★ *Niva* (*The Cornfield*): a weekly illustrated magazine.

Now, if you were each to visit this or similar places two hundred and fifty times during your lives, then the two of you would be responsible for the murder of one woman. Do you understand? Isn't it terrible? Two, three, five of you ganging together to kill one stupid, hungry woman! God, doesn't that horrify you?'

'I knew it would come to this,' the art student said, frowning. 'We should never have got mixed up with this imbecile. You think your head's full of great thoughts and ideas, don't you? Damned if I know what they are, but they're not ideas! You look at me now with loathing and disgust, but in my opinion you'd do better busying yourself building another twenty brothels like these than going around with a face like that. There's more depravity in that look of yours than in the whole street! Let's go, Volodya, to hell with him! He's nothing more than a moron, a complete imbecile . . .'

'We human beings do kill each other,' the medical student said. 'Of course that's immoral, but all these theories won't help. Goodbye!'

On Trubny Square the friends said goodbye and went their ways. Left to himself, Vasilyev strode down the boulevard. He was frightened of the dark, of the snow that was falling in large flakes, wanting to blanket the whole world, it seemed. He was afraid of the lamplight dimly glimmering through the snow clouds. An inexplicable, cowardly fear gripped him. Now and again he met passers-by, but he timidly kept out of their way, under the illusion that women, only women, were coming towards him from all directions and staring at him from all sides. 'It's starting,' he thought. 'I'm having a nervous breakdown.'

VI

At home he lay on his bed, shaking all over. 'They're alive, alive!' he said. 'God, they're alive!'

He indulged in every kind of fantasy, imagining himself first as a prostitute's brother, then as her father, then as the woman herself with her thickly powdered cheeks, and all of it horrified him.

For some reason he felt that he just had to solve the problem there and then, and at all costs. He felt that it was *his* problem and no one else's. He strained every nerve, overcame the despair inside him and sat on the bed, head clasped, trying to think how he could save all the women he had seen that day. Being an educated man, he was very familiar with the correct procedure for solving all kinds of problems. And for all his agitation he strictly adhered to that routine. He recalled the history of the problem, its literature, and between three and four o'clock in the morning he paced his room trying to remember all the modern methods of saving women. He had many good friends and acquaintances living in rooms at Falzstein's, Galyashkin's, Nechayev's, Yechkin's. Among them were quite a number of honest, selfless men. Some of them had tried to save women.

'These few attempts,' thought Vasilyev, 'can be divided into three groups. Some have ransomed a woman from a brothel, rented a room for her, bought her a sewing-machine and she has become a seamstress. Whether he wanted to or not, her rescuer has made her his mistress and then departed the scene after graduating, handing her over to another decent chap as though she were some object. And the woman has remained fallen. Others, having redeemed a woman and also rented a separate room for her, have bought the obligatory sewing-machine and started her on reading and writing, given her moral tuition and supplied books. As long as this was interesting and novel for the woman, she has stayed with the man and got on with her sewing. But later, growing bored, she has started entertaining men behind the moral tutor's back. Or else she has run back to the place where she could sleep until three in the afternoon, drink coffee and eat as much as she liked. A third group, the most zealous and selfless of all, have taken a bold, decisive step. They have married the girl. And when that shameless, downtrodden, spoilt or stupid animal has become a wife, mistress of the house and then a mother, this has so transformed her life and outlook that it has become hard to recognize a former prostitute in this wife and mother. Yes, marriage is the best and perhaps the only way.'

'But that's impossible!' Vasilyev said out loud and slumped on to the bed. 'I'm the last kind of person to marry! One has to be a saint for that, incapable of hatred or revulsion. But let's suppose that the medical student, the art student and myself overcame our apprehension and married. Supposing they all married? What would be the outcome? The outcome would be, while they were getting married here, in Moscow, the Smolensk book-keeper would be corrupting a new batch of them, and this other batch would come pouring into this place to fill the vacancies, together with girls from Saratov, Nizhny-Novgorod, Warsaw . . . And what about those hundred thousand prostitutes from London? And from Hamburg?'

The oil in his lamp had burnt down and it had begun to smoke. Vasilyev did not notice. Once again he paced backwards and forwards, still deep in thought. Now he framed the question differently: how could one remove the need for prostitutes? To achieve this, the men who bought and murdered these women should be made to realize the whole immorality of their role as slave-owners and be duly horrified. It was the men who had to be saved.

'Science and the arts won't be any help here,' Vasilyev thought. 'The only way is by "spreading the word".'

And he began to imagine himself standing next evening on a street corner, asking every passer-by, 'Where are you going and why? Why don't you fear God?'

He would address apathetic cabmen: 'Why are you hanging about here? Why don't you protest, show your indignation? Surely you believe in God and know that it's a sin for which people go to hell? So why can't you speak up? I know they're strangers to you, but please understand that they have fathers, brothers just like you . . . yes!'

Once, a friend of Vasilyev's had said that he was a gifted man. People are usually gifted in literature, drama, the fine arts, but his special gift was for human beings. He was keenly, marvellously sensitive to all forms of pain. Just as a good actor reflects the movements and voices of others, so Vasilyev could reflect another's pain in his soul. He would weep at the sight of tears. Among the sick, he himself became ill and would groan. If he saw an act of violence he would feel that he was the victim, would behave cowardly, like a child, and run off panic-stricken. Other people's pain irritated and stimulated him, reduced him to ecstasy, and so on.

I don't know whether this friend was right, but when Vasilyev thought that he had solved his problem his mood became inspired. He wept, laughed, spoke out loud the words he was going to say the next day and felt an intense love for those who would accept his teaching and join him on the street corner to spread the word. He sat down to write letters and made vows . . .

All this was like inspiration in that it was short-lived – Vasilyev soon became tired. The very weight of numbers of those prostitutes from London, Hamburg, Warsaw pressed down on him as mountains press down on the earth, and made him quail and panic. He remembered that he had no gift for words, that he was cowardly and faint-hearted, that apathetic people would hardly want to listen to him, a timid, insignificant third-year law student, and that true evangelism involves actions as well as sermons.

When it was light and carriages were already clattering down the street, Vasilyev lay motionless on his couch, vacantly staring. No longer was he thinking about women, or men, or spreading the word. His entire attention was riveted on the mental anguish that was tormenting him. It was a dull, abstract, vague kind of pain, rather like a feeling of hopelessness, despair and the most terrible fear. He could point it out – it was in his chest, below the heart. But he knew of nothing with which he could compare it. In his life he had suffered severe toothache, pleurisy and neuralgia, but all that was nothing compared with this spiritual pain. With that kind of pain, life was repellent. The dissertation, the fine work he had written, the people he loved, the rescue of fallen women, together with the memory of all that he had loved or had been indifferent to only yesterday, irritated him now as much as the clatter of carriages, the scurrying of servants, the daylight. If someone were to perform some great deed of mercy or dreadful act of violence before him at that moment, both would have equally revolted him. Of all the thoughts lazily drifting through his mind only two did not irritate him: one was that he had the power to kill himself at any moment and the other – that the pain would not last more than three days. The latter he knew from experience.

After lying down for a while he stood up, wrung his hands and stopped pacing the room from corner to corner, moving in a square, along the walls, instead. He looked at himself in the mirror. His face was pale and hollow-cheeked, his temples were sunken, his eyes had become bigger, darker and less mobile, as if they belonged to a stranger, and they expressed unbearable mental suffering.

At noon the art student knocked at the door.

'Grigory, are you in?' he asked.

Not receiving any reply he stood there for a moment, pondered and then answered himself in Ukrainian dialect,

'Ain't no one thar. 'E's darned well gone off to that looniversity, blast 'im!'

And he went away. Vasilyev lay down on his bed, covered his head with the pillow and started crying out with pain. The more abundantly the tears flowed the worse his mental anguish became. When it grew dark he thought of the night of torment that awaited him and he was overwhelmed by the most dreadful despair. Quickly, he dressed, ran from his room, leaving the door wide open and, without aim or reason, went out into the street. Without asking himself where he was going he swiftly went down Sadovy Street.

It was snowing as heavily as yesterday, but the snow was thawing. With his hands in his sleeves, shivering and starting at the clatter, the bells of horse-trams, and passers-by, Vas-

ilyev walked down Sadovy Street as far as the Sukharev
Tower, then to the Red Gate, where he turned off into
Basmanny Street. He went into a tavern and drank a large
vodka, but this did not make him feel any better. After
reaching Razgulyay, he turned right and strode down side-
streets where he had never been before. He reached the old
bridge where the River Yauza roars past and from where
one can see the long rows of lights in the windows of the
Red Barracks. To relieve his mental torment with some
new sensation or other kind of pain, and not knowing the
best way to go about this, Vasilyev unbuttoned his overcoat
and frock-coat, weeping and trembling, and bared his chest
to the sleet and wind. But that brought no relief either.
Then he bent over the railing on the bridge, looked down
at the black, turbulent Yauza and felt a strong urge to
throw himself in, head first – not from disgust with life, not
to commit suicide, but to replace one pain with another,
even if it meant being broken to pieces. But the black water,
the darkness, the desolate snowy banks terrified him. He
shuddered and moved on. After passing the Red Barracks
he returned, went down into a small wood and then came
out on to the bridge again.

'No, I'm going home! Home!' he thought. 'It will be
better there.' And home he went. Once there he tore his
wet overcoat and cap off and started pacing along the walls,
never tiring. He kept this up until morning.

VII

When the artist and the medical student called next morning, he was dashing around the room groaning with pain.
His shirt was torn and his hands bitten.

'For God's sake!' he sobbed when he saw his friends.
'Take me where you like, do what you want, but hurry up,
save me, for God's sake! I shall kill myself!'

The art student was very taken aback and turned pale.
The medical student too was close to tears, but remembering
that doctors had to keep calm and collected in all

eventualities, said coldly, 'You're having a nervous break-down. But don't worry, we'll go to a doctor's right away.'

'Wherever you like, only quickly, for God's sake!'

'Now don't get excited. You must take a grip on yourself.'

With trembling hands the art student and medical student dressed Vasilyev and led him out into the street. On the way the medical student told him, 'Mikhail Sergeyevich has been wanting to meet you for ages. He's very nice and knows his stuff. Although he only graduated in 1882 he has a huge practice already. He's very matey with students.'

'Get a move on, hurry!' Vasilyev said.

Mikhail Sergeyevich, a stout, fair-haired doctor, greeted the friends solemnly, with an icy civility, and he smiled on only one side of his face.

'Mayer and the art student have told me about your illness,' he said. 'Very glad to be of service. Well, now, please sit down.'

He made Vasilyev sit in a large armchair near the table and moved a box of cigarettes over to him.

'Well, now,' he began, smoothing the knees of his trousers. 'Let's get down to business. How old are you?'

He began to ask questions, which the medical student answered. He asked if Vasilyev's father had ever suffered from any particular illness, if he was a hard drinker, if he was unusually cruel or had any other peculiarities. He asked precisely the same questions about his grandfather, mother, sisters and brothers. When he learned that his mother had an excellent voice and had sometimes been on the stage, he suddenly livened up and asked, 'Forgive me, but can you remember if the stage was an obsession with your mother?'

Twenty minutes passed. Vasilyev grew bored with the doctor smoothing his knees and harping on the same thing.

'As far as I can tell from your questions, Doctor,' he said, 'you want to know if my illness is hereditary or not. It is *not*.'

The doctor went on to ask if Vasilyev had had any secret vices at all in his childhood, whether there had been head injuries, strong enthusiasms, idiosyncrasies, obsessions. It's possible to avoid giving answers to half the questions posed by diligent doctors without endangering one's health in the slightest, but Mikhail Sergeyevich, the medical student and the art student all wore expressions that seemed to say: if Vasilyev fails to answer just one question, then all is lost. For some reason the doctor wrote down the answers on a piece of paper. When he learned that Vasilyev had graduated from the Natural Sciences Faculty and was now a student in the Faculty of Law, the doctor became very pensive.

'Last year he wrote a first-class dissertation,' the medical student said.

'I'm sorry, but please don't interrupt. I can't concentrate,' the doctor said, smiling on one side of his face. 'Yes, of course, that has a part to play in the case history. Intense mental effort, over-tiredness . . . Yes, yes. And do you drink vodka?' he asked, turning to Vasilyev.

Another twenty minutes passed. In a low voice, the medical student began expounding his theory as to the immediate cause of the attack and then told him that he, the art student and Vasilyev had gone to S— Street the day before yesterday.

The indifferent, restrained, offhand tone in which his friends and the doctor spoke about women and that miserable side-street struck Vasilyev as most strange.

'Please tell me one thing, Doctor,' he said, trying not to appear rude. 'Is prostitution an evil or isn't it?'

'My dear fellow, who's disputing it?' the doctor said, his expression seeming to say that he had long ago solved all these problems. 'Who's disputing it?'

'Are you a psychiatrist?' Vasilyev asked rudely.

'Yes, I'm a psychiatrist.'

'Perhaps you're all right!' Vasilyev said, rising to his feet and starting to pace the room. 'You could well be! But I find it really amazing! The fact that I've studied in two faculties is considered a great achievement. I'm praised to the skies for writing a dissertation that will be ignored and forgotten in three years' time. But because I can't discuss fallen women as nonchalantly as I might talk about these chairs, I'm given medical treatment, called insane and pitied!'

Vasilyev somehow felt dreadfully sorry for himself, his friends, for all those he had seen the day before yesterday, and for the doctor. He burst into tears and fell back into the armchair.

His friends gave the doctor an inquiring look. His expression suggesting that he considered himself a specialist in this field, the doctor went over to Vasilyev and, without speaking to him, gave him some drops to drink. Then, when he had calmed down, he made him undress and started testing the sensitivity of his skin, his knee reflexes, and so on.

Vasilyev felt better. When he left the doctor's he felt ashamed of himself. The clatter of carriages no longer irritated him and the heavy weight beneath his heart grew lighter and lighter, just as if it were melting away. He held two prescriptions: one for potassium bromide, the other for morphia. He had taken all that kind of thing before!

He stood in the street and pondered for a moment. Saying goodbye to his friends he lazily trudged along to the university.

MORE ABOUT PENGUINS, PELICANS, PEREGRINES AND PUFFINS

For further information about books available from Penguins please write to Dept EP, Penguin Books Ltd, Harmondsworth, Middlesex UB7 0DA.

In the U.S.A.: For a complete list of books available from Penguins in the United States write to Dept DG, Penguin Books, 299 Murray Hill Parkway, East Rutherford, New Jersey 07073.

In Canada: For a complete list of books available from Penguins in Canada write to Penguin Books Canada Ltd, 2801 John Street, Markham, Ontario L3R 1B4.

In Australia: For a complete list of books available from Penguins in Australia write to the Marketing Department, Penguin Books Australia Ltd, P.O. Box 257, Ringwood, Victoria 3134.

In New Zealand: For a complete list of books available from Penguins in New Zealand write to the Marketing Department, Penguin Books (N.Z.) Ltd, Private Bag, Takapuna, Auckland 9.

In India: For a complete list of books available from Penguins in India write to Penguin Overseas Ltd, 706 Eros Apartments, 56 Nehru Place, New Delhi 110019.

CLASSICS IN TRANSLATION IN PENGUINS

☐ *Remembrance of Things Past* **Marcel Proust**

☐ Volume One: *Swann's Way, Within a Budding Grove* £7.50
☐ Volume Two: *The Guermantes Way, Cities of the Plain* £7.50
☐ Volume Three: *The Captive, The Fugitive, Time Regained* £7.50

Terence Kilmartin's acclaimed revised version of C. K. Scott Moncrieff's original translation, published in paperback for the first time.

☐ *The Canterbury Tales* **Geoffrey Chaucer** £2.50

'Every age is a Canterbury Pilgrimage . . . nor can a child be born who is not one of these characters of Chaucer' – William Blake

☐ *Gargantua & Pantagruel* **Rabelais** £3.95

The fantastic adventures of two giants through which Rabelais (1495–1553) caricatured his life and times in a masterpiece of exuberance and glorious exaggeration.

☐ *The Brothers Karamazov* **Fyodor Dostoevsky** £3.95

A detective story on many levels, profoundly involving the question of the existence of God, Dostoevsky's great drama of parricide and fraternal jealousy triumphantly fulfilled his aim: 'to find the man in man . . . [to] depict all the depths of the human soul.'

☐ *Fables of Aesop* £1.95

This translation recovers all the old magic of fables in which, too often, the fox steps forward as the cynical hero and a lamb is an ass to lie down with a lion.

☐ *The Three Theban Plays* **Sophocles** £2.95

A new translation, by Robert Fagles, of *Antigone, Oedipus the King* and *Oedipus at Colonus*, plays all based on the legend of the royal house of Thebes.

CLASSICS IN TRANSLATION IN PENGUINS

☐ **The Treasure of the City of Ladies**
Christine de Pisan   £2.95

This practical survival handbook for women (whether royal courtiers or prostitutes) paints a vivid picture of their lives and preoccupations in France, c. 1405. First English translation.

☐ **Berlin Alexanderplatz** Alfred Döblin   £4.95

The picaresque tale of an ex-murderer's progress through underworld Berlin. 'One of the great experimental fictions . . . the German equivalent of *Ulysses* and Dos Passos' *U.S.A.*' – *Time Out*

☐ **Metamorphoses** Ovid   £2.50

The whole of Western literature has found inspiration in Ovid's poem, a golden treasury of myths and legends that are linked by the theme of transformation.

☐ **Darkness at Noon** Arthur Koestler   £1.95

'Koestler approaches the problem of ends and means, of love and truth and social organization, through the thoughts of an Old Bolshevik, Rubashov, as he awaits death in a G.P.U. prison' – *New Statesman*

☐ **War and Peace** Leo Tolstoy   £4.95

'A complete picture of human life;' wrote one critic, 'a complete picture of the Russia of that day; a complete picture of everything in which people place their happiness and greatness, their grief and humiliation.'

☐ **The Divine Comedy: 1 Hell** Dante   £2.25

A new translation by Mark Musa, in which the poet is conducted by the spirit of Virgil down through the twenty-four closely described circles of hell.

ENGLISH AND AMERICAN LITERATURE IN PENGUINS

☐ *Main Street* **Sinclair Lewis** £3.95

The novel that added an immortal chapter to the literature of America's Mid-West, *Main Street* contains the comic essence of Main Streets everywhere.

☐ *The Compleat Angler* **Izaak Walton** £2.50

A celebration of the countryside, and the superiority of those in 1653, as now, who love *quietnesse, vertue* and, above all, *Angling*. 'No fish, however coarse, could wish for a doughtier champion than Izaak Walton' – Lord Home

☐ *The Portrait of a Lady* **Henry James** £2.50

'One of the two most brilliant novels in the language', according to F. R. Leavis, James's masterpiece tells the story of a young American heiress, prey to fortune-hunters but not without a will of her own.

☐ *Hangover Square* **Patrick Hamilton** £3.50

Part love story, part thriller, and set in the publands of London's Earls Court, this novel caught the conversational tone of a whole generation in the uneasy months before the Second World War.

☐ *The Rainbow* **D. H. Lawrence** £2.50

Written between *Sons and Lovers* and *Women in Love, The Rainbow* covers three generations of Brangwens, a yeoman family living on the borders of Nottinghamshire.

☐ *Vindication of the Rights of Woman*
Mary Wollstonecraft £2.95

Although Walpole once called her 'a hyena in petticoats', Mary Wollstonecraft's vision was such that modern feminists continue to go back and debate the arguments so powerfully set down here.

ENGLISH AND AMERICAN LITERATURE IN PENGUINS

☐ *Nostromo* **Joseph Conrad** £1.95

In his most ambitious and successful novel Conrad created an entire imaginary republic in South America. As he said, 'you shall find there according to your deserts: encouragement, consolation, fear, charm – all you demand – and, perhaps, also that glimpse of truth for which you forgot to ask.'

☐ *A Passage to India* **E. M. Forster** £2.50

Centred on the unsolved mystery at the Marabar Caves, Forster's masterpiece conveys, as no other novel has done, the troubled spirit of India during the Raj.

These books should be available at all good bookshops or news-agents, but if you live in the UK or the Republic of Ireland and have difficulty in getting to a bookshop, they can be ordered by post. Please indicate the titles required and fill in the form below.

NAME _____ BLOCK CAPITALS

ADDRESS _____

_____

_____

Enclose a cheque or postal order payable to The Penguin Bookshop to cover the total price of books ordered, plus 50p for postage. Readers in the Republic of Ireland should send £1R equivalent to the sterling prices, plus 67p for postage. Send to: The Penguin Bookshop, 54/56 Bridlesmith Gate, Nottingham, NG1 2GP.

You can also order by phoning (0602) 599295, and quoting your Barclaycard or Access number.

Every effort is made to ensure the accuracy of the price and availability of books at the time of going to press, but it is sometimes necessary to increase prices and in these circumstances retail prices may be shown on the covers of books which may differ from the prices shown in this list or elsewhere. This list is not an offer to supply any book.

This order service is only available to residents in the UK and the Republic of Ireland.